THE BENT POLITICIAN

by Jon Wycliffe

This edition first published in paperback by
Michael Terence Publishing in 2024
www.mtp.agency

ISBN 9781800947054

Michael Terence
Publishing

One

It'd been a hell of a day. Mark Spivey had been trudging the streets of the business area of town all day, only to receive encouragement to the tune of nil. His feet were wet and cold and they ached. As he scrubbed them doggedly on the ancient coconut mat outside the front door of the student flat, its crushed layer of dust began turning to mud. He felt that if he'd had a magic lantern, his genie would have collapsed in a useless heap. He plodded up the stairs and opened the door. The stench from the Chinese takeaway below seemed less intrusive than usual; the damp coldness seemed to have absorbed some of the reek of greasy glutamate permeating the room.

Despite the awful surroundings, his mood rose a little when he saw a small pile of mail from another world, lying on the splintered boards behind the door. Just trash circulars or bills, but one he saw was actually addressed to him. It was a communication from another more congenial universe, a letter. On the envelope were the words, "Enclosed a gift for you, blessed by Archbishop Jwara."

He tore it open. It had come snail mail all the way from Africa, blessed by Archbishop Jwara of the Catholic Archdiocese of Durban, Isifundabhishobi sama Katholika sase Thekwini.

The letter began, "Dear Mr Spivey, Your donation to the Zulu Missions - sent off as soon as you can - is a gift of life to the children of Africa - protecting them from killer diseases and providing them with essential food to grow and fulfil their potential…"

The rest was all about cash. The smallest donation mentioned was £18 or he could contribute as little as £3 per month. Failing that, he could always re-jig his will to leave a fixed lump sum. Some bloody gift!

Contrary to what you might expect, that letter gave him hope, but more importantly inspiration, even as he delved into his back pocket and grasped his total worldly wealth of £1.72p and a one euro coin he was saving to defraud the launderette. The letter provided the inspiration for a route out of destitution, an almost biblical revelation, A CHARITY!

He sucked the stunted index finger of his left hand that still sometimes tingled from beyond the end of the stump and his tongue was where his finger tip should be. He would not go to a charity and beg, he would set up his own, by himself, for himself. His conscience would not be pricked just as his fingertip would never again be pricked.

His world was a tough place just like Archbishop Jwara's, but he decided at that moment it would not always be this way. His days of knocking on doors in search of jobs that did not exist were over. He would get a return for his crap degree, from his second-rate university, in the third-rate, bum town, in clapped-out middle England. The last thing he'd get was pathetic faith in pathetic religion. His god already lay in his pocket and it was empty.

As he'd figured a way to pay the debt for his bum degree, the £2,000 he owed, he sang to himself,

My pocket is empty, it's been too long
I used to be healthy and fit and strong
But now I'm hungry and feel very weak
The rich with their laws in my pockets do sneak.
They stand and watch as their bellies grow fat
They stand and they grin like the old Cheshire cat
They laugh at our lives both mine and yours
They're pleased we are hungry and scrubbing their floors.

Fuck that, his inspiration was to turn begging into a commercial operation. Here was a real chance to pay back their poxy loan which wouldn't happen stacking shelves at Tesco for seventy quid a week, when one room in a shared student flat over the stinking Chinese was costing 40 quid that he had as much chance of getting as flying.

He knew charity law was as full of holes as a leaky colander. It was suddenly clear that all he needed to do was find a few of the holes and set them leaking in his direction.

It wasn't a new idea; anyone could start a charity they just needed to start collecting! Then get registered or maybe the other way around. It mattered from a theoretical point of view, but who was going to complain about volunteers offering their valuable free time to help others in distress? In practice, it could well be argued that running a charity was a form of organised begging, but the law in England dictates that *begging* is only going on when an individual in the street asks for money, for nothing! An act of *charity* takes place when people with a surplus give a portion of their wealth to the deserving poor, from the kindness of their hearts! Define poor and define deserve, especially deserve. Now decide who deserves what. There's an interesting legal conundrum or any kind of conundrum! What a load of sentimental bollocks, he thought.

His inspiration lay in a plan to help others. Ho ho! He would take a little *commission* for his efforts. Muslims and old-style Christians regarded charging interest on money lent as immoral. Is it really *wrong*? Archbishop Jwara did not think so, and what about The Archbishop of Canterbury? Did he dress like a bum? Not likely, he was very, very pretty - if you like that sort of thing. Mark knew that in the UK the Vagrancy Act was brought into being in 1824. Just nine years after the end of the Napoleonic wars, vagrancy and begging under the act - it's the Law! Still! - were created. Poof! A crime. Soldiers one day, criminals the next at the stroke of a pen by some fat-arsed politician in a big leather-upholstered chair in Whitehall. Send them to the hulks or the Antipodes. Problem solved. Poof! Gone. Hallelujah! God's in his heaven, no more tramps. What kind of morality was that? All the King's men one day, then, abracadabra, criminals the next.

He asked himself, am I a criminal? He was clear in his mind that so far he'd conformed, apart from his sexuality and whose fault was that if not God's? Was God a bastard? He certainly wasn't married. Was he, she or it a eunuch? Did God know he, she or it was God?

Mark? He had been more-or-less a model citizen. OK, maybe as a student he got drunk and caused a nuisance on occasion, but when have students not done those things? He thought it was almost a tradition that young people kicked over the traces at times. Consider Boris Johnson and the Bullingdon Club. Had Johnson grown up in London's East End, he'd almost certainly have begun his career being bullied by far bigger bullies than himself and in a Borstal Institution rather than Eton. Would he have his ebullient personality then?

Mark asked himself what he thought might be the fundamental questions; was his real problem that his arse wasn't fat enough and his mind not corrupt enough?

In the 1830s, soldiers were considered the lowest of the low and their lives were worth almost less than nothing. The Great Lord Wellington called the soldiers he commanded, "The scum of the earth." How much had things changed? Mark thought he was one step away from vagrancy and begging and well on the way to being branded a criminal. Scum of the earth? Bollocks to that. He hadn't worked his arse off for a crap degree for fuck all, he was looking for *his* payback.

The devil still took the hindmost and the only way forward was to push to the front with pockets full of cash. His student days were over, the greatest lesson he'd learned was that in the modern world, his world, the loudest voice sings to the tune of silent cash. He'd learned cash may be a benefactor or a robber, it is impartial. The controllers of cash are seldom saints. Think the Money Lenders in the Temple. He wanted his just desserts and stuff anyone in his way.

The problem now was how in hell could he raise the money to start a charity? Cash, filthy lucre, money, and the rich man's world. What was it that cash would buy that would net the cash he needed to get his charity off the ground? The answer was in his hand, a begging letter; though better expressed, an appeal letter. Words were all important when dealing with the law. Words, words defined the truth. The fundamental aspect of any document produced by a lawyer ties the truth into knots controlled by the rich and powerful, and their dodgy (corrupt? immoral? irreligious?) lawyers and accountants. He saw himself tying the knots to suit himself. This was how he'd make his iffy degree pay for itself. Dancing words could make the law dance in any direction the author wanted, and they were going to *sing,* as well as dance for him. He needed a plan, a means to get his hands on some leaflets at negligible cost. His experience at the half-baked university provided the answer. It lay in the building where he got his half-baked degree.

He was vaguely acquainted with the designer in the university's printing plant. He knew the guy fancied him. At least he thought he'd seen the signs, just expressions that those of his persuasion felt as much as knew. The only way to find out was to approach him and ask. *If* he could be persuaded to do a favour?

Mark thought they might 'get on' in more ways than one. Maybe even "get it on." If he could hook him, he had an ally for life because they both knew too much. They would be attached by circumstances that joined them at the hip like conjoined twins.

Mark made a cup of tea, cooked himself a cheese and mushroom omelette then went to bed with a book of quotes from Oscar Wilde. He'd not felt so chipper since before his father took an overdose and died. That was when he was just fourteen.

He awoke the next day feeling better than he had for months. He showered, breakfasted, put on his best CHARITY shop suit, wearing-in his only pair of charity shop proper shoes, he didn't look exactly stylish but at least he felt presentable and off he went. He had a plan, and now a *mission.* He walked directly to the university library. He still had a valid card. He went straight in and down to the basement. He wasn't there for books, he was interested in the printing plant. He'd never been in there before.

There were NO ENTRY signs on the double doors. He wasn't sure why he hated no entry signs. His thoughts ran to - they could, fuck off with their No Fucking Entry. What the hell were doors for if not entry? He saw no more reason for himself not entering than anyone else and if anyone attempted to stop him, they were facing a serious argument.

The no entry sign put him in a pugnacious mood. As it happened, the place appeared to be empty. It was oppressive with a low ceiling and no windows, a modern dungeon. The lights glared in his face the ceiling was so low. It was a horrible place. He thought what a great torture chamber it would make, as he pinched his ear lobe, hard, enough to hurt.

Not all the lights were on and the machines were silent, even so, the place was crushing. He could imagine the awful ear-blasting, jaw-clenching noise echoing around the bare white emulsion-painted concrete walls when the machinery was running. Almost a copy of one of Hitler's wartime bunkers, filled with bizarre, electronically-generated, mind-bending noise. The sound of his old charity shop leather shoes echoed eerily on the austere, grubby, grey-painted concrete floor.

In a far corner stood a partitioned section that he guessed was the design and origination room. He strolled nonchalantly in, massaging his sore ear lobe and there stood the very man he was looking for. The man turned to face him with a slightly puzzled expression, though very civilly and said almost obsequiously,

'Can I help you?'

Mark smiled and held out his hand, 'Mark Spivey. I'm hoping this is the beginning of a mutually-beneficial relationship.'

He believed in being brass-faced when pushing his luck. Confidence was everything.

The designer gave Mark a puzzled look, neglected the outstretched hand and replied, 'Oh Kaay?'

Mark held up the stump of his finger before the man's face. The response was quite simple, 'UGHhhh.'

'Not pretty is it? I left the rest of it in the Pie Factory in town, when half asleep on nights, trying to rustle up cash for my student room. I'm still working on negotiations for compensation. I've got a crap law degree from upstairs. You could say it indirectly caused the loss of the end of my finger. The uni shrink says she thinks I've got PTSD, Post Traumatic Stress Disorder. She's saying it's sent me a bit crazy, but I'm not so crazy that I'm not going to squeeze every bloody penny I can out of the bastard Pie Co. The whole business has given me an idea though.

'I got a third for my degree and my bloody minced-off finger was part of the reason for my crap degree, and a crap degree is almost worse than useless for getting a job. People with firsts from top universities are having trouble getting jobs with the recession. There *are* no bloody jobs. Take a look at this.'

He held out the African letter. The designer gingerly took out the letter from its envelope with an expression almost of fear, implying Mark was indeed, crazy. He paused, read it quickly and nervously asked,

'What has a letter from some dodgy charity in Africa got to do with your missing finger?'

'It's given me an IDEA! A charity.'

The designer repeated his 'Oh Kaay' and paused with a mystified frown. 'So, a charity? What d'you mean?'

'Not any charity, MY Charity.'

'I don't understand. You haven't got a charity surely?'

'No, and that's the very reason I'm here. You might think Gulliver's Travels has always been a children's story but really it's a comment on the world we live in. The only way I can start a charity and get away with it, is essentially with begging letters, but I can't call them begging letters, I have to make an *appeal.* Call it an appeal and it's OK. If you say, I am begging, in writing you'd probably be OK too legally because you are not homeless! It's only when you're on the street holding out your hand asking for money that you're definitely breaking the law. That's why there are lawyers because the law is a tricky business. It's put there for the benefit of the haves, and to the detriment of the have-nots. The have-nots are the little people like us. The haves put the law together to maintain the have-nots in their have-not station in life, ring-fenced in current parlance.

'National Insurance provided by the state ostensibly takes care of those who are unable to look after themselves. The words 'taken care of' make it sound as if their station in life is where they belong because they can't look after themselves. If this were not the case, the haves could not hang onto their status so easily. If life was a football match, the haves' goal would be half the size of the have-nots' and the referee would be in their pocket, in football parlance.

'You're a designer and know about printing. With what I know about the law and Gulliver's Travels, plus what you know about printing, we could start a charity. No one would be the wiser. Get it right and it's a licence to print money. That allows us to jump the wall between the Lilliputians and the Brobdingnags. The Lilliputians are us, the Little People. That's us. The Brobdingnags are the big people. They are the people who own the schools, the factories and the government.

'Charities are all about the law and pretty well the only way you can start one legally if you're broke is with begging letters. I read somewhere about some African guy in Nigeria who runs his own private jet on the proceeds of a religion he operates. Billy Graham made a fortune from religion. Charity, Religion, National Insurance, what's the difference? The only other name is begging! Put your money on the plate so the sodding priest can lord it over you every Sunday and smile at you pompously all week while sitting about getting fat. Have you ever seen a skinny priest? Or a starving civil servant?

'We won't be begging, we'll be making an appeal. There's no *real* difference, just a legal difference. By adopting the legal approach of an appeal, we'll be able to climb the fence between the haves and the have-nots. It'll make the haves' goal bigger for us and sidestep the bent referee, the bloody debt collector or the po-faced bank manager who'll give you money when you don't need it and tell you to piss off when you do. What do you say? Maybe I don't sound so crazy now, eh? We all need money and working in a dump like this is hardly living at all, is it? More like a sentence.'

The designer was listening with full attention now. Mark had him thinking. He'd really got his salesman's hat on and he was going to convince the designer through sheer determination. Mark was a believer; he'd ***make*** the designer believe.

'Stuck here in this bloody dungeon every day can't be anyone's idea of fun. It's not even a reasonable means to exist. I don't know about you, but I'd rather be dead. If we work together and pull it off it could lead to a way out for both of us. You handle the nuts and bolts and I do the admin. It could be a winner. It could make us both winners. I've even thought of a name, The Institute for the Alleviation of Suffering from Industrial Injuries. A right mouthful and as specific as the length of a piece of string. That's important, plenty of flexibility and ties us down to bugger all. It's got a neat acronym too, IASIA. Smooth or what? Cool as dry ice. What are you thinking now? Not quite so crazy, eh? I could put together a claim against this place, for *you*. I really could!

'It has given you depression; it is such a shitty environment, it's sent you crazy. Find the right quack to support you in court and you'll have a case. You could give evidence in court with a stammer and a tick, it'd be a rrrr-ight llll-laugh. It really could work too. Put in a claim for half a million for pain and suffering and permanent disability making it impossible for you to work. I'd take it on. It'd take years to get through the courts. It'd cost the earth but it'd scare the shit out of the university and a whole lot of other commercial/industrial operators too. Not because it's wrong but because it could cause turmoil across industry nationally and even abroad; thieves robbing the thieving shysters in the stock exchange and parliament, rough justice. I like it. The more I think about it, the more I like it.'

The designer was following Mark closely now. It wasn't difficult to see how unhappy he was working in the torture chamber dungeon. Even without the machines running, it *was* a hostile environment.

'This basement has a whole lot in common with a jail,' persisted Mark. 'The only real difference is you get more parole but they make you work and dance to their tune.'

'You're not wrong there,' burst out the designer. 'My boss acts like a bloody warder. I call him Herne. His name's Fred. He thinks I'm nuts. I think he's as thick as the walls of Fort Knox. Herne was a pagan god of the hunt. It's Fred who's nuts, you'd have to be to spend 15 years in this hell hole, chasing silly buggers like me, to suffer a life of boredom and stress, with all the departments saying we're too slow or moaning this or that is wrong or there should be a comma here and not a bloody full stop. *You're not wrong.* This place gives me what my mother called the willies.'

They laughed, but it was not a humorous laugh, it was an odd, edgy laugh. They felt it in common. That was the moment Mark reeled him in. They both knew Mark had got him.

'D'you fancy discussing some more details in a more congenial atmosphere out of this dump? It doesn't just give *you* the willies,' suggested Mark.

'Have I seen you in The Black Boy?'

'You might have. Want to meet there, tonight? I'm Mark,' he said offering his hand, 'and you?'

'Kevin. You're on.'

They shook. 'Seven OK?'

'Suits me.'

'Seven it is. I'll see you later, Kevin. I'll set about writing some stuff for the appeal letter.'

Mark went home and sat jotting ideas and thoughts about getting started. He was setting out a list in his mind as he made his way home. Looking back, he could remember feeling nervous about what he was taking on, but he was pretty much committed and without really thinking about it he'd got someone else involved, so he could hardly back out now. He was exhilarated too, nothing ventured nothing gained. All he had left to lose was his freedom and what was that? Freedom to stack shelves in Tesco. No freedom at all. A life of mindless boredom alleviated by getting pissed on Friday nights to forget the prospect of Monday.

THE LIST

1) Leaflet - letter. Pulling heart strings for donations. Research.(Where? how?).
2) Book-keeping, records, office, OFFICE, Security, Expenses, Accountancy.
3) Finance £££ finance, finance £££.
4) Bank account.
5) Aims and objectives. Constitution.
6) Trustees.
7) Transport & storage. Ambulance chasing? No win no fee?
8) Grants?
9) Publicity.
10) Presentation, a lecture on what I'm doing and why, I have to believe and present that belief, convincingly, to others. Confidence is key (new wardrobe).

He'd succeeded with Kevin. Others might prove more difficult but getting established should help!

The list brought home to him how much was involved and made him realise exactly what it was he was taking on. He needed to take it one step at a time or he'd sink in the enormity of it all.

His biggest problem, as ever, was raising finance. Why couldn't he be a poor little rich kid? Life would be so much easier but at the same time so much less exciting and exhilarating.

He went into town to try on some clothes with a view to deciding exactly what image he was going to project. Just what would his new persona be? Life was an act and he was an actor not like the other 99% in a fog of indecision. He'd take life by the scruff of the neck and mould it in an image he'd create.

Two

Mark arrived at the Black Boy Club just before seven. It was Saturday, but too early for a crowd. He ordered a lager shandy. He wanted to keep a clear head. It wasn't long before Kevin came in, carrying his portfolio and saw Mark sitting in a corner on a bench seat.

Kevin came over, put the portfolio on the seat beside him and asked, 'What are you having?'

'I'm OK, thanks.'

He went and got a drink, came back, put his drink on the table, and then opened his portfolio on the seat. A big woman with short, bobbed hair, wearing tight jeans across her generous backside and a denim waistcoat over a well-filled grey tee shirt, approached them.

'What's all this then?' she asked. 'Working on a Saturday evening Kevin? Reeling in the pennies are we?'

'You got it, Sonny,' he laughed. 'We're looking for an escape route, from a combination of poverty, drudgery, abuse and exploitation.'

'So, are you going to introduce your friend?' she asked. 'Have I seen you in here before?' she asked Mark.

'Could be.'

He'd not shown Kevin his list yet, but Kevin interjected, 'Sonny, meet Mark. We're just starting work on a project that could be a life-changer if it pans out.'

'Huh, talk's cheap. So, what is this life-changing project? Are you going to start forging tenners?' she asked with a look that projected a cross between a sneer and laughter.

'Ask Mark, it's his idea.'

'So, what is this wonderful scheme?'

Mark thought she was a natural-born bully, but sex dysphoria will do that to some people who can't decide who or what they are.

'You can laugh all you like at the moment, but you wait till our charity's pulling in the cash, then you'll laugh on the other side of your face - darling.'

Mark added the darling to wind her up and let her know he could give as good as he got. It took the wind out of her sails.

'Huh,' she replied. 'What do you know about setting up a charity?'

'Not a lot but I'll tell you when I've done it. I was about to show Kevin a list of things we need to get done, for a start.'

'OK then, let's have a look?' she scoffed.

Mark gave Kevin a look of resignation, as he faced him, palms up. Kevin glanced at Sonny who wore an expression indicating bored cynicism. Mark glanced at Kevin implying, don't involve me, you deal with one another, then he put his notepad on the table with the list showing and Sonny and Kevin leaned in together to see. They obviously knew each other well.

'So, you really are serious?' said Sonny looking up from the notes with an incredulous expression,

'Bloody right I am,' replied Mark. 'I'm in deep financial shit from my degree course and this looks like a viable way out. If it's possible to pay for an air ambulance with a charity, it ought to be a piece o' piss to pay off my fees. I'm bloody sure I'm a much more deserving case than a knackered donkey, and no way am I ready for any sodding knackers' yard yet.'

'I might be able to sort you out with an office,' she said, casually, 'if you really are serious. I work in the council's housing department and sometimes we kind of overlap with commercial property. You probably know there's an area in the town earmarked for regeneration, but it'll take years before anything happens on the ground. In the meantime, it puts a blight on the whole area. Some buildings lie dormant for years getting more and more dilapidated. You may think the council is a washout, but there's more to be sorted out than you'd ever imagine. Starting from the ground up, there are sewers and ground water drainage and that involves surveyors. Get that wrong and everything falls apart before you've even started.

'I'll have a poke around for you if you like. As a charity you might even be in line for a peppercorn rent, everybody gains in the long run. Whatever happens, even if you only get premises for a year or two, dirt cheap, everybody wins. Things keep ticking over instead of falling apart completely, and having to start again from scratch.'

Mark stood with a stunned expression. 'That'd be great. Just having a proper office would up our credibility, at a stroke.'

'I'll see what I can do,' she said. 'At the moment, I need a pee.'

When she'd gone, Kevin said, 'She's a right handful, but her heart's in the right place and she's no bullshitter. If she says she'll do a thing, you can depend on it. We've known each other for years.'

He showed Mark what he'd come up with regarding the APPEAL Mark had to stop thinking in terms of begging letters. Things were moving so fast, he couldn't believe he'd only had the idea the night before.

The three of them chatted together most of the evening. Mark explained that probably the first thing they needed to do was set up a Company Limited by Guarantee. This would be the best way for their committee to limit their liabilities if the whole business went belly up. Mark made it clear that that was always a possibility, even if it was just a trick to unload the bad bits and shift the good stuff elsewhere. Once you started looking at businesses, you soon began to realise that as often as not the owners were looking for any means by which to screw more cash from them. Ethics were the last thing at the forefront of anyone's mind. Ultimately, businesses are just money-making machines for the owners and the most successful ones screw every last penny out with not the slightest compunction about consequences for anyone or anything. Capitalists live to work and wallow in money. Workers work to live. We choose our poison and live with the consequences. Capitalists can't afford a conscience. This was Mark's philosophy.

If Sonny and Kevin were up for it, they could jump on board. If the boat sank, Mark would always have the law as a life-raft. They would need to keep proper books and record expenses just like any other business. When all's said and done a charity is just a business like any other with employees where appropriate and a responsibility to carry out the aims and objectives set out in its memorandum of association without fear or favour, ostensibly…

Obviously, it would be Mark's job to sort out what it was they were going do, and how to make - and he meant MAKE - the books balance. Lecturing might be a good start, and lecturers who are any good don't come cheap. Mark smiled at the thought.

Once Sonny settled down and relaxed, letting herself be herself, she turned out to be quite fun with a bitter sense of humour. They finished quite early. Between the three of them, they all had quite a lot to think about. It turned out that Sonny was already the secretary of the local Constituency Labour Party and this might, if they played their cards right, fit in well with what they were aiming to do with IASIA. Kevin and Mark went back to his place, which wasn't fancy but so much more pleasant than Mark's. With neither of them even really thinking about it, Mark stayed the night! When he awoke, Kevin was gone from the bed but Mark could hear the clatter of crockery from the kitchen. He slipped on his shorts and padded through to the kitchen. The kettle was bubbling and Kevin was busy laying out odds and ends for breakfast.

'What do you fancy? I'm veggie so it's either cereal or fruit, and there's only a gone-over tangerine, a banana or a slightly soft apple,' he laughed. 'You know what it's like when you live alone everything comes in half dozens at supermarkets, so when you get to eat it, it's nearly always a bit past its sell-by. You'd think their main objective was to get us to waste as much as possible.'

'Coffee with milk and two sugars and a couple of slices of toast with marmalade'll do it for me if that's OK? Give me an hour. I'm a slow starter. Morning's not my best time and it's Sunday. It's been a crazy week. At some point I'll give my mother a ring, I usually call the old bag on Sunday morning.'

'What's she like, your mother?'

'Don't ask! You think Sonny's a handful, put my mother and her together and they'd probably fight like cat and dog. Then make up and be all sweetness and light. Till the next fight. My mother is tough, but she's had to be. She's a cow! My father died when I was fourteen and I've got two sisters both younger than me and she's managed by hook or by crook. She's a receptionist at a glamorous firm that makes glue near Tottenham in London. She's friendly with the head of sales where she works. She's another old bag who sometimes comes to stay. That helps.

'All in all, though, she's a right cow, nothing I ever do is ever right. She was the same with my father. He was never good enough and it was my mother who pushed my father so hard he ended up so far in debt and so depressed he took an overdose. She's part of the reason I left London. Nothing I ever did was ever right. There's no way she's gonna kill me though, I'm gonna make a packet, wave it under her nose and tell her to piss off. Just like in the joke: "Hello *darling*, I won the lottery. Pack your bags." "What?" "Pack your bags. I won the lottery." "What? Why? Where are we going?" "*We're*, not going anywhere. Pack your bags and piss off. *I* won the lottery."

'I'll rub her nose in it the way she's rubbed mine and my father's. What about your folks?' Mark asked.

'I come from Derby. My father worked in the engine sheds. Started as some sort of errand boy and worked his way up to a kind of foreman in the stores and purchasing. He's not very well these days. Had a stomach ulcer, when he was a kind of under foreman and his boss wound him up all the time. The stress nearly killed him, but his boss died. He got over the ulcer and in a funny sort of way it was the best thing that happened to him. The management gave him his boss's old job, and he never looked back. He got more money and less hassle. By that time, I'd left home. I'd got good 'A levels' and an acceptance at Central St Martins. I got an Upper Second. I even won a prize in a competition for designing a Martel Brandy label. Got pissed for a week on some of the most expensive brandy you can buy.

'In those days we still got grants for university, so I didn't owe much when I finished. I got acceptances for a couple of jobs with good agencies in London. The work was creative and interesting but always there was pressure. To do my best work I need to have my heart in it, and having someone looking over my shoulder all the time just destroys any creative spark and tears all the pleasure out of it. I got fed up with chasing my tail, paying the earth for accommodation and just getting around in London. Ride a bike and chances are you'll get crushed; get on a bus and as often as not it's hardly any quicker than walking and getting a car if you could afford it, is hardly any quicker.

'I got offered a job back here in the Midlands nearer my parents. My Dad wasn't well. He was just getting old by then. My mother got what they thought were fibroids, but turned out to be cancer. She had a hysterectomy but it was too late. She died about three years ago. My job was with the ads department of a newspaper that was taken over. I was made redundant. That's when I ended up in the shit-hole in town. My father's in a care home. He's lost it. He's got Alzheimer's. One minute he's fine, the next minute he's away with the fairies. He'll end up being a full-time job. He's still active and has already gone walkabout a couple of times while I've been here. He'll need to be locked in soon or there's no telling where he'll end up, could be under a bus or frozen to death in the middle of a field.

'The cash from the house has nearly run out, and soon I'll be worse off financially than when I left school. Happy Days. We're gonna make this charity business work or I'll finish up just like you, in deep shit. You were so right about the dungeon. That place is bloody killing me. Ninety per cent of UK students wander about in a dream with no idea about what they're really doing, and most of the foreigners with just about enough English to know the difference between A and B aren't even too sure about where the hell they are. Even some of the lecturers don't know their arse from their elbow. Sorting out copy for exam papers isn't what I want to spend my life doing. I didn't do a Fine Art degree to be some sort of semi-qualified typesetter in a fucking dungeon. What I'd really like to do is something involving real art even if it is just curator in a gallery.'

'Jesus,' said Mark, 'you sound even more pissed off than me. I'll phone my mother, then maybe we'll look at some ideas for our appeal.'

He was feeling both elated and yet drained, things were moving so fast.

'OK if I make more coffee? I need a boost to get me moving this morning. It's Sunday. We could always go to church!' Kevin laughed at the prospect, then sang,

'All things bright and beautiful.
All students great and small.
The staff so wise and wonderful.
They drive me up the wall. Gaahh!'

'I could put the One Euro I was saving to defraud the launderette onto the collection plate for the glory of the established church. Stuff that!' said Mark. 'Tomorrow I'll see if I can't get some bloody temp work. The situation with my bank card is getting desperate to the point where they'll put a block on it. I don't want to apply for bankruptcy.'

'That bad is it? You're not the only one. I heard a story a little while ago about an ex-student who had a bankruptcy party. It was the talk of the English Department for a while. Tough times, it's not much different for everyone. Thatcher's squeezing us like lemons. See how things go next week. Sonny might come up with something. I have a feeling once she gets the bit between her teeth she won't let go in a hurry. She's OK is Sonny.'

'I need cash. I'll get some money somehow.'

'You phone your mother, then let's have a look at putting together these appeal letters.'

They cleared away the remains of breakfast and Kevin opened his portfolio. By lunch time they'd put together a simple appeal letter and Kevin said he'd laser print 100 copies by Monday night then they'd decide where and when to start distributing. It would have to be a pilot and if they got just one reply, they'd be "Over the Moon."

Mark checked and discovered a service supplying a poste restante address and company registration, complete package, for £55 that they could use instead of their office address. Things were still moving even if at a more sustainable pace. Mark told Kevin to hang fire on the printing until they had the address and company documents. That the bills were already beginning to pile up worried Mark. He could not go to the bank, it would be just a waste of time, and he was DESPERATE for cash.

He managed to get some temp work for a week, order picking on nights. It was disruptive for everything else but took the worst of the pressure off his bank card. He was a zombie by the weekend but on Saturday he went to the Black Boy to catch up with Kevin and Sonny. They were just a week into the IASIA project, and that was the night he met Lydia, Lyd to her friends. Lydia, among other things, was a dominatrix. Statuesque would fit the bill as a description. Full-breasted, well-built and broad-hipped with a crowning glory of flowing, copper-coloured hair. At just short of 6 feet tall she was an imposing woman. She lived, on and off, with Sonny, so he'd heard from Kevin. Together they were sugar and spice. Put another way you might say they matched like acid and alkali, they neutralised each other when together, but get them apart and either was formidable.

Given that his financial situation had improved, at least in the short term, Mark felt a little more relaxed than recently, until

Lydia came on the scene. Lydia was the informal leader of women regularly involved in the sex trade. Many of the women whose main income was derived from the cravings of males, were not simple prostitutes. A significant proportion of men wanted to be at least dominated and quite often gently tortured or degraded, and in this area of the business, Lydia was not only the most successful but also the leading S&M exponent. Her most important local client was the Chairman of the City Council, who Mark had heard, liked to be forced up and down stairs carrying an iron ball and chain while being prodded and beaten with a cane! Mark had heard the rumours but thought each to their own. He had his own quirks and foibles after all.

Lydia operated her business from premises in the area of the town that Sonny said was due for re-development. Lyd lived about three miles away, near a pleasant park and a small shopping area catering for those with expensive tastes. Most of the houses nearby were large, semi-detached, three-storey Victorian villas. Lydia's was a four-bedroomed bungalow surrounded by about an acre of gardens and a view from the back across a stream and then open fields. The gardens were kept in spectacularly good order by a full-time gardener. The gardener in question, who sometimes doubled as her chauffeur when Lyd chose to go out in the Bentley, was notorious as her slave, whether that involved sex or not was nobody's business other than Steve and Lydia's. Steve was said to be happy and seemed to be, in his role.

There were two cars housed in the three-car garage, the other being a Porsche which Lydia generally drove herself when the mood took her. Steve, gardener-cum-chauffeur lived in a tiny two-room cottage surrounded by trees near the gate. As well as his other duties he acted as gateman. Lydia, so Sonny told him, treated him like "dirt" and he simply accepted that he was her "slave." It was a kind of ritualistic relationship difficult to understand but it takes all sorts, as the saying goes.

Lydia seldom came to the Black Boy during opening hours, although she was part-owner. Mark learned later that she was either the owner or partner in property and businesses all over the town and beyond. He never discovered how far her tentacles reached. He soon understood she was not a person to be trifled with. She had influence all around the Midlands and could make life difficult for anyone unfortunate enough to excite her displeasure. She wielded power through knowledge over almost everybody who was anybody. Through her business network, she knew more about the local community and beyond than almost anyone. It was rumoured she only had to whistle and the manager of one of the largest banks in town would be dancing in attendance. Lydia was rich and could pull rank over all and sundry.

Sonny had mentioned their little project to Lydia and stirred her curiosity. Kevin and Mark were savouring their Vodka Red Bulls in the Black Boy when Sonny arrived to tell them they'd been invited to the function room upstairs. When Mark asked what was going on, she simply said,

'Don't look a gift horse in the mouth.'

They trekked upstairs, intrigued as to what was happening. They were surprised at the size of the room for a start, it was big enough to accommodate a small stage upon which stood a boardroom table. Lydia sat at the head. They moved towards the steps. Lydia rose and came towards them. She was wearing tan suede leather flared trousers with matching high-heeled, platform sandals, a white puffed sleeve silk shirt with a slim black velvet bow tie and a suede bolero that matched her trousers. Mark guessed she was wearing half his yearly income.

'Come Up. Take a seat.'

They did as instructed. Sonny made swift introductions.

Lydia began, 'I hear you're setting up a rather interesting project and need finance to get off the ground. I'm in business and always interested in new ventures that sound as though they could be lucrative. So, Mark, would you like to tell me how you envisage your new enterprise developing?'

'Well really I came out tonight for a bit of relaxation and I've had a couple of drinks after a shattering week. This is a surprise but I'll do my best. I've just finished a law degree and got a Third, partly because I lost the first digit of my left-hand index finger,' holding up his stump. 'But no one is going to take this into consideration. I might have got an Upper Second but if-'

'If ifs and ands were pots and pans there'd be no need for tinkers,' said Lydia smiling. 'I understand.'

'The top and bottom of my situation is there's no way I'm going to get a reasonably paid law job with the economic situation as it stands, so I need to do something else, even without the disadvantages caused by the loss of the end of my finger. I've been thinking about alternative ways of making money and the best I've come up with is a charity. I don't know how much Sonny has told you, but I'm inclined to think I've sold the idea to her. We haven't really got very far yet but I've already set up a company registered under the name of IASIA, The Institute for the Alleviation of Suffering from Industrial Accidents. It covers a pretty broad spectrum of suffering, from physical to mental health problems among working people and their families, and even friends and associates within the confines of legal definitions.

'These are always open to being picked over from a legal position. The law is never fixed, it can always evolve as social definitions and culture change. Homosexuality has only recently been made legal, as you are no doubt aware, and rightly so, given that the law before the change was well known as the Blackmailer's Charter and people are what they're born to be and have no say in the matter.

'A charity such as I'm suggesting could (a) raise all sorts of legal questions and (b) provide employment for those willing to promote a more insightful approach to health and safety in the workplace. That could be looked at with benefit for a start. By fighting cases that were clearly unjustly treated, and raising the awareness of the public to cases where the law is presently unjustly administered - Homophobic police forces are probably more common than not, as you're no doubt aware - IASIA would serve to promote a much-needed reappraisal of the law as it exists and this area could prove to be extremely lucrative for exponents.

'The law in the UK at present needs updating. You could argue I'm setting out on a crusade for a more enlightened legal system relating to industrial and employment health and safety. The nuts and bolts of what I'm proposing are, in essence, an appeal for money to promote a campaign for the sort of legal changes I've just outlined. Those ideas raise all sorts of questions about how our society is run and could cause us to look at all sorts of borders in our society that might benefit from a reappraisal.'

Lydia leaned back in her chair and said, 'Well Mark, the way you just expressed yourself has impressed me. I think we could fruitfully discuss your ideas in more depth. And Kevin,' she continued, 'how do you see your role developing in all this?'

'Er well, I'm not very well prepared either but I'll do my best. The ideas are Mark's, my job will be to present them in simplified graphic form. That's what I'm trained for, and I think I'm good at what I do. At present my real talent isn't being used. I feel as though I'm wasting my time laying out exam papers and requisition forms at the university's print plant. I'm a graphic artist. My degree is in Graphic Art and as such my job is to express ideas graphically, in the form of montages, cartoons, caricatures, spoofs, you name it. If it has a graphically creative aspect I can represent, then that's how I'll set out to present it.'

'Sonny, you say you think the ideas are good, and you're interested in getting involved,' said Lydia. 'How do you think you can contribute?'

'I can use my influence in the council, the unions and the local Labour Party. I believe I can sway the attitudes of locally powerful people in the public sector towards a better understanding of social minorities and as such make a real contribution locally, and hopefully in the longer term, nationally to the policies of the party as a whole.'

Lydia rounded off the impromptu meeting, 'Well, what more can I say? OK. We'll leave it there for tonight, but in general terms, you can count on my support! Does anyone want a drink? Steve, open the bar.'

As the board table disappeared, replaced by a disco, other people started to arrive. Mark recognised the Bursar from the university and one or two other local notables as well as a local MP, known to the initiated as Noddy, because of his association with a well-known local churchman known as Big Ears who was renowned for his unbelievable stupidity and big mouth, that he invariably, put his foot in. The enemy was there in force it seemed, but no doubt it was a case of SunTzu's axiom, 'Stay close to your friends and closer to your enemies.' The drink prices were reasonable and Mark set about circulating and getting smashed. It had been a stressful few weeks, he felt he deserved a break.

When he awoke, it was early, just getting light, his head throbbed, his brain was a brick and a bricklayer was knocking it square and level on a mush of mortar. His outlook was foggy, as though shrouded by net curtains. Beneath all this lay a dreadful gut feeling of foreboding. He had no idea why, but he knew something had gone seriously awry. He stumbled to the toilet bowl to empty his stomach then took a couple of mouthfuls of water from his cupped hand to rinse his mouth. That improved his situation. He lurched to the kitchen in search of coffee with a desperate need first to clear his palate of the taste of vomit, and second his head of the reverberating brick.

He rinsed a dirty cup from the drainer and took more water with a couple of paracetamol. He switched on the percolator and then belched, returning the foul tase of vomit to his mouth but clearing his mind with the thought that he sounded as disgusting as he felt.

It wasn't till 10.30 a.m. that Kevin rang. 'How're you feeling?'

'Like shit.'

'Can't say I'm surprised, telling Noddy he was a homophobe. Asking out loud if he'd got new glasses because he was going blind through 'pulling his pudding', and was he wanting to take us all back to the Victorian era, all crippling women with lace-up corsets and black silk as an affirmation of support of Queen Victoria, split crotch knickers for God knows what, the destruction of the NHS, and a return to backstreet abortions, syphilis, and TB.'

'Jesus, did I say that?'

'You did; don't you remember?'

'The last thing I remember was that little bloke Steve giving me a Happy Pill.'

'You also said, very loudly, or maybe even shouted, quote: Mrs Whitehouse is a narrow-minded old bag who needs to take the lock off her chastity belt and have a bit of fun with some slap and tickle now and then, and stuff the bloody god squad.'

'So, what happened then?'

'Noddy and Big Ears and some of their cronies got up and left, grunting and moaning about being disgusted. Then you got on the stage and started singing and dancing to the words, if not the tune, of Singing in The Rain. Then staggered off the stage and slurring but loud: Goo' nigh' aaw' Ahh don' fee' too goo'. I followed you, but you told me to, Fu'off. I saw you go into your flat and left you to it. I thought you might take a swing at me, so I left you to sort yourself out on your own. It seems it was the right decision. God knows what'll happen now.'

'Did that woman Lydia do or say anything?'

'I was expecting her to be well pissed off, but if anything she appeared to be the opposite, pissing herself laughing.'

'Oh well, Que Sera Sera. All we can do is keep our fingers crossed. If I'm honest, at the moment I couldn't give a shit. I'm just about ready to die.'

With that, Mark put down the phone, had another glass of water and went back to bed.

He crept out of bed at about seven in the evening, still feeling a bit sorry for himself, though he was over the worst of the hangover. He was feeling hungry and the Prince of Wales around the corner did a speciality of cottage pie and gravy on Sundays so he decided to treat himself and fuck the future. Tonight, he'd forget everything for once and then he might at least sleep undisturbed by money worries for at least one night and Please God, feel almost human in the morning, especially as he'd take a good steady walk before turning in at around his normal time.

Mark's body clock was still a mess after working twelve till nine all through the last week, and then putting himself through last night's fiasco. He wasn't looking forward to the coming week, probably another week of nights with aching feet and his stomach not knowing whether it was on its arse or elbow. He wasn't in an optimistic mood. He lived up to his promises to himself and was in bed after a good meal at the pub and a steady hour-long walk, though he still wasn't really tired so he read some silly magazine articles till around midnight.

The alarm woke him at eight. He got up, shaved, showered, and was surprised to discover he felt reasonably normal. He was just preparing to phone the temping agency when the phone rang. He thought it might be Kevin, so he was surprised when he heard Sonny's voice simply saying,

'Can you be at Pinfold Street at 10.30 this morning? We've got an offer of office premises just a couple of doors up from the Duke of Granby pub.'

'What? I'll be there. You are serious, not pissing about?'

'I don't piss about at half eight on a Monday morning,' she growled. 'Get there.'

So off he went. He arrived early and wandered up and down sizing up the area as a possible address for IASIA. It was not ideal, he'd have preferred the legal district, but having said that, he thought the parking situation there would have been a good deal worse than here and obviously it would depend on the building, the offer, and not least upon rental cost and other factors.

Sonny arrived on time with a guy Mark had never seen before. They met outside the Duke of Granby. It looked slightly seedy and unkempt but not unduly so, just pretty much as might be expected given the area. As they exchanged greetings, a beautiful young Asian woman walked demurely past, her sari wafting the smell of curry. Two steps on she slowed, hawked like a navvy and spat in the gutter. They shared expressions of shocked amazement.

After composing themselves, the guy, whom Sonny had not yet introduced, said,

'Could happen anywhere I suppose. Simply different cultural, social and ethnic backgrounds. I wonder where she's from?'

He extended a hand to shake. His hand felt cool but clammy and his grip was a bit sloppy. His rather blotchy face gave an appearance of mediocre health, his hair was thin, wispy and lacklustre, and his voice seemed an octave too high. He was twice Mark's age and struck him as drearily unattractive.

As they shook hands, Mark said, 'Probably a sad story hiding in there somewhere, but then again, maybe not. Appearances aren't everything.'

The guy began walking away from the pub with a slightly shambling gait, apparently assuming they would follow, which they did.

'Who's this twat, Sonny?' asked Mark. 'Where's he from?'

'His name is Malcolm Stimpson and he's from Sankey's estate agents. He's been sent by Lydia. She thought your performance the other night was a riot. Said she wished she'd said some of what you did, herself. She hates Noddy and Big Ears and shares your feelings about Mary Whitehouse. She was glad to see the back of them, but she wasn't impressed with your singing. Not a good idea for you to do that in public, keep it for the bathroom.' Her face wrinkled as she gave a little hissing laugh of disapproval. 'Lydia's not what people anticipate when you get to know her. There are lots of sides to her, so you can never take for granted that she'll do anything you'd expect. She's a professional standard saxophonist, for a start. She thinks twice as fast as those of us she approves of, and she's thinking so far ahead of the rest they think she's a weirdo, which I suppose in a way she is. If she wanted to, she could put on a show that'd make that disco pillock look exactly what he is.'

'I take it you don't think much of him then, but off the scale about her.'

'That's about right. She's so good at everything, it makes you sick. Everything she touches turns to gold.'

Mr Stimpson stopped, turning on his heel. 'This is it, number 45 Pinfold Gate.' He opened the ill-kempt door with a big old-fashioned key and they went in. The room was big and bare but for some odds and ends of rubbish, and everywhere was covered in dust and dirt.

'How long since it was in use?' Mark asked. 'And how long has it been empty?'

'Well, that's one question really,' said Stimpson. 'And the answer is about two years. Well, nearly three.'

'Gift horses and mouths,' said Sonny.

Downstairs there was the shop where they were currently standing, and a further two rooms with a staircase at the back leading to the first floor. Further back, outside, beyond a Victorian blue-bricked yard stood a two-storey workshop-cum-washhouse with heavy double doors and a solid brick floor. In the corner stood a nineteenth-century, brick-built, coal-fired, cast iron-lined boiler that had probably been illegal to use for about a quarter of a century or even before the war. At the side of the main building facing onto the street was a covered entrance wide enough to accommodate a good-sized van and with great heavy

Victorian double doors with iron bars allowing air and light in above head height at the top. The whole place was in a neglected condition, still solid but in desperate need of a fresh coat of paint. As a building, it was beyond his wildest dreams.

Upstairs, the room facing the road was twice as wide as the room below because its floor covered the side alley. A grand marble-surrounded, Art Nouveau tiled fireplace graced the chimney breast on the opposite wall. Everything was filthy and neglected and had not seen occupation for years. Towards the back were a further two rooms between which ran a poorly-lit stairway continuing to an attic floor above. This was clearly designed as servants' quarters with a low ceiling and sloping walls following the contours of the roof. Patches of damp black mould showed on the ancient plaster. The whole was pervaded by an air and odour of dereliction.

Mr Stimpson chattered breezily while sporting a jowly, hangdog, half grin around crooked, yellowed teeth, as they moved through the sad building. They climbed down to the first floor and stopped in the impressive front room which Mark guessed was at least four times, and more, the size of his present accommodation over the Chinese Takeaway.

Stimpson looked at him. 'What do you think?'

'It's way bigger than anything I might want, and it needs a fortune spending on it. It needs a new roof for a start and heating this room alone would cost as much as heating a whole six-roomed terraced house and it's blighted because of the council's plans so I'm told.'

Stimpson smiled. 'That's the point, with vision and determination, the blight could be removed, and the value at least trebled in a stroke. The owners need tenants to begin. That would be the first step towards removing the blight. Tenants who were willing to cope with inconvenience in the early stages of rehabilitation of the building might gain significant benefits in the longer term for having endured discomfort and nuisance in the short term. With respected tenants operating growing businesses, this whole row could be regenerated. This is the sort of policy looked upon with favour by the government, both nationally and locally. These buildings were constructed by people of substance in the early to mid-nineteenth century and represent what some would consider, an important chapter in the history of the city.

'These doors are so wide because this house was built when crinolines were fashionable. The timber used, if you could buy it today, would cost thousands, and the quality would not be as good. The end walls are twice as thick as modern walls. As a result, soundproofing is excellent, added to that is the fact that the rooms are so big and internal insulation can be added with an insignificant loss of space. These houses represent state-of-the-art design by respected architects whose appreciation of sound structural engineering practice was in some ways, better than today because costing was less significant. Builders were more skilled and paid proportionally less.

'This house is halfway to a bloody castle. Regeneration saves money and can be money well spent. If the council can be convinced that this is the right policy to follow, this whole area of the city and this complete street could be an asset rather than a liability. Add to that the elegance, and its historical, design significance and you have a major asset. This is the owner's vision.'

'So, who are the owners?' asked Mark.

'In effect, ownership is syndicated. It's a syndicate representing various areas of expertise that have joined forces to purchase the whole street to see it completely regenerated. The level of investment anticipated is significant. The council has been approached and without any formal agreement, come to accept the proposals based on the expert knowledge of the people involved. My firm represents members of the syndicate. Unofficially you understand, and not to be quoted, some members of the council are willing to make a financial contribution. Legal deniability, to which you, with your legal knowledge might contribute, the creation of trusts, for instance, will be put in place.'

He smiled and nodded towards Mark with widened eyes and an expression that did not quite, include a wink. 'What do you think?' he continued. 'I'll give you some time to consider, and perhaps discuss possibilities with Sonny and Lydia. No rush but if this is to go ahead you need to think in terms of total commitment. I make no secret, it is a major decision and as with any business, there is an element of risk. However, we represent participants who are already committed, and are already successful in business.'

'It looks like a fantastic opportunity, but it's a big step and we need to think about details and discuss how our plans fit with the plans and aims of your syndicate,' replied Mark. 'Give us a couple of days to come to conclusions regarding basic details, and then, all being well, we can work from there.

It took three days to sort out a time when Lydia, Sonny, Kevin and Mark could meet. They had a key to 45 Pinfold Gate provided by Stimpson and they'd agreed to meet there despite its dreadful condition. On arrival, they discovered that some basic cleaning and clearing of rubbish had already been carried out by community payback people whose services Sonny had organised through the council. These tasks were allocated, as punishment and re-education of people convicted of minor offences, in preference to and as a cheaper option, than a short prison sentence or a fine they were often in no position to pay. Mark and company operating as a Charity qualified for this sort of assistance despite being such a young organisation. Sonny, who was involved in the allocation of this sort of work in her role as a council employee, had also managed to acquire an old dining table and some chairs from a different charity that distributed donated furniture to those in desperate need. Ever thoughtful, she had even brought some cups and a big flask of coffee.

Lydia took pride of place sitting at the head of the table. 'Well,' she said, 'here we are at the inaugural meeting of our charity, IASIA. First things first, I propose we elect Sonny as Minutes Secretary. All agreed?'

They all raised their hands.

'Good. Now other officers. Is everybody happy to accept me as Chairperson of the Board of Trustees?'

Again, they all raised their hands.

'I'll take that as unanimous. Next, I suggest Mark take the position of Legal Secretary. Is everyone happy with that?'

Up went the hands. Mark sat feeling slightly bemused at the pace of things, looking dumbfounded with a blank expression of mild shock.

'Last but not least,' continued Lydia, 'I suggest Kevin as Advertising and Promotions Director. Agreed?'

Again, the hands rose obediently.

'Right. Next business. Premises! Here we are. I'll bring you all up to speed as regards this building where we're sitting.' She waved her hands airily. 'We've had approval from the council regarding the erection of scaffolding for replacement of the roof. Sankeys have surveyed the building and pronounced it sound, though with the proviso that all services need complete renewal. New plumbing and electrics will have to be installed. The brewery that owns The Duke of Granby has been contacted. A meeting has been arranged and we have to convince them that our plans for the street will change the nature of the area. The planning department has agreed to the extension of their car park. These changes will bring a better class of customers to the pub and change its function from a local drinks venue to a food and drinks destination. I think they realise that with the right level of investment, upgrading it to a far more profitable venture for a relatively small outlay will be a better commercial option than effectively selling to the council for the simple value of the land. From our point of view, this in itself will contribute to our plans for the area.

'Kevin might be able to help by providing some visuals of the way we envisage the development looking on completion. Would that be possible do you think Kevin?'

'It's not something I've done before but I'll come up with something and you can all have a go at picking it to pieces. Do remember criticism is easy, creation is hard, and I'm a delicate flower.'

'Never mind dear we'll treat you gently,' Sonny said with a smile.

'Jokes are OK,' Lydia interjected, 'but remember we're here on business, there's serious money involved and there's a lot to do. This is no time to mess about!' She was making clear that this was a serious business involving real money some of which was almost certainly hers. She was boss!

She continued, 'We've worked out a plan for this building that will make it more or less the lynch pin of the whole project. We propose to make the ground floor a copy shop. The council have agreed in principle and next week they will carry out the work of connecting three phase electric, in conjunction with the electric company.'

Mark raised his hand. Lydia glanced at him with a frown, 'Yes Mark?'

'Who is going to foot the bill? That's an expensive job.'

'The council has agreed to pay as part of the regeneration scheme.'

'So, has the regeneration scheme been approved?'

'It is approved in principle, though not yet before a full council meeting. It will be. We anticipate that we can generate enough work through the investors' businesses, to turn a profit almost as soon as the plant is up and running. Beyond that, the charity arm will generate a significant amount of work and my business will contribute to that as well.

'We need to sort out some effective accountancy. That's a key issue we need good creative people not necessarily easy to find. Mark, you might be able to look around among any contacts you may have at the university?'

'I'll see what I can do but I can't guarantee anything. Although there's an overlap with law, it's not my speciality. Where is the cash coming from for the printing equipment?' he asked.

'We can get that through the local council's allocation from central government of seed funding for new small businesses.'

'Sounds good to me,' Mark replied.

'No doubt it will sound even better when you hear that it is suggested that both you and Kevin be directors of the new company with responsibility for getting it up and running. You'll presumably have to employ a trained printer at the very least. Also, we will need to come up with a name for the company. We'll leave that to you. All told we estimate the development will create at least ten jobs in the short term, and considerably more over time.

'Right,' Lydia continued, 'First floor where we are sitting. It is proposed we divide this into three self-contained offices with a joint service area containing a basic kitchen and separate toilet area all accessed from a new enclosed staircase totally separate from downstairs. This floor will contain three offices. At the front where we are, will be IASIA. In the centre, the printing services admin, essentially the publicity arm of IASIA. At the rear, PR Services which I will be responsible for. Any questions?' She gave a Cheshire Cat grin.

'What will PR Services do?' Mark asked.

'Surprisingly enough, PR services.' Again the Cheshire Cat grin. 'The new roof we expect to take approximately a fortnight depending on the condition of the underlying structure. That's one of the problems of dealing with old buildings until the basic structure is brought to light, we don't know for sure what we have to deal with. However, we have had surveyors checking and the prognosis is good. Now all we can do is wait and hope. Generally, things are going as well or better than could be expected; everything is moving fast which means we have effectively a fait accompli. Any opposition within the council will be hampered because so much has been accomplished already. I think it's fair to say everything is moving forward better than might have been anticipated, even a couple of weeks ago. The scaffolders begin tomorrow. I think that covers everything I need to say. Are there any questions?'

'What is the intended use of the top floor?' Mark asked.

'Ah, yes, we have something of a quandary there, in that there needs to be a fire escape which would probably require some major works but we are looking at the options. The obvious use is to make it into some sort of living accommodation.'

That was as far as they got, and the meeting finished. Mark was not sure how he was feeling about the way things were going. It was a hell of a lot to take on board and he felt he might be losing control of what, he felt in the end, was his pet project.

Three

Everything was going well, almost too well. Mark was nervous and felt something had to go wrong soon. He'd sorted out some income from a government scheme that helped those setting out to start a business. It was only equivalent to the dole but better than nothing. Now all he could do was wait until the building was usable. There was little progress that could be made beyond preparation towards the time when the building was habitable. Despite all going well, he was feeling slightly depressed after the excitement and exhilaration of everything moving at breakneck speed and now the pace slowing to a crawl. He decided to spend some time at the university library looking at the law relating to company structures and ways and means of avoiding tax.

At the suggestion of Sonny, he joined the Labour Party, the fortunes of which were looking good with the new Blair leadership and the dropping of Clause IV from the manifesto. He was feeling a need for things to do. He spent the day in the university library and concluded that some of the best ways of avoiding tax had already been achieved by becoming a charity and second, by making the organisational structure as opaque as possible by the simple expedient of connecting so many different entities as to make the whole such a puzzle, that for the powers-to-be to unravel it all would be so time consuming as to make it an unenviable and probably unviable task. Creating legal structures of this nature should not be too difficult if an organisation had several owners who swapped ownership on a spasmodic basis.

It was Wednesday at about nine thirty a.m. when he was pretty much at a loose end and the doorbell rang. He opened up to be faced with two big guys whom he thought he recognised. He felt rather threatened.

'Lyd sent us,' said the frontman.

'Would that be Lydia from the Black Boy?'

'Yeah, she said somethin' about collectin' for charity?'

'Oh, she's not spoken to me about it.'

'Yeah, well we work like contractin' on days, doin' it when we're not workin' 'er doors.'

'Ah, I thought I'd seen you before. You're doormen at the Black Boy, is that right?'

'We run security at clubs around the town. Best value, minimum trouble, proper service, deal wi' the Old Bill when things get awkward. We got pull wi' the Old Bill. Minimum trouble all round. They help us out when things get sticky an' we do the same for them when things need dealing with - on the quiet like. Dy' know what I mean? Unofficial nod, nod,' he said with a leer.

'So why are you here?'

'Well, Lyd' says y'need some collectin' doin'. Kinda' security work. Y' know?'

'So, what do you mean? I don't really understand.'

'Bloody 'ell. Do I 'ave to write it on a fuckin' blackboard? The sweatshops round 'ere are usin' illegals, an' if they don't cough up for charity, then we see to it. They get raided by the Old Bill. We give the Bill the nod, an' they make their presence felt "for a drink". Then we go round an' see 'em, let 'em know the score an' if they don't cough up, they get a second visit from the Old Bill wiv' real consequences. See. an', all above board, an' kosher. You an' us go 50-50. Job done. You claim tax back cos it's a charity, receipts the lot, an' everything's above board an' no strings. Everyone's a winner. Even them wot donate get a better place in fuckin' 'eaven. Got it? OK.'

'I see. So, what do you need from me?'

'All we need's identification, what shows we're kosher; got it? You fix us up wi' passes saying 'oo we are an' where we're from an' Bob's yr' uncle. OK. All we need's a receipt book wiv' the charity name on an' some ID, an' we're up an' runnin'. Ow long d'you reckon it'll take to get some paperwork sorted?'

'I'll have to see, and think about it, er but a couple of days should be OK. Give me your number and I'll get back to you. What's your name?'

'I'm Mick and this is Drew. People call me Shanker, and sometimes Mick the Flick.' Mark hardly saw the movement as a flick-knife blade appeared from his hand. 'Don't think too long or Lyd' won't be 'appy,' he said with another leer.

'I'll need passport-type photos. Get me them and we'll see about sorting it out, OK?'

This scenario led Mark to a chain of thought about the law and its grey areas. Demanding money with menaces is a nasty offence. Blackmail carries a maximum prison sentence in the UK of 14 years. Threatening to expose lawbreaking on one level may be regarded as menacing, but it discourages lawbreakers from continuing their illegal activities. It puts everyone in a quandary. It was putting Mark in a specific quandary. Ultimately, he decided he'd risk it. He was desperate for cash and fate had handed him an opportunity to solve his short-term cash worries. Fuck it! He'd take a chance and put his fate in the lap of the Gods. Apart from anything else, he didn't fancy the consequences of getting on the wrong side of either Shanker or Lyd' and perhaps marked even by the Old Bill as a potential problem.

Mark rang Kevin telling him he needed to see him as soon as possible. He said he'd see him on his way home and arrived at about half past five. Mark let him in and put the kettle on.

'So, what's going on now?' Kevin asked.

'You'll never guess how quickly things are getting heavy.'

'Why? How?'

'Two guys came around at lunchtime, Mick and Drew. They're doormen at the Black Boy working for Lydia and apparently running a sideline "collecting for charities." Mick's nickname is Shanker. He carries a flick knife and he hinted that's why he's called Shanker. They'll collect from sweatshops employing illegal labour, threatening police raids if they don't cough up some cash for Shanker's chosen charity.'

'So, what's that got to do with us?'

'*We're* the chosen charity.'

'Oh, I see. That is seriously heavy. So, what's it got to do with me?'

'You're elected to create the identity cards and a receipt book for our own private extortionists, Mick and Drew.'

'So, this really is getting serious. What's the legal definition? Is it demanding money with menaces?'

'This is where the law gets complicated,' Mark replied. 'Collecting for charity is perfectly legal but where do menaces start? Is a dirty look menacing? Is dropping a peanut on the ground and crushing it with a boot menacing? It's all about nuances. If it ever came to court it could be a touch-and-go matter but given Mick and Drew's association with the police, if it got that far there'd be red faces in all sorts of places. All in all, our risks are slimmer than Mick and Drew's and they're connected to the police as is Lydia when it comes to a pinch. When push comes to shove, I don't think we've any option; we're already in too deep. All we can do is keep our mouths shut and plead ignorance.'

'OK. Can't say I like it but if you think it's a risk we have to take, then I suppose I'll just keep my fingers crossed and zip my mouth. I'll just need photos and addresses and we can use the address at Pinfold Gate for IASIA. Shit! So, it's really happening.'

'Who's going to ask questions? It's a bit of a gamble, but nothing ventured nothing gained, and I'm the front man when all's said and done. One thing's for sure, I don't want to fall fowl of Lydia or Shanker and Drew and even the Old Bill. I wouldn't have thought anyone else does.'

They walked down to the Earl of Granby to see what it was like. They decided it was a dump and left to get an Indian carry-out then went on to Kevin's flat, watched a naff film, shared half a bottle of cheap red and went to bed. Their relationship was developing in a most satisfactory fashion, it seemed to Mark.

Kevin had to work, so was up before Mark again. They chatted briefly before Kevin left and Mark told him he'd try to get photos of Mick and Drew, and if he could, he'd ring and meet for lunch in the uni cafeteria. What with one thing and another it took a whole week before they got Mick and Drew's paperwork sorted, but it was only two hours before the shady pair came back with two hundred pounds, half would be for them, with a cut to Lyd. Mark and Kevin's half was a hundred, 50-50 straight split. Kevin and Mark went to the Black Boy to celebrate. Sonny was already there.

'I hear we have a reason to celebrate?' she said.

'Where d'you hear that?' Kevin asked with a crooked smile. 'What are you drinking?'

'OK. I'll have a pink vodka, but let's not get too carried away, we need to take this step by step.'

'What do you mean?'

'We need to think of our next step.'

'So, what d'you think it should be?'

'There's a constituency Labour Party meeting on Wednesday. Mark needs to get there and get his face known. You up for that Mark? You've got a qualification in the practice of law. A law degree is useful in politics and with the right specialisms, law and politics fit like a hand and glove. The Tories think they have the law sown up, but things are changing and there's room for new faces with a slightly different outlook. There are opportunities in education as well as health and safety at work.'

'What do you mean?' Mark asked. 'My degree is in Economic Development.'

'Our economy is moving away from manufacturing into services and probably the biggest service industry, where we lead the world, is education. The technical colleges are becoming universities, and we're earning foreign currency from governments abroad, sending students here for an education. If we can get into the education sector now, then we can begin to make a real input into the national economy. The Labour Party with Tony Blair at the helm is leading the charge in both health and education with the Private Finance Initiative. There are lots of opportunities for those with the wit to take them. The cash from your charity, Mark, is just the beginning. Play your cards right, and the opportunities are almost endless. Lydia is pointing the way. Your next step is to get to the Union Association Rooms on Queen Street, on Wednesday at seven. I'll be there to introduce you. OK?'

Mark began to realise, that in effect, he was being groomed, and he needed to take care to watch his back. It was not difficult to understand that his best defence was knowledge of who was doing what with a view to making money, and whether or not the activities were shady, and other than that, downright crooked. He'd moved into an area where the law was complicated, but there were those going with him who would be every bit as vulnerable as himself, so his biggest protection was that knowledge. It's said possession is nine points of the law and his only real possession was his knowledge of the law and the people who administered it. In Stalin's Russia, Lavrenty Beria the head of the security service, operated on the basis of blackmail and murder; his files were said to cover information involving around 10% of the population. Fear was his stock in trade. The Law is ultimately based on fear of retribution! Mark based his philosophy of life on covering his back. If in doubt, deny and obfuscate. If the worst comes to the worst, hide behind ill health. If the worst came to the worst there were always MA&D's palms that might be crossed and ultimately dumped.

By Wednesday, Mick and Drew had collected another four hundred pounds, two hundred of which were his and Kevin's.

The split this time would be 75-25. Kevins's contribution was more-or-less nil and he had no idea of the cash involved. Mark felt an unaccustomed flush of generosity, and if he were honest, he thought Kevin was bloody lucky to get as much as he gave him. Mark would not be that honourable in the future. Let's face it, he thought, he was the brains, and carried the bulk of the risk and responsibility. He was also a confirmed pragmatist; money was talking and its voice was growing louder.

The next time Mark visited number 45, the roof had been replaced and the building was watertight. The services were connected, and all the major work was on the way to completion; all that was needed now was more or less cosmetic. There were stud walls to go in and plumbing to finish but Mark had decided to lay the foundations for the office of IASIA and made a phone line a priority. Exactly ten days after getting Mick and Drew collecting, Mark received the first call from Smyth and Smyth Solicitors. Darius Evangelou, owner of Smyth and Smyth had agreed to accept him as a trainee on the basis that he worked from Smyth's office in the town one day a week, and they were already working on the case relating to his finger. The connection between Mark and Evangelou had been engineered by Lydia, who already had dealings with Evangelou. Darius had accepted a deal whereby Mark had joined his firm and would receive 10% of any profit from the business he brought in through IASIA.

Mark's office at No1, First floor, 45 Pinfold Gate was just functioning. It must have been the least salubrious in town, furnished with a used office chair, cheap second-hand desk, a filing cabinet and a phone still being shaken with vibration and noise, as well as showered with brick dust from ongoing building work. The client was a man who had been surveying work done on a major building site in the city. He was employed by the architects to make sure that the work done was to a satisfactory standard. He'd been wearing all the required safety clothing when he slipped backwards through a safety gate with a defective latch as he leaned against it. He'd sustained multiple injuries namely a cut on his arm requiring nine stitches, two broken ribs and a broken jaw. He was lucky not to have fallen further because he'd been left hanging in the air when the hood of his jacket snagged on a scaffolding clip. The accident had caused him psychological damage as well as physical. It was a case made for IASIA. They had been recommended by a building workers union through the Labour Party branch and Sonny.

Mark offered to accept the case on the basis of no win, no fee, and the standard 25% of any settlement after an initial consultation. The union rep who'd called him said a donation to funds would be appreciated when the claim was settled. He'd been recommended by Sonny. To say Mark's life was growing more complicated was an understatement. He rang Darius to let him know of the development. Darius instructed him to come to his office in the town on the following Friday as they'd agreed. Mark would spend Friday each week as a trainee at Smyth and Smyth. He'd be earning a pittance through Smyth and Smyth though he would, by agreement, be operating through IASIA and earning that way, with Darius's cognisance, and to a degree, assistance. Mark knew the arrangement might have legal flaws, but he thought it unlikely anyone would complain because qui bono would be at play unless someone decided they wanted to make his or Darius's life difficult. Mark decided all he needed to do was keep his head below the parapet.

Friday, Mark duly arrived at Smyth's office. He was wearing his recently acquired suit bought from a charity shop in the town for the handsome sum of a fiver. It was rather dated but never-the-less good quality and little worn. He was still watching the pennies despite his newfound, relative, wealth. He hated debts that incurred interest and he was determined to pay his off as soon as he possibly could. The future was looking bright, especially compared to six months ago. He'd not met the receptionist before and she greeted him with a curious glance as she introduced herself as Florence. She was tall, dark and thin. She carried herself with the cool self-assurance of one accustomed to respect, not cold or arrogant, but very well-spoken and self-assured. Her desk was covered with post-it notes neatly arranged in between three old-fashioned telephones, one of which she picked up to communicate the news that he had arrived.

She put down the phone and said, 'Mr Evangelou will speak to you now. His office is first on the right through the hallway.'

The whole building exuded an air of well-maintained Victorian solidity with thick carpets, wide, moulded wainscots, elegant ceiling roses, and expensively moulded plaster coving of a past era, when the law was practised only by those of a suitable background, with stiff painful celluloid wing collars, black silk ties and silver-bound, mother-of-pearl collar studs, under heavy dark barathea three-piece suits.

He was not going to be intimidated. He was beginning to make money, and money was what this place was about. Long, indulgent lunches, expensive wines and obsequious service. Mark saw himself looking forward to the time when he brought the arrogant old farts up to date, and he got his slice of lean bloody rump with trimmings.

They had only met once before in the room above the members' bar at the Black Boy with Lydia in attendance when their deal had been agreed with some input from that ubiquitous lady. Now was a formative beginning as to how their relationship would develop. Mark was not defensive, simply wary, observant, and non-committal.

Darius began with, 'You'll be working with our Prakash who deals with private and co-ownership property and property conveyancing. Generally, not the most demanding area of the law, but good for a basic grounding, maybe, for your first year and then perhaps moving on to other areas as we might see fit.'

He picked up a phone and called Prakash, down the corridor, who appeared at the door a few seconds later. Mr Evangelou introduced Mark and he followed Prakash to his office. Mark's initial impression was that Prakash had the air of an unaccomplished has-been. He clearly had some kind of skin complaint that caused white blotches on his already rather unprepossessing countenance. His hair was dyed black to the blackness of greasy soot and coaxed into place with the very same grease. His office was at the far end of the hallway. It was windowless, lit by two fluorescent tubes, embedded in a discoloured white polystyrene-panelled ceiling. Cheap contract carpet covered the floor and Prakash's heavy old industrial steel desk dominated the room. A pair of grey steel-framed cheap office chairs stood before the desk. Another small desk bearing a distinct likeness to Mark's desk at 45 Pinfold occupied a corner. There was an ugly dull greyness about the decor of the room.

His position was clearly to be at the bottom of the pecking order. He'd accept that at present, but straight away he knew he had no intention of letting such a state of affairs continue for any significant length of time!

Four

It was 3.30 pm, Friday. His day had been uninteresting, if not boring. Prakash sparkled like - as Mark's mother would say - a wet fart in a windstorm. His feet were itching to feel the pavement. It was obvious Prakash felt the same, and then everything changed. A young woman walked through the door.

'Hello Prakash,' she said. 'Thought I'd come and see our new trainee. You're the man, Mark isn't it? I'm Sara, Sara Evangelou, the big boss's daughter. So, take care.'

With an archly gleeful smile, she leaned across the desk exposing her cleavage as she thrust her hand forward to shake. At that time, he'd not found many women particularly attractive but something stirred as she grabbed his hand and thrust her chest forward to make it clear she wore no bra. Their hands stayed clasped for a longer moment than necessary. Her hair was cut in a bob. She was not tall, but there was a vivacity about her. She was slim and athletic-looking. She wore tight-fitting, black riding britches accentuating her hips with soft brown leather laced boots and a khaki hacking jacket with a reddish brown big check and a white silk blouse. As she leaned across the desk, the jacket fell open and it became even clearer she wore no bra. He was taken aback, almost shocked. He felt aroused.

She smiled, flicked out her tongue wetting her lips, and said, 'Party tonight, I was twenty-three on Wednesday and my party is tonight. You wanna come and help me celebrate?'

He was unusually dumbstruck, lost for words, and didn't know what to say. He was dumfounded even shocked. He'd seldom felt so uncomfortable. He was in work clothes that were not his real self.

'I'd like to come,' he said, 'but I need to go home and change, and get comfortable.'

'Come as you are. You look awfully respectable, too bloody respectable. You can have a shower and freshen up, dump the jacket, undo the waistcoat and swagger when we get there.' She did the tongue-flick thing again with almost a smirk. 'You can come with me now, Dad won't mind. If it's not done by Friday afternoon, it'll wait till Monday. It's a bit early but he won't bother.'

Mark was normally careful watching his back, but she'd taken him by surprise. He didn't have time to think and he wasn't used to dealing with girls. His sisters were younger and he'd not really had much to do with them. He didn't quite see them as girls. On the spur of the moment, he agreed.

'Ok then, if you're not bothered about my formal attire.'

She giggled and said, 'It's not the clothes I'm after. Come on then.'

He followed her out saying good night to Florence on the way, who gave him a surprised, questioning look as they passed. He followed Sara around to the back of the building where there were four parking spaces and five cars. A red Triumph Spitfire was blocking three other cars. She opened the driver's door and moved forward so that he could open his door and get in. She was a competent driver, pushing her way into the early Friday afternoon traffic with casual panache.

'D'you smoke?' she asked.

'No. I couldn't afford it if I wanted to.'

'D'you want to see if you can roll me one? There's tobacco, weed and papers in the glove compartment.'

'It would be a waste of time. I couldn't do it if I was standing still, let alone sitting here in your car.'

He felt unusually uncomfortable and dominated, even slightly dismayed. The atmosphere did not improve as they sat in silence in slow-moving traffic.

'OK, I guess I'll have to wait till we're home.'

He felt she was laughing at him. That brought mixed feelings, annoyance with an unaccustomed disturbance. Home, it turned out, was a large detached Victorian villa with a gravelled, U-shaped drive to the front and a gravelled driveway to the side. She parked at the side of what appeared to be an annexe that might have been a gatehouse or originally servants' quarters. He got out and followed her through a side door that led into a hallway with stairs leading off to a second floor. He followed her up and she opened the door to a bathroom with a bidet, toilet, bath and shower.

'What d'you fancy, bath or shower? There are towels in the cupboard, take your pick.'

Mark began to relax, looking around to get his bearings, then sat on an ottoman by the wall at the end of the bath to undo his shoelaces and remove his shoes. He tucked his socks into his shoes and was looking for somewhere to hang his jacket but found nothing, laid it on the ottoman and was undoing his shirt when the door opened. It was Sara dressed in nothing but a bathrobe.

'God, don't take all day. Come on, stand up.' It was his mother all over again. He stood as she said, 'I'll help.'

With practised ease, she undid his belt and trouser button and slid down the zip, bending to slide his trousers to his ankles. Then she stood allowing the belt of her robe to drop causing it to fall open allowing him to see she was naked. She looked at his shorts where his burgeoning erection was becoming evident.

'Ah,' she said, 'I thought you might not just be queer.'

She dropped to her knees, pulling down his shorts and taking him into her mouth. It was clear she was no stranger to such activities. She rose up, kissed his lips and forced her tongue into his mouth. He responded with his.

She leaned away from him asking, 'Do you know what 69 is?' as she threw off her bathrobe sat on it and pulled him down towards her. He was bemused by the whole business, but, by now excited. 'I'm six and you're nine,' she said as she lay beside him and took him in her mouth again. She moved her head back saying, 'Well, aren't you going to join in? I hate one-way streets and shaved this morning thinking about you.'

He responded and so did she, indicating pleasure with a high-pitched groan as she took him into her hand. This lasted just a few seconds before she rolled away and then turned back towards him, as he began to rise from lying on his back. She leaned across, placed both hands on his shoulders pushing downwards, then she mounted him and began moving rhythmically back and forth. He pulled her towards him and rolled them over together so he was on top and fully excited. He moved quickly to a climax, then withdrew, and lay beside her exhausted, feeling something close to panic. He'd completely lost control. His first thought was exhaustion. Like the exhaust pipe at the back of her car, switch off the engine slam the doors and fuck off. He laughed nervously at the ridiculousness of what went through his head.

She said in an accusing voice, 'Too fucking quick. I need a smoke.'

'Too fucking quick is right. What are we doing? I hardly know your name. Where's your father?'

'Don't worry about him. He can piss off. He's a bastard.'

She picked up her bathrobe and put it on roughly tying the belt to express her annoyance. 'I'm gonna get a smoke.'

Mark was shocked at what had just taken place. He'd lost control. He went into the shower to try to flush away the reality of what he'd just done, to wash his hands of the responsibility and eliminate his vulnerability.

Sara came back into the room carrying a tobacco tin. She put it on the ottoman, slipped off her bathrobe and stepped into the shower with him. She put her arms on either side of him and slid her hands under his crotch, giggling. He felt undermined again.

She stuck her finger up his arse, asking, 'Is that your' first time?'

'With a woman? Yes.'

'So, how did you first find you were attracted to men?'

'The vicar got me to masturbate him in the vestry before choir, then sucked me off, and I felt kind of ambivalent but a part of me liked it.'

'How old were you?'

'Maybe twelve, thirteen. I'm not sure.'

'And you've got a thing going with Kevin. How serious?'

'How d'you know so much about me?'

'Aha, I was there when you made such a fool of yourself and those arseholes Noddy and Big Ears. So just how serious is the thing with Kevin?'

'I hadn't really thought about it. It's as much a business arrangement as anything, and a bit of fun, kind of convenience, though having said that, it's not the most subtle way of expressing it. We get on OK. How do you know all this? Is anyone likely to come in here?'

He was beginning to think clearly and feeling exposed and ready to be embarrassed, even dropped in deep shit.

'Only my mother and she won't bother us. I do as I want. We don't have much to do with each other. She carries on like a slave to my father. She's weak as piss after ten pints of water. He lets me do as I please until he thinks it's important, and then if he gets mad, he'll hit me. He hits her too. She's like a whipped dog. Says nothing, and fawns over him so he doesn't beat her. He's a bastard.'

She took his hand and placed his fingers on her crotch and sucked at his neck, saying, as she licked his ear, 'Massage me.' She was masturbating him at the front and rubbing her finger over his rectum at the back. 'Am I better than the vicar?'

Mark wasn't sure if he was relaxing, feeling almost drugged. The situation was so far beyond his experience, so bizarre that normal conventions had become irrelevant. He was confused thinking about the vicar too. He didn't really like him although he got Mark aroused.

'Better and worse,' he replied as he massaged her back and front, in return. Their arms were sliding against each other in unison. He'd never felt anything so erotic.

'Hmmm that's nice,' she said. 'You're learning fast. Dry us off and we'll go to bed.'

'What about the party?' he asked.

'This is the party!' she laughed, then started singing, 'It's my party and I'll do what I want to. It's my party an' I'm gonna party. Party-party-party, all over youuuuu.' She sang, and rather well. Then said, 'Just enjoy yourself and party *with* and all over *me,* if you want. We may be dead tomorrow. I'm gonna take you to bed and ride you till you cry for mercy.' Then she gave a little squeal of laughter.

That's what happened. They went to bed and shagged till they fell asleep and then woke, and did it again. Mark had no idea how many times. He was young then and still finding himself. It was morning when he started to slip back into reality, and he was surprised to find himself feeling almost normal. Sara was still asleep. He crept to the bathroom and got dressed. He was thirsty and padded to the kitchen for a drink. He discovered he was in a self-contained flat with a kitchen and sitting room. He imagined it as his. Bloody heaven, no stinks of Chinese food, and quiet. All he could hear was birds twittering outside. He found a coffee perc' and ground coffee. He was in another world. None of your instant crap. This was his first real glimpse of the world he wanted. He'd read "Room at the Top" not that long before and not thought about it at the time, but now he knew for sure what he wanted. He took Sara a coffee. It was seven-thirty, around the time he usually started his day. It had not long been light.

Sara looked at her bedside clock and said, 'Fuck, is that the time? It's still almost night. Where are my smokes? I need a ciggy.'

'Where the fuck am I?' he asked.

'What do you mean?'

'What's the address?'

'Where?'

'Here.'

Groggily, 'Oh, er, The Annexe. Seven, Willow Gardens.'

Bugger the expense, he called a taxi. He wanted out! He was going home to his shit hole over the Chinese. The taxi charged him seven quid!

He didn't usually spend that much in a week on food and drink. He made a coffee, instant crap. That's when it hit him. He was shattered. He went to bed. He awoke when Kevin rang, it was lunchtime.

'I need a catchup. I thought I might see you last night?'

'I had to go to a party. The boss's daughter at the solicitor's where I have to do my training, to get qualified. The day was a pain, the guy who's my mentor is as lively as the dregs of yesterday's lager. He's a bloody wet week. The boss's daughter came in at about three thirty and invited me to her twenty- third birthday party. I could hardly refuse. I got pretty pissed and slept over, a bloody duvet on the floor, I'm still aching. The house is a flaming mansion. The party wasn't great. I wasn't acquainted with anyone and I just got pissed. Had to get a taxi back this morning. Cost me seven bloody quid, and a bit of a hangover, but, I suppose the hair of the dog at the Black Boy's not out of the question. Say two this afternoon, OK?'

'OK, see you there, at two.'

He arrived a couple of minutes late and Kevin was already sitting at a table. Mark asked him if he wanted another but he shook his head, 'No thanks.'

Mark ordered a half of lager and took it to Kevin's table.

'So what's she like the boss's daughter?' Kevin asked.

'Given three guesses, I'd say she's tough as old boots, but I can't say for sure. I could hardly believe she's only twenty-three. I think she's pretty crazy, but I've hardly met her really.'

'What's Evangelou like? There are rumours about him. I've heard he's a bit of a scumbag, bit of a shit.'

'Oh yeah? Where d'you hear that?'

'Not too sure, just y'know talk, gossip, I guess.'

'So, what's the gossip?'

'Well, the word is, he farms his daughter out. What did she seem like? Did she seem screwed up?'

'Hard to say I didn't have that much to do with her really.'

'What were the other people like, the people at the party?'

'Generally speaking, out of our league. Lots of dosh. The house must be worth half a million.'

'What's with the lager, not your usual?'

'Is this the third degree, or what? I've got a little man with a hammer in my head and he's banging my brain from last night, and I thought I'd just have half of lager. Is that OK with you? Am I allowed? You're not my fucking mother, but you're starting to sound like her. Everything I do examined through a bloody magnifying glass. Give me a bit of air. Jesus!'

'OK, OK. I'm just interested in what's going on. I may be a junior partner but I need to know where I stand. I need to know what I'm involved in and how far it goes. We're sailing close to the wind, and I want to know if I've got a life jacket that's all. I've been hearing stuff about Smyth and Smyth and Evangelou.'

'All that matters to either of us, as regards Evangelou and Smyth and Smyth is will my time there get me qualified and allowed to practise? Mostly the Financial Conduct Authority is a load of bollocks because it regulates itself, so can't go wrong. Once my three years are up, as long as I don't get caught with my pants down, I'm in clover and you too. Part of the secret is opacity. The more fog, the more security. I'll be building a smokescreen. Anyone outside will need the tenacity of a leech and the deviousness of a Machiavelli, as well as a giant fat wallet to pay for the time to ferret through the smoke and mirrors.'

'So how would you, as you say, be caught with your pants down?'

'It's really simple. If someone could *prove* that I, or we, had done something blatantly illegal and been caught red-handed, we'd be in trouble. It can't happen because ninety-nine per cent of the time the law is not clear-cut. Proof has to come from the accusers. So far no one can prove we've done anything illegal, simply because we've not. Even Mick and Drew who you could argue, on the basis of extortion, have broken the law, but at the same time the government is aware that there are over a million illegals in this country, and as such they are failing in their duty to protect our borders from foreign incursions. It follows there are lots of questions that would be raised if Mick and Drew were arrested and charged.

'From our point of view, I've made them, MA&D Ltd, a limited company. They're chuffed to bits and think they've hit the Big Time. Any dealings we've had with them have been carried out through our respective companies. That starts to raise all sorts of other legal questions. So just think in terms of us being covered in legal bandages. These bandages act as a kind of armour. They're available to the people who've had either a silver spoon or the wit to work it out for themselves. Just think of yourself as lucky to have met me because I know what's what. Things might get sticky and expensive, but we would not be on our own. That's all I can say, there are risks, but there are risks crossing the road. Get over worrying. We'll cross bridges as we come to them.

'OK. 90% of the battle is confidence, bullshit baffles brains, the squaddies in the army knew what they were talking about. Look after number one equals the first lesson of survival. Darwin only told half the story. The survival of the fittest amongst humanity is based on legal shit as deep as the Grand Canyon and I've got it sussed. You, me, we're safe as can be expected. They catch us and start picking holes, they open a can of worms stretching from here to the moon, and they'll slap the lid back on so quickly they'll get friction burns. The reason is they're all involved up to their necks.

'That sums it up. If I don't get caught, you won't get caught. Next week, if all goes to plan we're going to need you out and about, looking at what we need to buy in the way of printing plant. Lydia will be calling a meeting in the next couple of days, and I have an idea we might be meeting some more of the people involved in her syndicate. All being well, the plot will thicken and the prospects for our wallets will thicken too. You happy now?'

'Sound's good. You want to stay over tonight?'

'Why not? If it's OK with you. I'll be coming to sleep, if that's all right. I'm going to walk off last night's booze and I need some sleep. I've an early start tomorrow. I want to check everything's up to speed at Number 45, and I'm meeting that twat from Sankeys there at nine.'

Five

Mark had to be up early because he needed to catch a bus into town. He was in IASIA's office by eight-thirty. There was still decorating to be done, but the electricity and water were on, and a functioning toilet. They were almost at a point where they could begin to work as a normal business organisation. Cash was still a major problem, but compared to three months earlier, the situation was much more stable. IASIA had a bank account, and the red side of his personal account, though still inadequate, was at least more or less balancing.

Stimpson arrived on time, letting himself into the ground floor. Mark heard him mounting the echoing, uncarpeted, stairs. The door to his office was open though he'd had locks fitted.

The first thing Stimpson said on arrival was, 'Ah, locks. We as landlords will require keys to all the premises.'

Mark's instant instinctive reply would have been, 'Over my dead body.' But he was learning to curb his instincts and answered, 'I'll get another key cut. I'd offer tea or coffee but I'm afraid we're not that organised yet. Only got the electric and water on yesterday, and the kitchen still isn't finished. I'm hoping that'll be done today, at least to the point where we have a sink and drainer fitted.'

'I'll see about giving the builders a push.'

'Good, that would be a real help. The other thing on my mind is some sort of tenancy agreement. It's only verbal at the moment, through Lydia, but I'd like something formal, so we all know where we stand, and there's no argy-bargy.'

'Fair enough. We need to meet with Lydia to sort that out. She's the prime mover in this whole business, at present.'

'You say at present. Is that likely to change?'

'Er. No. No. Just a figure of speech.'

'Good. I'm not too keen on the fact that I've not met all the syndicate members yet, and don't really know where the money is coming from for the whole project. Not that I'm complaining. Everything is coming together better than I could ever have imagined possible, six months ago.'

The more Mark spoke to this man, the less he liked him. He'd trust him like he'd trust a wineglass stem to hold up the Empire State Building. Blotchy, sweaty skin that he could smell, a flabby paunch and watery, pink-rimmed eyes. A physically weak appearance, that he felt would overflow into his psychology. An "Easy way out." person, with the backbone of a worm, and the slipperiness of an eel. He did his best to hide the fact that he felt repugnant at the very idea of being near him, though he felt the real atmosphere between them was as congenial as it would have been, between him and a drunk who'd just puked all down him. To say he was glad to see him go, was more than an understatement.

He spoke to the builders' foreman who told him that if he got a kettle and a teapot, there'd be a brew on all day. He set off for the charity shop that sold used household electrical goods.

Wednesday, that same week, the office kettle had been hot all day. At 7.30 in the evening, he was taking minutes at the Labour Party constituency meeting. There were a few old 1950s and 60s Stalinists trying to deflect the new world. The old world was taking back the reins in just the same way as it had been managed in Franco's Spain when the slippery old fascist died. The new elite of canny politicians and behind-the-scenes entrepreneurs joined forces to hoodwink Joe Soap or Jose Jabon, as in days gone by when all was an agrarian idyl, according to some 19th Century English poets. The left moved to the right, and the right moved left.

Everyone, even most Israelis, accepted that past mayhem and atrocities were best forgotten. Digging up the bodies and reburying them in more sanctified places, made for closure. Short memories were the best panacea for all concerned, and a new bright world beckoned after a new economic strategy was inaugurated following WWII. The consumer society was born. Money was aplenty, and corruption debts, and bankruptcy a side issue, inflation nibbled away at real value. But all was well with the world as both rich and poor in the West saw their wealth grow. So long as his grew fast, Mark didn't give a shit. Scruples? Expensive nonsense. Morals a waste of time, even a bit of a joke. Sex is fun or why did they make condoms you hardly knew you were wearing? Do we need babies that suck milk, and maybe later, blood? No chance. He'd drink tea or better champagne with the new left, PFI and print machines churning out cash from charities, local papers, or any other money tree. His father might or might not be proud, but he'd taken an easy way out and was six feet under by the time Mark was fourteen years old, and playing with the vicar, who was playing with him.

Bygones were bygones so who was Mark to be fussy? Sonny was the chairperson and understood the way the wind was blowing. Mark was happy to follow in her wake, a balmy breeze blowing in their favour. Regeneration was the watchword and the PM put regeneration cash on the table. Mark was gonna have his share, come what may. It was agreed that they would support the council in its bid for funding for a small printing plant to be installed at the newly refurbished community regeneration project centred at 45 Pinfold Gate. The facility would provide training for under privileged young people to encourage community cohesion through the publishing of community newspapers. The project would also provide a source of publicity for other, deserving community facilities.

Nutters were being released from mental hospitals to 'Care in the Community' another source of cash for those 'In the Know.' The drug trade was booming: speed, weed, morphine and cocaine, used throughout the war, now found their way onto the black market and a whole new criminal class was developing as a result. The law was having trouble coping, maybe not really understanding the seriousness of the problem or perhaps making too much money to bother.

Now Mark was beginning to understand why he had not yet met all the members of Lydia's syndicate. He wasn't the only one sailing close to the wind. He saw that what they needed now was the limit on the level of expenditure, that they might be allowed. He needed to get a clear picture of the amount that might be required to finance a small but fully self-contained printing plant. He'd get Kevin to draw up a plan for the machinery required, and come up with a ballpark figure of costs. Things were going to be quieter for a while. There would be a lull in activity, while they waited for the printing machinery to be, acquired, installed, and commissioned.

He'd been in contact with Shanker and Drew who told him they were running short of targets. That source of income was facing a drought. The case for the loss of the first digit of his left-hand index finger was moving slowly. He had decided to carry out the work himself. He had a law degree and making the claim would be a good experience. He knew that the going rate for such an injury might be in the region of three thousand pounds. There was the added loss of the quality of his degree and future earning capacity, quite how much that might be valued at was much more of a moot question. He was determined to push the Pie Co to the limit.

The PTSD angle had real potential. He was looking at ways he could present evidence of psychological trauma. He would get the uni nurse to write a letter. Whether or not he'd offer her cash for her trouble, he'd approach with great circumspection. He'd also look at the cost of an expert witness. At the same time, he could pick the brains of his lacklustre mentor at Smyth and Smyth. On a visit to the charity shops, he'd met with a fellow worker at the Pie Co. He worked there as a full-time employee and had broken all four fingers of his left hand when a hydraulically operated guard had malfunctioned and smashed his fingers. He had been unable to work for several weeks. They chatted and he was in the process of making a claim through a solicitor who would charge 25% of winnings. Mark convinced him he could do the work for 10% of any settlement. He could do it cheaply because he could run their two cases together. This would put the Pie Co in a difficult position. Two cases in tandem would not look good in the press, or with insurers. They might at the same time push the point that two cases running at the same time might reflect poorly on the Pie Co's health and safety provision, implying that the quality of their products might be thrown into question as well if management culture was poor.

He decided to concentrate the next few days on chasing these claims aiming for an out-of-court settlement, *significantly* above the norm. He was really beginning to get the hang of legal extortion. He rang the Pie Factory to discover the identity of their solicitors and insurers. He had little doubt they'd be more experienced than himself, but they certainly were not going to be as committed. Now he had two cases, the payout would almost certainly be bigger simply because the Company's insurance bill was likely to rise significantly unless they settled directly from their own coffers. They might even decide to pay over the odds because future insurance bills were likely to be a good deal higher. The whole business, like so much relating to the law, was little different to a lottery, where judgements and settlements were reached on a system based on little more than the throw of a dice.

Mark rang Kevin to let him know he needed to speak to him about the print plant and suggested he collect a carryout meal. Kevin could choose what it would be, Indian, Mexican or Thai, anything but Chinese, just the smell of his room put him off that. Kevin chose Mexican, which suited Mark, it would make a nice change. Mark also told Kevin that on the advice of Sonny, he was putting himself up for a seat on the local council. The first rung of the political ladder. He went to Kevin's flat with the takeaway to get some idea of the cost of the machinery they needed before they were up and running and printing. There were things involved that he'd not even considered. A guillotine for a start, to cut up reams of paper, and a folding machine as well as the obvious printing machine itself, and a plate maker, computers and software to feed the platemaker.

It was not going to be cheap even if they bought second-hand, and council projects do not usually do that. There were so many options, that it made the whole business difficult but they had decided to put together a package that would be ideal and disregarding cost, take a punt and see what the response was.

Mark was staggered at the conclusion they reached. Whichever way they looked at it, the bill was going to run to over £75,000 when the average three-bed semi house would cost around £20,000, but they'd agreed that that's the sort of money they were looking at. His heart sank, he did not think there was any way their syndicate or the council would be prepared to trust them with that amount of cash. Despite that, they went ahead and presented their estimates to Lydia.

Now Mark set to, aiming to sort out the best deal he could manage with the Pie Company. He'd talked to the nurse at the Uni and she'd provided him with a succinct letter pointing out that the stress and problems relating to the damage to his finger had caused common symptoms of PTSD, insomnia and a diminished ability to concentrate. She had contacted his departmental head and asked if there was evidence of a decline in the quality of his work and exam results that indicated a failure to reach expected standards after the damage to his finger. He had written to confirm that Mark's results had failed to reach expectations that had been estimated at a level of at least a two-two degree.

Added to this was a statement from the chief engineer of the Pie Company, at the time, who had resigned after the accidents. He maintained he had left as a result of insufficient maintenance staff to meet satisfactory standards required to reach the safety levels required in a modern factory. He had left the company's employment for this reason because he saw that he was being unfairly treated in that he would be bearing the responsibility for health and safety at the company when he had insufficient resources to carry out the work properly. In his words, 'I was just being taken for a Patsy. I could see it coming. Someone was gonna cop it.'

Armed with this evidence, Mark arranged to meet with the company's solicitor the day after they came up with the estimates for the print plant. He had to travel to London to see the man at his office. More expense, but he was determined that they would pay. He had learned from various people in the legal community that it was normal to ask for double the amount you were willing to accept and no less than 50% of your original demand. He had concluded that the two cases brought as one were worth at least £20,000 thousand each. So, he set his initial demand at £40,000 which he thought was suitably exorbitant even though he might use the threat of going to the media to smear the reputation of the Pie Co.

The solicitor he was to meet was called Giles Portman-Styles. He'd spoken to him on the phone and needless to say he had a terribly expensive accent. Mark took that as evidence he was expensive to employ, but that did not mean he was a tough negotiator. He intended to stick at £30,000. Take it or leave it. If he left it, he'd meet him in court. The receptionist asked if Mark would like a coffee while he waited. He was nearly twenty minutes early and she said that Mr Portman-Styles had not yet arrived. His appointment was for 9.20 am. If his negotiating skills were as good as his timekeeping, he was about to get a thrashing. Mark sat and drank their coffee. Good expensive fresh ground, while he waited for his tardy opponent. Mark finally got to meet Portman-Styles at 9.30. He was 10 minutes late and Mark vowed to himself that Portman-Styles's tardiness would cost him another thousand in the settlement. He'd stick at £31,000. Portman-Styles apologised for being late. Mark said nothing about having travelled a hundred miles and still managed to be early. He made his point by being blunt,

'I was here on time for the business, can we get on with it?'

'Right, what sort of settlement are you looking for?'

'£41,000.'

Portman-Styles took a gulp of expensive ground coffee and Mark could see he was close to spluttering. Mark almost laughed when the reply came.

'What is your Christian name, Mr Spivey?'

'Mark,' he replied, 'and the settlement I'm looking for is £41,000.'

Portman-Syles gulped another mouthful.

It struck Mark at the time that had he been Styles's secretary, he'd have offered to get her boss a double espresso!

'You think that is a realistic figure?'

Mark said. 'I'm willing to haggle, but it seems to me, this is no ordinary case. For a start, there are two claimants, both with very real claims. In a normal situation, each of those claims might be expected to settle for around £20,000. For actual physical damage, approximately £8,000. Then the pain and suffering aspect, another £6,000. Then long-term damage, both mental and physical.' Mark held up his stunted finger. 'Every time I see this, I get annoyed. I get angry, my blood boils because it was totally unnecessary. The Pie Co were cutting corners and I paid the price, and now I want every penny I can get in recompense for their failure to pay due attention to their employee's welfare. Add to that the fact that Mr Smith feels the same. He is still suffering because he cannot work, and has a baby on the way, all of which is making his life far more difficult than it needs to be, all as a consequence of the Pie Co's lack of proper care and attention.

'I think it only reasonable that the settlement be punitive, to ensure that in future they act more responsibly. As a result, under normal circumstances, when we might expect a settlement of around £20,000 each including an extra £3,000 for costs above and beyond a simple payment for essentially bad luck. Then £20,000 each would seem perfectly reasonable. I'm sure you can do nothing but agree.'

He coughed, looked at his coffee cup, picked it up and attempted to take another mouthful but it was empty, then said, trying to hide his discomfort,

'So, you've just made a case for a settlement of £40,000 for the two cases, which I would regard as totally unrealistic.'

'Yes,' replied Mark, 'but here we are looking at two cases combined into one which adds an unusual aspect to the case. It's moving towards a mass claim situation, which puts the company in a far weaker and more awkward position, showing a clear lack of attention paid to the welfare of their employees and even possibly their customers. Let me ask, tell me, did anyone eat the end of my finger?'

The blood drained from Portman-Styles's face. He picked up his cup, only to realise for the second time, it was empty. Putting it down, he looked directly at Mark and asked,

'So what is the lowest figure you'll be prepared to accept?'

'£36,000 for the pair.'

'I'll need to take this back to the company. I'll be telling them this is unrealistic and if this is your last word, we'll be heading towards court, which obviously changes everything.'

'So you have a clear picture of my position. I'll leave it to you to discover the position of the Pie Co.'

On that note, Mark headed home. He'd put the fear of God into Portman-Styles. He'd not expected such a truculent approach to negotiations. Mark was happy. The meeting had gone much as he'd hoped. Portman-Styles had expected to come to a quick agreement, and Mark had gone to his office in a pugnacious mood spoiling for a fight. Portman-Styles now knew he was facing a battle. Mark could not have made it clearer, he had plenty of ammunition and fully intended to use every last bullet, with no quarter given. In the school Mark came from, a fight was a fight, and as expressed in the vernacular, a real fight meant, kick bollock, and bite.

When he arrived home, there was post-it note on his phone "call Lydia". He rang her immediately.

'You're making waves,' she said.

'Am I allowed to say, good?'

'I've had a call from Mr Dolby who is chairman of the board of the Pie Factory. He's not happy about your approach to Mr Portman-Styles at Fleishman Grabalov. He's looking to negotiate an out-of-court settlement and is unhappy about your blunt line of attack. He's contacted Darius at Smyth and Smyth. You should have talked to Darius before going bull at a gate.'

'That's all very well, but not many law students working on a night shift lose a chunk of their finger in a mincing machine without proper guards. Followed by another regular employee getting his hand crushed in another improperly guarded machine, who the law student happened to pick up as a client. So, what do we know about Darius and Portman-Styles?' Mark asked.

'Apparently, they have "A good working relationship." We can only assume they work together on a "You scratch my back" basis. I have an on-going relationship with Darius and none of us wants to upset any apple-carts. You need to speak to Darius before you do anything else. OK? Call him in the morning, and go easy. All right?'

Mark needed to speak to Darius about the surveyor case, anyway. Monday morning and he was back at Smyth and Smyth chatting to Florence while he waited to see Darius. After exchanging pleasantries, she said with a look expressing approval,

'Well, you seem to be finding your feet at an uncommon pace.'

'I didn't spend three years working for a law degree to be overawed by actually practising. No doubt I'll make mistakes, but there's no better way of learning how to avoid mistakes than by making them. It may be a matter of doing it the hard way, but it's got to be the fastest. My mother has always said I'm in too much of a hurry.' He held up his stunted finger.

A phone rang on the desk. She picked up and nodded to him.

'Darius is ready for you now.'

He waved his finger stump saying, 'Quick but not always comfortable.'

She pulled an Ooh Ahh face, then smiled. Mark preferred talking to her than to Darius. He was not particularly looking forward to this interview, but it put him on his mettle. He would be careful, watching his back. He had a feeling Darius would be wanting his pound of flesh. Mark knocked and went into his office. He smiled as he said,

'Good morning Mark. How's it going, keeping busy? I hear you're making an impression.'

'Good or bad?'

'I suppose you might say a bit of both.'

'I'm an optimist, so shall we start with the good?'

'Well, first and foremost you are doing extremely well showing initiative and flair for our sort of work. If you are truly going to make a success, we need a benchmark to define success. Ultimately it has to be measured in monetary terms from a business point of view. The law is a business, but it is more than that. You are already showing that you will turn a profit for our business, though you do need to display perhaps a little more circumspection and forethought. You are rather impulsive. You have shown initiative in bringing in business but you need to be more interactive within our organisation, more communicative, you understand?'

'I think you are saying I need to inform my mentors about what I'm proposing to do and get feedback before acting?'

'I couldn't have put it better myself. There are procedures and processes within the system that make it work. Your three years of training will enable you to get a good grounding in what these procedures are, and why we adhere to them. As your training progresses, you will begin to understand.'

'I think I'm beginning to understand already, but could you be more explicit?'

'If I say it doesn't do to tread on people's toes, does that begin to make it clearer?'

'Essentially you mean I was rather blunt, even rough with Mr Portman-Styles because in some cases you have common interests. Would that sum it up?'

'Well, I suppose, that in a very broad nutshell, would express what I'm trying to say. We are all in the same business, and it is competitive, but, and it's a big BUT, we do not want to be cutting off our noses to spite our faces, as you might say. Ultimately, we need to look towards our opponents' point of view and consider ourselves in their position, because the time will almost inevitably come when we find ourselves in *their* situation.'

'I agree that I have a tendency to be direct even blunt but, I find it difficult not to be. I say what I mean and mean what I say. If you need me to handle Portman-Styles with kid gloves because you have an ongoing business relationship with him, then it seems to me that the three of us need to get together and come to a conclusion we can all live with. Given that I am representing myself, you can't really expect me not to take off the gloves and fight with all the ammunition in my arsenal, and let's face it I have plenty. So where do we go from here?'

'I understand your point of view, I'll have a word with Giles and see if we can't work something out. One thing is sure, it's in no one's interest to go to court. Any value that is in the case, would be thrown away in costs: that is the reason just 2% of these cases come to court, people get bloody-minded and forget what the argument is about. Ultimately, it is the settlement value to all concerned. Think about that, and I'll see what I can do.'

Mark knew that the truth of the matter was they were at an impasse. Darius had to make a choice, and Mark had to gamble on the fact that Darius would not take measures to control him. Mark popped in to see Prakash, who said,

'Didn't take long for you to start ruffling feathers.'

'Can't make an omelette without breaking eggs.'

'You enjoy an argument and have an appetite for trouble. You're an extremist. You will either do extremely well in this business or fail miserably.'

Mark thought typical boring old fart, all the get-up and go of a wet sponge.

'I have no intention of failing. There are a lot of opportunities at the moment. I'll see you on Friday.'

Mark went back to 45 Pinfold Street. The first thing he did was try to ring Lydia to discover if there was anything he should know about what was going on. She either was not around or simply not answering. Mark tried Sonny. She answered,

'Come to the Black Boy at six. Can't talk now.'

Mark called the main office of the building firm where the surveying accident occurred and explained to the receptionist that he was representing the firm dealing with the claim relating to the surveyor falling through the scaffold gate.

'Ah, Mr Evangelou?' she said.

'No, I'm Mr Spivey. I work for Mr Evangelou. I'm in charge of the case.'

'Oh sorry, I was under the impression that was Mr Evangelou.'

'Mr Evangelou is my superior but I'm dealing with the case.'

'I'll put you through to Mr Tillotson.'

'Thank you.'

'Tillotson speaking.'

'Good morning, it's Mark Spivey here of Smyth and Smyth. I'm dealing with the case of the surveyor, Mr Carter, who was injured in an accident at your site at Bloggs Bottom.'

'I've been speaking to Mr Evangelou regarding that. I thought he was dealing with it?'

'I don't know exactly what Mr Evangelou said to you, Mr Tillotson, but although Smyth and Smyth are the company dealing with the case, the client is mine and although Mr Evangelou controls Smyth and Smyth, it is I who is dealing with this client and consequently, although I may be a trainee, I do have a degree in law and have every right to know what is going on with the case, because ultimately, the client is mine.'

In his mind, although he was putting his traineeship in jeopardy, he was damned if he was going be pushed around by anyone, boss or no. The client was his, and he was going to work to get the maximum settlement, no matter what Evangelou was setting out to do with the builder and his insurance. He was fairly certain there was some sort of collusion going on, otherwise, why was he being cut out from knowing what was happening? Follow the money, Latin, "Cui Bono", "Who is the criminal who gains?" One way or another he'd find out what was going on! The first thing to do was find out which insurance company was insuring Tillotsons Builders Ltd and exactly what their policy covered.

Mark had already spoken to Mr Carter who two months after the accident was still unable to work, and ascertained that Tillotsons were liable because they were the main contractor. However, when the claim was settled they could then claim against the scaffolding firm, whose equipment was at fault. The scaffolders were a small outfit that was already in receivership when employed by Tillotsons. Obviously, Mr Carter an independent contractor to Tillotsons knew nothing in this regard. As a result, Tillotsons would bear first responsibility for the claim and their insurance premiums would be liable to a prohibitive increase. Mark needed another interview with Mr Evangelou! Whose side was he on? The claimant Mr Carter or Tillotsons, or even Tillotson's insurers? The case could even go back as far as Carter's insurers. The law in a case such as this was a jungle. Mark wanted to play Tarzan, but Cui bono, which was the most lucrative route for Mark to take?

Mark made a cup of tea and took a wander around No 45. He needed to let his subconscious do some thinking for him, and then let things take their course. The builders and decorators were still working, but the whole place was beginning to look totally different from the day he first saw it. For the most part, all structural elements were finished. The main room on his floor was starting to reach the point where it was returning to its former glory. The great fireplace was looking as imposing as originally intended. The great heavy doors and wide wainscoting spoke of their rich old ancestry, although still in undercoat. It still smelt of paint and plaster but was so much more pleasant than the room he was living in over the disgusting Chinese takeaway. Their future waiting room would create the sort of impression they could not have dreamed of a year ago. It would give Smyth and Smyth a run for its money. This was a part of town on the up.

Mark left the office at lunchtime feeling buoyant and went for a pub lunch in town, then took a tour of the charity shops. He bought a black, lightweight fine merino wool, roll-neck sweater by a West End manufacturer, a crew neck sweater, also black, to wear over the roll-neck, and some mid-grey winter weight slacks. Bought new at main street retail outlets he guessed the total value to be around £100. He paid £15 for the lot, a good afternoon's shopping and relaxing. He was pleased with himself.

He went back to his smelly room and changed into his new clothes then made his way to meet Sonny at the Black Boy. All being well, his shopping days at charity shops would soon be over but in the meantime, he felt more comfortable in his new outfit than he had done for some time with his tattered, old student wardrobe.

By the time Sonny arrived, he was on his second Vodka Red Bull and feeling more relaxed than ever. She soon changed that.

'What are you drinking?' he asked.

'Pint of Heineken, thanks.'

He got another Red Bull and her pint. 'So, what's the news?' he asked.

'Bad news first?'

'Go on.'

'Evangelou is going to give you the elbow. He's not happy with you giving him ultimatums.'

'How is it you know before me?'

'Lydia got you the traineeship, and he told her before telling you.'

'OK, but there's good news too?'

'There's a traineeship going at the council and you're a prime candidate because you're the Minutes Secretary for the local constituency of the party in power. If you can't be rich, be lucky. Ducky.'

'It's nice to know I have friends as well as enemies.'

'Shall we sort out your application now?'

'One question first. What do you and Lydia know about the Carter case?'

'So, you've guessed. Well, we got you the business and wouldn't mind a slice of the action.'

'Fair comment, what were you thinking?'

'Let's not count our chickens. We've had some advice but it's a bit of a lottery, so we're told. We need to see the result but a reasonable estimate seems to be a total somewhere around the £50,000 mark. IASIA's slice, £12,500. The best way to deal with the share-out would be to talk to an accountant. Lydia has contact with a competent man. The way things are going, we'll be needing someone soon anyway. By the way, the council has approved the costings for the print plant.'

She laughed as his jaw dropped. He hugged her and kissed her cheek. He was getting to know her quirky sense of humour and the pleasure she got from understatement.

'Steady, steady,' she laughed some more as she hugged him back and grabbed his bum with her left hand then squeezed his balls with her right hard enough to make his eyes water. She laughed even louder as he yelped.

He was still gasping and only just managed to say, 'This calls for a celebration, you bloody bugger.'

He walked unsteadily to the bar to order champagne! Just as he reached the bar, Kevin arrived.

'We're celebrating,' said Mark. 'The council finance committee has approved our application for funding for the print shop. We're in business!'

They shook hands and hugged.

***

God knew what time he got to bed. Lydia came with her slave, Don, who brought some coke. They went upstairs. The next morning it struck him coke would be the death of him if he wasn't careful. It was a hell of an evening but God he was paying the price now. As he looked at himself in the mirror while shaving, he realised he even looked older.

That night, he met Gunter who'd fled East Germany with his girlfriend Mila, when the wall came down. Mark never found out quite why, and he didn't care, but he liked him and he had a feeling he was a good guy. It turned out he was a good printer too, and it wasn't long before he became a partner. He was a slick trombone player who played jazz with Lydia, and Mila who played electric violin. They played as they celebrated. It was a wild night he knew he'd never forget.

That night his life changed for good. It was mind-bending! He was a bit shocked when Sara turned up as well, they just nodded as though they were just casual acquaintances. He felt odd about it but didn't give a damn. He was on a high. They'd got the cash. Now they had to get stuck in and use it. He could not believe his luck, but he set to work with Kevin. They negotiated hard and got the printing machine, a two-colour B2 (That's a bit bigger than four A4s) Free! Brand new, from a top German manufacturer. FREE for a £70,000 machine no less, but then he discovered it was £14,000 less than book because it was free for one year, after which re-payments would be around £7,000 per year excluding interest after purchase tax had expired. German manufacturers had found a way around the UK purchase tax. There's always a way if you look hard enough. A good chunk of the rest of the equipment came on the same basis.

It pays to understand the law! It did not take even two weeks before they were in limited production. The first item they produced was a beg — 'Wash my mouth out!' he thought - an *appeal* for funds to help support those unfortunates who had suffered through injuries to themselves or associates as a result of industrial activity; final arbitration for injuries either psychological or physical, and their dependents, as measured under capitalism in terms of CASH! Just like the song that was in the hit parade that week, "Give me money, that's what I want. Your love gives me thrills, but that don't pay no bills. Give me money, that's what I want!"

That week he did some more footslogging around the city, dishing out their first attempt at a flyer for IASIA around affluent areas where some residents might feel conscience-stricken enough to 'give us a handout' like in the 1930's US depression song "Hallelujah I'm a Bum". So, hopefully, he might get a return this time instead of just wet, aching feet and the feeling that he *was* a bum.

Lydia came in a couple of days later with the copy for a "Trade Magazine." It turned out to be mainly contacts for ladies of the night. Dare he say like herself. Who was he to judge others? We all have our place in society, chosen or imposed. He did have to say Mrs Whitehouse was welcome to her sanctimonious chastity belt. MA&D Ltd was settling down to provide a more reliable, steady flow after the initial surge, and the printing element of the business was also coming on stream through the copy shop, which Kevin and he had named "Hot Plate Press & Copy Ltd". When the injury settlements came to fruition, his financial situation might begin to look rather better than simply stable. He began to worry about hubris. Pride comes before a fall. He knew he needed to tread carefully or he might "Do a Noddy" and open his mouth, only to put his foot in it."

He'd sat down with Sonny and put together his application for the traineeship at the council. He needed to be wary of over-confidence; after such a spate of success and good luck, he needed to be confident, but circumspect, as Mr Evangelou would express it!

In the meantime, he needed to work to get everything up and running at the print plant. Bills were coming in now and they had to be paid. They had the bank account. In those days opening an account was easy but borrowing was not. The Bank of England was still operated by the government. It still belonged to everybody. The so-called High Street Banks would lend only if they were more-or-less certain it would be paid back - with interest, and everything was done through the bank manager who was "honest", boring, had a reasonable conventional education and the imagination of a concrete slab. His family was middle class and were happy with their lot. Bank managers were conservative with a lower case "c". To Mark, they were little tin gods like the vicar who deplored sodomy from the pulpit and practised it in the vestry.

He went cap in hand to the bank and explained the situation regarding IASIA, and the council funding for the project. He was suitably obsequious. He showed the manager his stunted finger and explained about his degree and the fact that he was fighting the case against the Pie Co that would ultimately pay a significant sum into his personal account and would contribute towards providing some future security for the bank's cash. He explained how they needed operating capital for consumables while they got things up and running and started generating capital. The manager agreed to an initial short-term (one year) loan to be drawn upon as and when required to a maximum of £1,000 at a yearly rate of 8%. It would have to do. He was a tight-fisted bastard, but it would allow them to keep day-to-day running costs in their hands and separate certain elements of the business from the overall business controlled by the council.

The council, he was already beginning to learn, was pretty casual with cash by normal standards, for the simple reason that it was not theirs. He was tending to come to the same conclusion regarding their solicitors. They did not fight the way he would, because it did not matter too much, one way or the other, whether they won or lost. The real legal talent, for the most part, went elsewhere where the nitty-gritty law was practised with all daggers drawn unless it was day-to-day drudgery of the nature of family work, conveyancing and the like.

He breezed through the interview for the traineeship without problems because he had contacts on the inside, as well as having spent a few months at Smyth and Smyth. Consequently, he already had a grounding in the real world of solicitors in private practice, an advantage against those who had always worked in the public sector, unless they were willing to bend the rules without getting caught.

They had their first operational control meeting of the directors of IASIA at Number 45. The first thing they did was to make Gunter up to a director. He was already producing paying work for Lydia and laughed wholeheartedly when he saw what was being printed on machines financed by the council. The consumables were paid for by IASIA which was paying a peppercorn rent to the council for the premises. The machines ran when direct council employees were still in bed, and no one was the wiser! As far as Mark could see the level of control exercised by the council over peripheral community-operated organisations such as the Community Print Shop, as the committee agreed it should be called, was quite minimal.

Mark was waiting for a suitable moment to slip the idea to Sonny that he might take one of the flats on the top floor of No

45. Everything was new, fresh and clean and there would be no sharing the kitchen, plus the rent was only marginally higher than what he was already paying for his one stinking room. Added to that was the fact that the heating was included in the rent.

IASIA's business was beginning to stabilise. When they could afford to allocate a regular proportion of income to promotion, they could come up with a reasonable prediction of income and an amount that could be allocated to actual charity work which at this early stage would not be much. Until they achieved this objective, they were guessing and forced to manipulate activities and accounting procedures to fulfil their legal obligations as a charity.

Charities could be run in various ways and the law governing what they did was flexible. The Charities Commission was just a gravy train for the commissioners, as The Audit Office had pointed out. So, thank heaven for the Commissioners' lackadaisical performance. Sources of IASIA's income might be regarded as questionable in law. The production of material advertising Lydia's services providing income for a charity was a case in point. Charities running shops and using the profits from sales of donated goods and voluntary labour were fine. Hmm! However, using the services of an advertising agency to bring in donations was moving towards a grey area.

By printing for Lydia's enterprise, IASIA was sailing very close to the wind. It was a problem. Problems were made to be solved and in this case, the solution was simple, another company insulating one part of the organisation from the rest. They started another company, MSP Promotions Ltd. to deal with any work that might be an embarrassment to a charity. The same people might do the work, on the same machines, in the same buildings, and be paid for it by the same customer, but they would be wearing different hats. It sounds silly but that's the way the law works. It was almost as creative as a Leonardo painting.

The mailing arm of IASIA was coming on stream too, and Mark decided to operate that as part of MSP so that it might generate income in its own right by selling delivery services to other firms wanting one-off leaflet distribution. He called the vicar at the local church who he knew spent some time delivering the church magazine himself. They arranged to meet at the Black Boy. He was not worried by its reputation as a gay club, which Mark thought was surprising, but obviously, times were changing. They introduced themselves and chatted and he made no secret of the fact that he was gay which was fine by Mark because he didn't fancy him anyway. They understood one another straight away. Mark liked them young, and he guessed Father Timothy was in his late forties. Timothy had two children, so he said, so he, like Mark, could play both ways. In essence, he got the idea that Tim's marriage was effectively a business arrangement.

They chatted about their relationships and how they worked. Tim told him that he and his wife managed to co-operate bringing up their children, by compartmentalising their existences. The truth is they fitted into a society where the love stories of poets and dreamers were pie in the sky. Reality is that people who live in close proximity almost invariably fall out on occasion, and a way through that for people like him and Timothy was through, what these days we know as an open relationship. They lived together as a kind of convenience, working and living as a couple, but also with lives segregated into compartments, together but apart.

At present, Mark's partner was for the most part Kevin, but they were both aware that it was a temporary arrangement. Mark's life was a cross between a helter-skelter and a merry-go-round. He'd seen Sara again and the sight had caused excitement and visions. He wanted to see and touch her and have her touch him with passion. He sometimes thought he was a mess psychologically but at other times, he felt that he was so much more alive than most people whose flat dreary lives, and flat dreary emotions, as well as second-rate sexuality seemed sad and banal.

Timothy told him that he had a working relationship with the Imam of a local mosque, Abdhalla who was also gay. In his own words, he said,

'He's a useful guy to know. He's got access to a source of top-quality Moroccan dope at excellent prices and might have access to good-quality coke too, if you're interested in a bulk buy. He's also in contact with quite a few attractive young men.'

Mark told Tim he did not smoke, making himself feel really righteous.

'Ah, you can always bake a cake!' Tim laughed. 'I'm having a private party in conjunction with a friend next week. You're invited, of course. It promises to be a relaxed affair of like-minded people.' He looked at Mark sideways with a nod and half-wink! 'In a village hall out in the county, not too far, but far enough. There might be people there you know!'

He adopted a knowing expression again and licked his upper lip with the point of his tongue. Mark hadn't even had a chance to mention direct mail distribution. He could see Timothy was up for action. He left in the knowledge that he'd made a useful new contact. He wouldn't trust him any further than he could throw him, but he already had pretty near enough on him to be able to twist him around his little finger. He was almost as good as money in the bank.

Back at Number 45, things had been moving. The longest message on the answerphone he'd ever heard was Sonny telling him a seat on the council had come up uncontested and the Secretary said the Labour Party would support him if he was willing to stand. The next meeting of the local party was in just two days and he would need to decide by then. He straight away called Sonny back to tell her he was up for the job. No money, just expenses, no problem. He'd be one of the youngest Councillors in the country. Eighteen months ago, he was a broke student and soon he'd be a Councillor claiming expenses and the Chief Executive of a charity that was on the up.

The first serious appeal leaflets were on the press, just a pilot, 5,000, four-fold concertina A6 in four colours throughout. They told a story starting with a gruesome accident and finishing with a successful claim helping to hold a family together through harrowing times. It pulled on the heartstrings like the bells of St Mary's tolling at a funeral. Kevin had done him proud. If it didn't make a return, Mark would be wetting his pants. It had to work. They were distributing twelve hundred and fifty in each of four different demographic areas. For the next few weeks, he'd be a bag of nerves. If it didn't work his finances could well end up in a worse state than when he finished at uni, it didn't bear thinking about.

His life was getting more hectic by the day. Some days he was putting in fifteen and sixteen hours and it showed; his eyes all too often were red-rimmed, and his skin felt dry. He sometimes wondered how long he could keep it up; he needed some time off. He'd almost had a premonition something was amiss, and then it came, a call from a police inspector Jerry Standing. He wanted to speak to Mr Spivey about Michael Smith and Andrew Johnson.

'Who?'

'You may know them as MA & D Ltd.'

'Ah, yes, we deal with that company.'

'I see, so what is your connection with them?'

'They're a promotional outfit that collects donations for our Charity, IASIA.'

'I see. Thank you. We may need to ask some more questions.'

'Fine. Tomorrow I'm away in Brighton for the Labour Party conference. I'll be back in a week. I'll speak to you then if necessary.'

Mark called Lydia. He got Steve, who said, 'I'll get her to call you.'

'Tell her it's important, very important, and next week I'm away at the party conference. I need the time off. I'm one of the speakers and I haven't even thought about what I'll be saying. Kevin will have to answer the phone here next week, and I'll be having a break.'

He rang the hotel in Brighton where he was booked in for two days. Luckily there were still vacancies for him for the following days, extending his stay to a full week. Kevin was still in the building at No 45. Mark ran downstairs and told him he was off there and then, and that the police were asking questions about the relationship between IASIA and MA&D Ltd. He was to say nothing. Mark would be away in Brighton for the conference; Kevin knew nothing about MA&D and had never met any of their directors. If there was anything the police needed to know, then they'd have to speak to Mark. As far as Kevin knew, Mark was the only person at IASIA who had had anything to do with them. Kevin knew nothing. He was to deny any knowledge of MA&D., as the Americans say, period. When he started to ask what was going on. Mark simply said,

'You know nothing, and you need know nothing. You are not implicated in anything to do with MA&D. Ask no questions, get no lies. Period. OK, I'm off to Brighton. I'll be back in a week. I need the time off anyway. Things can run themselves for a week. I'll be back after the conference is over. There's a lot going on and I'm hoping that the case regarding my finger will be settled, and there'll be more cash available for anything and everything. All you have to do is tell anyone asking that I'm away at the conference and will be back in a week. OK? Leave everything to me. Maybe you'd fancy a week off yourself? We'll sort everything out when I get back. I'm leaving immediately. Don't worry about anything, just take it easy and act dumb. You know nothing. Hear no evil, see no evil, speak no evil. Got it?'

'OK. I'm just the wicket keeper.'

'Excellent. I'm off. See you in a week. Don't worry about anything. We're covered.'

Six

Mark walked home. Packing took a few minutes, then he grabbed a taxi to the station and he was off. Anyone wanting him would have to wait; he was over his head and drowning with the pressure of the last few weeks. He was determined to forget everything but the conference and enjoy the week. He bought a Times and a local paper at the station. He sat with a disgusting coffee in the restaurant and went through the local paper first. There were references to a body found in a local canal. The body was identified as that of factory owner, Bilal Patel. The cause of death was unspecified, but the police were treating the case as suspicious. The investigation was ongoing. Mark knew nothing of Mr Patel or his business, nor did he want to.

He spent his time on the train journey to Brighton going through the news section of the Times for any reference to the case of the body in the canal; there was nothing. He intended to enjoy his time in Brighton if it was the last thing he did. He felt he had earned some rest and recreation time and he had every intention of raising his profile among the Party chosen. He would not be hiding his light under any bushels. He'd heard the Brighton cottaging scene was vibrant. He had a feeling there might be an element among the political class who would thrive on the theatricality contained in a political presentation. He thought this could be a breakthrough week in his political career, and the Old Bill could get stuffed. He intended to have a bloody good time and his burgeoning political reputation would help thwart any undue problems brought about through his 'tenuous connection' with MA&D.

At the hotel, it was obvious who was there for the conference; badges and emblems were everywhere, as was a party atmosphere. As soon as he'd unpacked, he went to the bar and chatted with various people, raising his profile amongst those he thought might be useful and those he might 'Get on With'. He sat in his room and rattled off a draft of his speech. He didn't believe a word of what he wrote but that's politics he thought, laughing to himself. Most people wouldn't understand it because it meant very little but was designed to convince people he was clever and he was on their side. The fact was that he didn't give a shit about the politics just so long as it advanced his career. That was good enough for him.

The Speech went like this,

'Our party at present limits its approach to the world which we live in to a concentration upon economic issues at an almost microscopic level. My aim as a representative of ordinary working people would be to broaden the spectrum of thinking about society and to be more inclusive of those people presently marginalised. It covers a pretty broad spectrum of suffering, from physical to mental health problems among working people, their families and even friends and associates within the confines of legal definitions. These are always vulnerable to being picked over from a tightly-defined legal position. If God didn't want homosexuals to be discriminated against, he would not have created them. The law should never be fixed. It can always evolve as social definitions and culture change. Homosexuality has only recently been made legal, as you no doubt know, and rightly so, given that the law before the change was frequently described as a blackmailer's charter, and people are what they're born to be and have no say in the matter. A charity aimed at promoting such a philosophy as I'm suggesting could (a) raise all sorts of legal and social questions.

'Some of the world's greatest minds have been deemed mad by their contemporaries. Namely, Isaac Newton, Alan Turing, Marie Curie (Sklodowska) and even, on occasion, Albert Einstein. Such a charity could (b) provide employment for those willing to promote a more insightful approach to health and safety in the workplace as well as overcome such sexism as Sklodowska experienced throughout her life. By fighting cases that were clearly unjustly treated and raising the awareness of the public to cases where the law is presently unjustly administered, I would serve to promote a much-needed reappraisal of the law as it exists. The law in the UK at present needs updating.

'You could argue that I'm setting out on a crusade for a more enlightened legal system relating to industrial and employment health and safety that goes way beyond the simple basics of trips, slips and falls to cover approaches to mental health and social exclusion on philosophical grounds, through the limitations of common culture today. The nuts and bolts of what I'm proposing are essentially an appeal for money to promote a campaign for the sort of legal changes I've just outlined. Those ideas raise all sorts of questions about how our society is run and could cause us to look at any number of borders, limitations and narrow-minded practices in our polity that might benefit from a reappraisal.

'As a representative of working people, I would advocate a much broader and more flexible approach to education in general, to include a broader, more open-minded examination of social development than the present concentration on economic aspects of life. Our society as we understand it, allows, as the common saying has it, "Money isn't everything." The Greek philosopher Diogenes had much to say about Greek thinking in his day, searching with his lamp during the day for an 'honest man'. Defining what it is that makes an honest man is still as big a conundrum as ever. Many of Diogenes's ideas are still as valid today. Honesty isn't a simple concept and the legal discussion required to come to a conclusion about what honesty is in our modern society is as valid today, as two thousand years ago.'

'Bullshit baffles brains as the saying goes.' This speech set Mark thinking about himself in relation to the Greeks and he concluded that although they invented democracy, it was democracy only for Greeks but Greeks regarded themselves as a superior race and that idea set them free from the view that all men are equal. Slaves were put on the earth to serve the Greeks. They believed, like Hitler, that some people were by nature superior to others, and that the Greeks were a master race and other species of humans were put on the earth to serve the

Greeks. There were Greeks and other species of men who were destined to be slaves to the Greeks. There were exceptions in that other men who learnt the Greek language and learned to write could become Greek because they were by nature, Greek. The rest were born to be slaves.

The modern world he thought was based upon Greek philosophy. There were those born to lead and those born to follow. They called it democracy. OK, it was democracy for the Greeks but the rest were sub-human. The followers were put on earth to do the bidding of the leaders. At various times, the leaders would become degenerate and lazy and lose the power to rule and this would create a vacuum in any given society and just as in any structure throughout the universe, matter attracted matter. The Greek philosophers got it right when they argued that Greece at the time of its existence was the centre of the world. It was the creative and structural centre.

All things, however, degenerate. Steel rusts and returns to its natural state, iron oxide, as it combines with oxygen. It was the same with societies, they come to fruition when an intellectual elite dominates. Just as fresh fruit ripens then rots. The Romans called a secondary level of society the plebeians. The plebeians carried out the craft tasks such as shoemaking, weaving, building, and metalworking that demanded the sort of training that might best be handed down from father to son, or mother to daughter. Plebeians were free, but only free to work at their craft tasks. Below the plebeians were slaves who carried out simple grinding labour; they emptied cesspits, fed the central heating systems, and did the mining and other mindless labouring tasks. This structure enabled the elite to dominate with their superior intellect. They could indulge all their fantasies and this gave them the ability to dominate the plebeians and slaves by always thinking one step ahead. The plebs were kept in order with bread (that they made) and circuses, the circuses being gladiatorial fights from which modern Spanish bullfighting developed.

Mark's right to go cottaging stemmed from his superior intellect which demanded that he indulge his desires as a member of the elite and reach his full potential as a member of the elite. He set about using his week at the conference of the Labour Party to assert his right to a position among the elite. On the first night, he attended his first homosexual orgy. He'd never felt so alive. By the end of the Conference week, he felt totally refreshed and invigorated. He'd had a wonderful week and was fully ready to pick up the reins again at No 45.

His room above the Chinese stank worse than ever after his week away. His new-found optimism after the spirit-lifting week away contributed to a determination to see his exit from the depressing aura of the stinking box. He vacated as swiftly as he could, to avoid the depression such a home engendered. Stuffing his dirty laundry into his old student rucksack, he made his way to No 45. Mounting the newly-carpeted stairs, he noted that the sound of his steps was muted. After having got used to the echoing clatter of the bare boards, now there was carpet. The smell was different too, fresher and more pleasant than the intrusive stink of fresh paint and damp plaster. Even the hallway stairs were so much more agreeable than those leading to his room over the Chinese.

He dropped his rucksack on the landing outside the office and climbed to the floor above. Entering the flat above the office, he was astounded at the style with which it had been modelled: a small but functional kitchen with a washing machine and tumble dryer, a bathroom tiled to the ceiling and a shower above the bath. There was a proper sitting room, and generous bedroom, even a reasonably-sized broom cupboard, that made him laugh because he knew he'd almost immediately fill it with a poor hoarder's rubbish. He decided there and then it was his. One way or another, he'd get the cash together for a deposit.

He went downstairs to the office and shuffled through the mail. Fleishman Grabalov LLP stood out. He ripped it open. Short and sweet: our clients The Pie Co. are prepared to make this final and private offer to remain unpublicised and entirely without prejudice or discussion, to close the following cases for a total and final settlement in both the matters of Spivey v Pie Co

Ltd, and Smith v Pie Co Ltd dealt with as one case exclusively and without prejudice in complete, total and final settlement of £30,000. To be paid directly to M Spivey Esc, sole representative of both, Mr Smith, and Mr Spivey. Fleishman Grabalov LLP. Signed G Portman-Styles.

Done! His short-term financial woes were over, £15,000, Bang! Directly in his pocket, tax-free, plus £1,500 taxable and £13,500 for John Smith. Before the business was over though he had to get Mr Smith's acceptance. He sat down to write an acceptance agreement letter for Mr Smith to sign, then rang him. He gave Mr Smith the news that the Pie Co had made an offer that he thought was as good as they were likely to get. Smith agreed, verbally, to accept. Mark told him he would give him a couple of days to consider and discuss with his partner. His response was,

'How soon will I have the money?'

Mark explained that once he'd signed and accepted the offer then the business was finished and there could be no going back. Again, Smith said,

'How soon will I have the money?'

Mark told him he could expect to have a cheque for him within a week of his signing the acceptance letter.

Smith said, 'Shall I come to your office now? I need the cash.'

Mark told him to discuss it with his partner first, and then he could come first thing in the morning if she was in agreement.

Smith replied, 'I'll be there first thing.'

Mark went downstairs with a spring in his step to see Gunter and Kevin. The first thing Kevin said was,

'The police are looking for you.'

'You do surprise me. I'll give them a ring, Have you got a number?'

He wanted to sound cool, brazen and confident, which was the way he felt, especially as he'd just received the message about his claim against the Pie Co.

Anything MA&D did was nothing to do with him. He knew nothing of their activities. He said nothing regarding the Pie Co settlement. The less said about that the better, especially as it was not yet signed. Better that they thought he was still nearly broke, then they would be thinking that it was a waste of time asking for any cash. The first edition of Lydia's magazine was completed, delivered and was away for distribution and sale. Work had begun on a council-funded news sheet singing their own praises, of course.

Efforts were being made to sell some advertising to contribute towards its funding. The contractors involved in the regeneration building work should be good for a sizeable chunk of that, with a little arm-twisting.

Mark made his way to the council offices to carry out his duties as a trainee solicitor. Again, his employers were being very flexible about his hours because things were being done quickly. He was willing to take responsibility as well as be accountable and take risks that dyed-in-the-wool bureaucrats baulked at. He was even teaching his lack lustre, gutless twat of a boss to fucking swear. The old saying, 'Possession is nine points of the law' is ninety per cent true, and councils possess ninety per cent of power in ninety per cent of cases. If they set out to flex their muscles, their relatively talentless employees' jobs were easy. Climbing the ladder of power just seemed to him to be taking the easy route. Luck no doubt played a part but determination and ability were every bit as important as well as good old-fashioned ruthlessness and manipulation.

His direct boss, Mr Wheatman's weaknesses were good old alcohol, and secretaries. Mark soon had plenty of evidence of his indiscretions and was thus able to exert power over him by the odd innuendo or pointed implication. Wheatman knew he was vulnerable, especially when faced with someone as aggressive as Mark who thought he was as gutless as an anaemic rabbit. When it came to the pinch, Mark knew he could push him around like a shopping trolley.

Mark rang Inspector Standing from his office at the council. Standing was out. He got the desk sergeant who gave him a private number for Standing. At the same time, he gave the sergeant another number through which Standing could contact him. He left it at that. By three in the afternoon, he'd done all he needed to and went back to No 45. He called Sonny but she was not available. He then called Fr Timothy, who picked up almost immediately.

Mark got the standard response, 'Father Timothy at St John's.'

'It's Mark Spivey. How are you getting on? I had a great time in Brighton, lots of action both political and social. Do you ever get to ecclesiastical events there?'

'No, can't say I've ever been.'

'Don't know what you're missing. Had a great time. How're things with your magazine? Our print shop and distribution are coming on song. Could probably help one another in various ways, I was thinking.'

'I don't know. I'll give you a call if Abdhalla has another shindig. OK?'

'OK, thanks.' Fair enough, so that's that, Mark thought and went home to the flat he'd occupied illegally.

Sonny called at about six. He didn't beat about the bush.

'I want to rent the apartment at Pinfold Street. Is that possible?'

'I don't see why not. What about the cash? You'd need a deposit.'

'All being well, I think that won't be a problem. I think I might have a bit of a windfall soon.'

'How soon and how much?'

'Within maybe three weeks, and enough.'

'OK, I'll see what I can do. You gonna buy me a drink?'

'If everything pans out as I hope, I'll buy you a few. You can come to my first party. I can't wait to get out of my room. You haven't been there, have you? It stinks and not figuratively. It's over a bloody Chinese takeaway, and I mean it really stinks of old, burnt, vegetable oil and monosodium glutamate.'

'How did things go in Brighton?'

'Brilliant. Had a great time. Shame you were working: maybe next year. I think you'd enjoy yourself. D'you fancy The Black Boy tonight? I'm buying.'

'OK, after seven.'

'Good. See you there then.'

He knew he'd have to be careful, he was already spending The Pie Co's money.

Seven

Tuesday morning prompt at nine John Smith turned up. Mark called Gunter from downstairs, as a witness. Smith signed and Mark assured him he would have his money within a fortnight.

He protested, 'Yesterday, you said a week: now it's a fortnight.'

'You're right. I'm just being careful not to make promises I can't keep. You'll have the cheque in your hand, all being well, by the beginning of next week, OK?'

'I'll be holding you to that. I need that bloody money. I need it now. I don't s'pose you know anyone who's looking for a labourer? I need another job. I've got skills but my fingers are still not really right.'

'Sorry, can't help you. If I hear of anything I'll give you a call. OK?'

Off he went. Gunter was still in the room. Mark took out his wallet pulled out a twenty and handed it to him.

'You saw nothing, OK? Shtum's the word. You saw nothing!'

Gunter smiled, 'I see notting, fine.' He made a gesture zipping his lip. 'Notting. I blind.'

Mark sat at his desk and wrote a letter to Labour Central Office stating that he would like to stand as a constituency candidate as an MP for the Labour Party. He included a post-dated cheque for £500 as a contribution to Party funds.

Mark set out to concentrate on the Surveyor's claim that was beginning to develop into a millstone. Problem number one was the fact that he no longer worked for Smyth & Smyth. He called Sara and got her answerphone. He simply said he had a problem and she might be able to help; give him a call. Next, he began calling solicitors' offices around the town, explaining his situation and asking for help. He made a list as he went through the phone book. The thirteenth he called gave him a positive response. 'So much for unlucky thirteen,' he thought. He explained his situation. He had a client but was not fully qualified, still a trainee at municipal offices, so not officially able to practise yet.

The solicitor told him to come round to his office so they could discuss his problem there. Mark went to the address he'd been given and finally discovered the office in a cul-de-sac behind a nightclub. There was a 20 x 10 cm plastic sheet over a printed sign: 'J Brown. Solicitor at Law' beside a hardboard-faced door that at some time in the distant past had been painted dark blue. That was so long ago that it had faded to a dusty, greyish, light blue. Beneath the sign was a cracked plastic bell-push. He pressed it. Nothing happened. Mark pressed it again several times. He heard scuffling noises on the other side. The image before him put Mark in mind of the beginning of a black-and-white B horror movie he'd seen as a kid.

The door opened, but without the squeaky groan he'd expected. Slowly revealed was an area about three feet square at the bottom of a dingy, dark, dirty, staircase. The stink of stale cigarette smoke hit him like an almost tangible fog. To the right was a door that might at some time have been white, but was now a nicotine-stained brownish yellow. Mr Brown looked through eyes that might be anything between sixty-five and eighty-five years old. He pushed open the yellowed door with a hand, the first two fingers of which were nicotine-stained to the colour mahogany. He croaked from a face whose skin resembled deeply-creased, thick, dry, brown wrapping-paper.

'Mr Spivey is it?' croaked the spavined face.

Mark had found the man he was looking for. He'd already explained what he needed. The main question he wanted answered was what percentage Brown would be satisfied with, if Mark did the work of representing the surveyor, Mr Carter? Mark talked him into coming on board with an offer of five per cent for which he'd have to do nothing except provide a front as a qualified solicitor. Mark handed him £25 in cash to keep him interested, intending to pay him nothing more beyond the odd tenner to keep him quiet. Brown was a nobody, just a backstop against difficult questions regarding his qualifications.

It was wet - wet and windy and it gave Mark great satisfaction as he went back to his warm, comfortable office at No 45 to call Mr Carter the surveyor in question. He explained he had been contacted by a person from the TUC who represented Chartered Surveyors at a national level and explained that he had recently graduated with a Juris Doctors degree and had already settled his first case with a 40% above average settlement. He further explained that he set his targets high and aimed to win above-average settlements, even though that might mean greater commitment, extra work and a closer relationship with clients to look more diligently into obtaining recompense for the stress and distress caused to claimants. Most solicitors would not set out to understand and consider these elements of a claim, essentially because as administrators of law they were too elitist and did not consider that ordinary people's feelings and psychological welfare were just as valuable as anyone else's, even theirs! Added to that, would be the fact that he was willing to take on Carter's case for a reduction in the standard fee of 25% to 22.5%, a better deal than he would get almost anywhere.

If the settlement was agreed at £50,000 which would be average for his case, then he would receive £1,250 more on completion, given Mark's terms. He was welcome to look elsewhere to see if he could find a better deal but Mark would guarantee he'd find it so difficult as to not be worth his trouble. If Mark achieved a settlement ten percent above average which was the minimum that he'd have his sights set upon, his payout would be significantly higher. Mark would look towards getting his case in the best court with the most sympathetic judge. He was aware of contacts who could manage that for him.

Mark had the feeling he'd reeled him in. He did not want to overcook his spiel. He left the call with a note to say, 'Call anytime night or day.' He thought he'd done enough for the day and went to the gents in the park near the theatre where he thought he might score, as a celebration of a good day's work done, and the conclusion of the Pie Co case. His luck wasn't running, and after a few minutes, he went home. He opened the door to his room. His, own, lovely new room. He poured himself a vodka and blackcurrant, downed it in one, and went to bed alone.

On Wednesday morning early, he heard the bell ringing in the office below. He quickly donned slacks and a tee shirt. Arriving at the door, he was met by a man who produced a badge and introduced himself as Inspector Jerry Standing of the local constabulary.

'To what do I owe the honour?' Mark asked.

'We're investigating a suspicious death.'

'All I can say is it wasn't mine, and I know no one who has died lately, either suspiciously or otherwise, so why are you speaking to me?'

'We need to know what your relationship with MA&D Ltd. is. We have evidence to suggest that people connected with that company may have a connection with the deceased.'

'I see. Well, all I can say is that MA&D Ltd, act as promotors of our Charity IASIA.'

'Have you ever met a man named Michael Sherrard?'

'I believe I have. I think he came to the copy shop, just as we were opening, looking for some identity cards. That's how come his firm started doing promotional work for IASIA. We got chatting, he told us what he did, and we saw a mutually beneficial opportunity. We've done some business, but not a great deal. I only actually physically met the man just the once.'

'I see. Well, we may need to take this further, if so, I'll be in contact.'

'Right you are, inspector, whenever you feel the need, you know where we are.'

That was that. Mark rang Lydia to let her know that he'd had a visit from the local constabulary asking questions about any contact between him and Michael Sherrard.

'Has that anything to do with me?' she asked.

'I just thought it might be as well you knew. I didn't want you getting any surprises. We've not spoken for a while. I also thought you might be pleased to hear that Gunter is doing an excellent job.'

The rest of the week settled into mundane work of no major consequence until Saturday morning. He'd illegally moved into Flat No.1 at No. 45. He'd dragged an expensive double mattress up three floors, topped it with a half-open sleeping bag and duvet and a new feather pillow for the best full night's sleep - in surroundings he controlled - ever. His contented slumber was broken by the doorbell on Saturday morning. He staggered down the three flights of stairs to be confronted by Sara. The difference between their recent night time activity was very apparent. She was dressed in a bedraggled evening dress and looked slightly the worse for wear, while he was wearing a tee shirt and hastily-donned jeans.

He wasn't in an eloquent mood, 'Jesus are you OK?'

'No, I'm fucking not.'

'Come up,' he said, as she threw her arms around his neck. 'There's no furniture, but I've got coffee and mugs and milk and sugar.' He showed her to the bedroom asking, 'Shall I get coffee?'

She simply nodded, as he went to the kitchen, filled the kettle and spooned some instant into mugs. There was milk in HIS fridge. He slipped a splash of milk into her cup as well as his own with a dash of sugar and carried it to the bedroom. She'd propped the pillow against the wall and sat using it as a backrest. He passed her a cup. He walked around the bed, put his cup on the floor and sat beside her. He took a mouthful put his mug by the mattress and caressed her forearm. She put her mug beside the mattress and pulled him towards her with her arm around his neck. He returned her embrace and they lay together clasping one another tightly. He didn't know how long they lay together like that but it was a while.

'What happened?' he asked eventually.

'I went out with Sonny for a night on the town. We drove to Mottingly and were going to go to Starqueens. We hadn't thought about it but there was a football match on and the traffic was a joke so we turned around to come back and stopped on the way at the Oast House. It was packed with football supporters from Manchester or some other yahoos united. We'd gone into the bar to maybe get a drink and had just decided it was a pig pen and were leaving when a drunk called Sonny "a fucking dyke" and spat at her. She stuck her finger in his eye and he fell over. I started to run for the door, kind of dragging Sonny, but there were bouncers there, and they stopped us and called the police. The police came and took us back to Mottingly in a riot van. At the police station, I told them I was a solicitor, and they were making a mistake. After that, they eased off, but they kept us waiting at the nick all bloody night, not in a cell or anything, just in a front office waiting room. This morning the next shift came on and gave us a cup of tea, then told us we were free to go. So, then we had to get a taxi back to the Oast House to get the bloody car. We just had a shitty night and Sonny hurt her finger, poking the drunken shit in the eye. We didn't even get pissed, and I'm shattered worse than if I had a grade-A hangover.'

'D'you want any breakfast?'

'All I want is sleep.'

'Fine, I'll go downstairs and do some work and leave you to it.'

He kissed her cheek, got dressed properly and went downstairs to do some routine paperwork.

Sara went home at around lunchtime. Her departure heralded a period of consolidation. Little of great moment happened until after several months had passed when a short letter arrived from the Party informing him that should he still wish to stand, the selection committee had agreed to adopt him as the candidate for a constituency south of the Thames, that had never been won by Labour, but it was the first step towards a parliamentary seat. His main concern up until that point had been the Carter case. The defendants were dragging their feet, as only defendants' solicitors can, clocking up their hours while doing and achieving the minimum real progress, other than increasing their bill. Sara and Mark had developed a working relationship that was advantageous to them both. She learned to be more brass-faced when dealing with clients, the opposition, and authority, while Mark learned to push a little less hard when dealing with almost anybody.

The printing business was becoming more stable and earning an increasing, and steady income as was IASIA. Gunter had taken on a trainee who was doing well. Kevin and Mark still spent the occasional night together after warming up at the Black Boy. Mark's finances were growing steadily more secure. He heard no more regarding the body in the canal and any connection between it and MA&D Ltd and himself. Lydia explained to him that the local Chief Inspector of Police had placed it among the unsolved cases' files because of the lack of any significant leads or evidence. Quite how she had got this information he did not inquire. He went to a couple of sex parties organised by Imam Abdhalla where he made a number of useful contacts, one of whom was employed by the so-called Vice Squad as a participant rather than investigator, which he found quite amusing, especially as he was one of the ugliest men Mark had ever encountered. The poor chap had a face that would have disfigured an ape. Fr Timothy didn't appear either, quite why he never discovered. Maybe men friends were going out of fashion among the clergy.

He'd negotiated a five-year lease on his flat with the council and furnished it quite sparsely but comfortably and his situation as a trainee solicitor at the council had settled down in a satisfactory way with his income from that rising steadily. He could almost feel himself getting fat.

He spent time over the next few weeks travelling backwards and forwards to Isleminster where he was the new Labour candidate showing his face, telling bad jokes and buttering up the faithful, telling them that nothing was impossible, just keep the faith in the old red flag. Under the circumstances, he was well pleased with an increased Labour vote of nearly 5% that most of the people who mattered thought was a very promising result. His star was rising! Thatcher's was declining, and Mark thought John Major had the charisma of a two-day-old codfish on a supermarket slab. The future was looking bright. He felt he was backing the right horse. This year's Party Conference was coming up and he'd been asked to appear as a speaker, again, at a couple of side events on European Trade and the Computer Revolution which was hardly his area of expertise, so he'd have to do some brain picking and polish up his hottest line in bullshit and crap jokes.

The Carter case had dragged on with little progress and Carter was beginning to annoy him. His finances were looking more stretched than they had for a while because his lifestyle had gone, "up market" a good deal. He could now more-or-less buy clothes fitting the image he expected to project. That fact was making him feel more comfortable and confident, even though he was still a man of the people, despite the bulk of the people being mindless plebs.

He made a resolution to see the Carter case brought to a conclusion. Mr Carter, despite his broken jaw and cracked ribs, was getting stroppy. It was a difficult and complicated case but Mark determined to push flat out for a resolution because his commitments in the constituency and the House were demanding more and more of his time, as well as expanding his social calender. He wanted the case out of his hair and the cash would not go amiss. Carter would take what he got, and like it; especially as he was pushing hard for a resolution.

Mark had made his decision. Yugoslavia was falling apart. It was an opportunity for those with foresight to take their place in the world. There was real money to be made. He was here to grab that opportunity with both hands and with the grip of a man of destiny.

Eight

He called Tillotsons Builders' MD and asked him if he'd had any estimate of the value of the claim. Mark hinted that he might be willing to negotiate to get the case settled because it had dragged on for so long. Tillotson told Mark he'd ring back.

Mark wanted the cash desperately because there were refugees coming to the UK from the Serbian-Croatian conflict. He knew the government was clutching at straws looking for accommodation for a major influx of refugees. He knew of a local hotel with around 400 hundred rooms and an exhibition hall right on the edge of his old city's regeneration area where things were now moving along sweetly at No 45 and IASIA.

The hotel had been built in the late 60s in a flush of economic optimism. It had never made a profit, but although it was in poor condition, considering its age, it was structurally sound and most importantly, it was for sale. It was valued at little more than the cost of its demolition, cheap very, very, cheap under the circumstances. If he could fill it with refugees at the going rate for government accommodation, it could return the expenditure within a matter of months. It was an opportunity too good to miss. He knew Lydia rented part of the building for her present activities, and as such it would be a real, long-term, asset for her. If he could set up a consortium, the potential profit might set him up for life, stuff the Nolan principles. He was almost drooling at the prospect. He simply had to raise cash to buy the place. The first step had to be the Carter case, a resolution! And cash in the bank to buy his slice of the Langland Hotel.

He called Imam Abdhallah. He had a sudden urge, a vision to whip and sexually abuse a pathetic young homosexual man, to see him grovel. Despite his need for cash, he needed this release, beyond anything, to stay focused on his objective. It was an uncontrollable urge though he was hardly aware at the time. He needed the release that the total domination of a pathetic creature, abject, weeping, totally subdued, an inspiration to achieve his destiny, his place in the world, a man, a master, an Alexander, next to God.

He called Lydia telling her he wanted to meet privately over a matter that could be to their mutual advantage, and which needed to be dealt with quickly or the opportunity might be lost. She agreed he should visit her the following evening at her house.

He called Tillotsons Builders and asked to speak to the MD. The response was,

'You want to see me grovel? You want to see me broke? Well, you can fuck off. I'm sick and tired of the whole bloody business, the fucking hire-purchase bastards, who give when you don't need it and charge extortionate interest when you do, and that includes your lot. Bloody solicitors sitting on their fat arses, charging an hour's work for writing a poxy letter that takes five minutes so they can have their two-hour dinner breaks and moan when we stop work cos it's pissing down with rain. I'm gonna fight you bastards to the death, even if it kills me. I've got work to do, I'm trying to run a profitable business and make a reasonable living, and you bunch of arseholes are making it impossible.'

At that, he put the phone down. Mark almost laughed. He could see the guy's point of view. He'd had similar feelings himself at times. He knew the feelings of frustration with his university and the Pie Co. The builders was not a large company, and all reasonable actions had been taken to ensure the health and safety of the employees. It was the system that had failed, not the MD of the building firm. Of course, his frustration was explicable under the circumstances.

Mark called him back to make placatory noises, pointing out that he could see Tillotson's point of view, and suggesting that they should meet to come to a mutually-acceptable solution. The fact was the system had failed, and this created a problem at both ends of the spectrum. Mark was unusually placatory. He wanted the case concluded every bit as much as the building firm's MD. He wanted his own cash from the case, while the builder wanted to get on with his work of making a living in the building industry. Mark argued they should meet and discuss ways by which a resolution could be reached. This, he explained, could be achieved by sidestepping the faulty system that had caused the problem in the first place. They would need to co-operate to reach a mutually acceptable conclusion that was legal, and advantageous to both sides while sidestepping the mess created by the stupid Government regulations that might as well have been created by a monkey. If they could work together, they could overcome the impasse in a mutually beneficial way. How about it?

Tillotsons was a small outfit with limited resources. The necessary equipment was finally purchased after years of blood, sweat and tears. Tillotson spent close to a hundred hours at work most weeks just to stay afloat. His wife had thrown him out and was constantly after him for cash for the kids, who were still in education, and all he wanted was to be done with the "bloody millstone of an injury claim from a prick who shouldn't have been allowed near a building site because he must be blind, dumb, daft and stupid to fall the way the silly bastard did."

Mark put the question directly to him, 'How much could you afford to settle for?'

'Do you know how much I have in the bank at the moment?'

'Ten thousand in the red?' Mark said.

'More like fifty, but it is going down even with the bank squeezing me like a fucking lemon. I have a couple of good contracts on the go that should finally put me in the clear, and out of the thieving, bastard, bank's clutches. I've nearly finished paying for the yard and offices; that'll mean the end of outgoings of more than five hundred a week that I won't have to shell out. I'll own the office and yard outright. That'll be the biggest millstone I won't have to bloody-well carry. On top of that, there's the plant. There's some left to pay on that, and that'll be paid off soon. That'll be another hundred a week not going out on bloody finance at extortionate fucking rates.'

That was the moment Mark put it to him,

'What about bankruptcy? Have you ever discussed that with a lawyer or accountant?'

'I'm not bloody bankrupt. If I sold the lot, I'd have money in the bastard bank, but I wouldn't have a fucking job. I've spent the last thirty years building this business. You think I'm gonna throw all that away now because some bloody pillock didn't have the nous of a crippled frog?'

'It all depends on the way it's done. Who is your accountant?'

He gave Mark a name.

'I'll give him a call and see if we can't get together, and sort out a plan that'll work for everyone, even the fucking crippled frog.'

It was all Mark could do to stop himself from laughing out loud. He carried on though, 'There are more ways of skinning a cat, OR using the law than most people appreciate. We may be able to help each other, despite the fact we're supposed to be at daggers drawn.'

He'd not convinced Tillotson but at least they were communicating. It was a start.

Abdhalla called to tell Mark that he'd arranged an appointment with a couple of gay young men who were willing to do almost anything for 5 grams of coke. He agreed to come if Mark could be ready with some cash for the said coke. He told Mark he'd pick him up and they'd go to his bungalow out in the country.

Mark called Sara. He'd hardly seen her for a couple of months. He told her he'd like to see her the following Sunday. He had a proposition for her. He wanted her in more ways than one. He wasn't sure why, but she did have an attraction for him. These thoughts got him aroused. He went to the men's toilet in the park. When he arrived, there was no one in there, but a young man came in who gave the impression that he was looking for business. He came to the stall next to Mark's. Mark gave him a sideways look. The guy shook his dick as if to shake off excess piss, then started to masturbate. Mark looked back and shook his prick without pissing, He was onto a winner.

'Nice day for it,' Mark said.

The guy answered with, 'Fancy a walk in the park?'

'You're on.'

They zipped up and Mark followed him out. He stopped a few yards from the cottage entrance with his back to Mark and his left arm slightly away from his body palm open towards him. Mark grasped the proffered hand, squeezed it and began to walk; almost immediately, two uniformed police appeared at both sides of them. The guy disengaged his hand as the officer beside him said,

'You are under arrest. Soliciting in a public place with the intention of engaging in a sexual act.'

The guy beside him shook his hand free saying, 'I'm a police officer, you'll need to accompany us to the station.'

'Incitement?' replied Mark. 'You've got no chance. I'm a solicitor.'

'Name and address, date of birth and nationality,' said the cop.

Mark supplied the requested information and then said, 'Under the code of conduct act, incitement is a criminal offence. If you take me in, you'll be letting yourself in for a whole wagon-load of trouble. Of course, you could always come home with me, you're not bad-looking and we could have some fun.'

'Fuck off and don't let me catch you at it again, you filthy bastard,' said the two-faced copper.

'Tut Tut,' said Mark, 'discrimination, threatening behaviour and misogyny. You really do need to do some serious mugging up on your code of conduct.'

'Fuck off. We'll be watching you,' said the officer.

'What's your number? I'll be keeping an eye out for you, too. You can take that any way you want,' Mark replied with a grin.

Mark went back to his office and called Abdallah. The events of the last few hours had set him feeling even more randy. Abdallah gave him a couple of numbers to ring. He had some coke in stock and took a room at the local Travelodge. The youth was very obliging, even though Mark didn't hurt him much, largely because he was so out of it on the coke Mark had given him it made the whole business somehow unsatisfying, even, almost a farce. The coke had rendered the sad youth past feeling normal pain, which took the edge off Mark's pleasure. The whole episode collapsed into squalid disappointment and anticlimax, even a fiasco.

Sara came to Mark's place on the following Sunday morning as arranged the previous week. They had been collaborating on one or two cases at the council where they were both working. She generally dealt with family law matters whereas Mark specialised in finance. In some situations, the two areas overlapped and there were occasions when it was helpful to them both to discuss points of law that were open to interpretation. They went into town for lunch. Mark paid then they went back to his flat.

'It's really quite OK now, isn't it? Carpets, furniture, quite civilised,' she said.

Mark crossed the room and opened the drinks cabinet. 'Ta rah. You get drinks now, even ice if you want, and if you fancy a sniff?'

She crossed the room and gave him a full-on kiss. He felt the blood suffusing his dick. She rubbed his crotch and said,

'Bed.'

It was Monday morning before they got down to the business in hand. Mark explained about the Langland Hotel and the coming influx of Serbian and Croatian refugees as well as his growing influence in the Labour Party and the coming election. He told her the old story, If you can't be rich be lucky. Luck is what you make it; it does not come out of the blue, it takes vision. He was feeling so full of himself, that he didn't see her turn away to stop herself from laughing. He had a plan to fill the Langland Hotel's 400 rooms with refugees at the going rate of £25 per night per immigrant at two to a room for six months at a cool £560,000 per month. Six months, and they'd have collected three million clear if they allowed £60,000 a month for expenses which was generous. 700% in six months was a *very* reasonable return.

Lydia was in for £100,000 and she was feeling out Stimpson the estate agent who she had wrapped around her finger. Personally, Mark wouldn't touch him with a bargepole, less guts than an anaemic flea. He wanted nothing to do with the putrid twat. He could eat him for breakfast but the very thought made him want to puke and he'd trust him like he'd trust a starving rat with his favourite pork pie.

He was going to London, there were people there he needed to see. The right people in the right jobs, with the right politics and most of all, the right access to filthy lucre. They were in London. Most of all he wanted to see a junior minister called John Smith of all names. Mark had heard that Mr Smith was looking for investment opportunities and owned property in Spain that could be mortgaged to provide cash towards the purchase of the 'Langland' and a return that would pay off the mortgage in less than a year. A bonus was that Mr Smith was a great one for parties, especially his kind of parties; that was a part of the reason for the house in Spain. The attitude to sex was very different over there.

Mark called him to let him know he'd be "in town" and would like to see him about a mutually beneficial proposition. Smith agreed to meet outside Portcullis House and take him into

Bellamy's which was inside the parliamentary estate, and subsidised on top of an MP's basic salary and expense accounts. He was surprised to discover a Vodka Red Bull was cheaper than in an average Midlands pub. Roll on the day when he could impress his friends and acquaintances by inviting them in with a member's pass, a nice little perk that most people didn't realise was available to MPs. He topped up his drink with plenty of ice, feeling some annoyance because he needed to keep a clear head, and pitched his proposal to John who had enough influence in the right quarters to fill the Langland three times over, at the government's (the electorate's?) expense, or so he said.

Mark was wary and determined to maintain control and a majority share in the Langland. He wanted ultimate command. He was aware there were pitfalls, and he was looking for leverage over John; he wanted his back covered. John's position was on the other side of the house to his. Despite his name, filthy lucre rearing its ugly head again, and though in general terms, their common objectives remained the same, all any individual had to do was *appear* to uphold some kind of plausible position regarding the objectives of the Party. Take John Major's Private Finance Initiative, (PFI). There were ostensible reasons for it, but the truth was a simple sellout to the banks. Who gives a fuck? No one but the loony left. That night he went to John's party and who should be there but the PM-in-waiting from Mark's side of the Commons, a microcosm of the gangland culture that held sway in the 'House'.

Mark went and shook his hand and wished the Party luck at the next election. He did not think the PM-in-waiting was embarrassed. He smiled, and Mark thought it was genuine.

'What seat are you standing for?' he asked.

Mark told him. 'Well, if we're to win, that's a seat we need. I have a feeling I'll be seeing you in the next government. He raised his glass, 'To us, the Party, and the next election.'

'To us, and the Party, all being well,' responded Mark. 'The future is the time to party with, "THE PARTY," whatever the media throws at us, and we're stronger there than many people realise.'

Mark's future was looking brighter than ever. The next PM had the morality of the starving rat with the pork pie. Did Mark give a fuck? He was already living in the real world. He thought this must have been 1986 or early 87 and all he wanted was for the party leader to keep up the *good!* work. He got pretty rat-arsed and went to bed with a junior minister of the opposition. It was a pleasant, though tiring night. They chatted a lot, among other things, and consequently Mark was shattered in the morning but never-the-less he went back to Bellamy's the following day to show his face to some of his colleagues, in the opposition, and got slightly drunk again with "hair of the dog" to celebrate, his blossoming future.

He returned home to find a phone message,

'Hi, it's Lilith. That's what I'd like to be called now. You may have new responsibilities. I think I'm pregnant.'

He was dumb! Dumbfounded! He had not even considered the possibility. He put the phone down. The phone rang again. He took it off the hook and left it unanswered, then went and poured a Glenmorangie. (His tastes were still moving up-market with his income).

The shock demanded extreme measures. He returned the phone to the cradle. It rang again almost immediately. He picked up.

She said again, 'It's Lilith! Now. I'm certain, or at least, more or less certain, I'm pregnant and I'm certain it's yours. You might not believe it, but there have only been a couple of others and they were more-or-less plants from my bastard father. He's a piece of shit, a devil compared to Jimmy Saville. You might not be a knight in shining armour, but I know, I do what not many women can, I turn you on, and you do it for me too. God only knows why, and I'm not too sure I want you for the father of my child, but I'm stuck with it, and you. You might think I'm railroading you, but I'm not. I think we deserve one another.

We're two halves of a mould that was made in heaven or hell, take your pick. There's no getting away from it, it looks as though I'm two months gone and I still want you. Heaven knows why. Shall I come around?'

Mark stammered, 'I- I- I have to go to the Black Boy for a drink with Kevin and Gunter tonight. I've hardly seen them for a couple of weeks and there are matters we need to catch up on, but if you want to come around later tonight, we can talk then. I guess I'll be back at 9.45. How does that sound?'

'Ok. No rush. There's still seven months before anything really changes.'

Mark was in shock, but surprised at the way he felt. The prospect of having children had never really occurred to him, but he found that a part of him was pleased, although he needed to get used to the idea of what his responsibilities might be, under the circumstances. The idea that one day he might have children, that someday he might be a father.

He'd never had much to do with his own father. He always seemed to be away, or working, and never seemed to want to be around his family anyway, appearing preoccupied and introverted. It was only now Mark began to realise he was probably depressed. Mark was upset when he killed himself, and he blamed his mother. He felt she treated him in the same way she treated his father. She just had a knack of niggling that got under his skin. He sometimes thought not just metaphorically. After his father died, he developed psoriasis on his knees and elbows, and when he was stressed with exams, it invariably got worse. He sat his 'A levels' wearing soft cotton gloves with ointment to control the constant soreness and itching on his hands. Within months of his leaving home, the psoriasis cleared up completely. It had never returned. He had a gut feeling his mother was the stress factor.

He was distracted during the meeting with Kevin and Gunter, but as far as he could tell, everything was going well. There was enough work for Kevin to have placed an ad for a print finisher, that would enable more work to be carried out in-house. He simply made it clear that he'd let them get on with their side of the business, while he continued to deal with the introduction of lucrative work. He didn't think of himself as a salesman, although had he analysed his real situation, he would have realised that's what his real function was. He was selling an idea that selfishness was good and moral, an idea that everyone should adopt. Being a bastard was certainly working for him, why not everyone else? It was bastards who "came good" and gained respect and money.

Mark's greatest concern was centred around the way he was going to deal with the Carter v Tillotson case. It was complicated to the point where he wished he'd never taken it on, and being a bastard wasn't even an option. He was beginning to feel like Tillotson. The case was a bloody millstone. He was constantly mulling over ways that he could deal with the situation without it ending in court; that would be in no one's interest, certainly not his.

Mark arrived home at 9.45 pm as agreed, to discover Sara/Lilith had let herself in. He had no idea she had a key, it made him edgy.

'When did I give you a key?'

'Oh, I don't know, months ago, don't you remember?'

'No, but no matter. If you're pregnant, and it's mine then it's fine, I guess, especially if you're thinking in terms of marriage. I wouldn't want to think I fathered a bastard, even if I'm a bastard, and even dare I say if you're a bastard, not necessarily in the biblical sense if you understand my meaning. I'm not too sure I'm cut out to be a father. Maybe like my own. Marriage would be good for the image I suppose, given that we're both flexible about our sex lives and get on OK as working partners, then I'm game if you are. Good for tax purposes too and our social appearances as well.'

He grabbed her with an arm around her waist and with the other hand groped her arse saying, 'Bed,' before pushing his tongue between her lips as she pulled him close, her breath coming in gasps. On consideration, he realised it was a rather unconventional proposal, but they both knew what they were doing.

They christened the new king-sized bed with the extra firm mattress he'd just bought. The sex was satisfactory, if somewhat exhausting and the bed excellent. It was as good a night's sleep as he'd ever had. After breakfast, he told her about the situation regarding the Carter v Tillotson case and how it was dragging him down just at the time when he needed the extra cash to carry off the Langland deal. She suggested they get Tillotson and his wife around a table and see if they couldn't work out some sort of deal whereby the Tillotsons avoided tax by restructuring the company so that everybody gained. Mark told her he had thought much the same and that it might be an avenue worth pursuing. She suggested they speak to an accountant and company law specialist. She promised she would ask her father about experts in that area.

Then they discussed their forthcoming wedding. Mark's only thought was more bloody expense, but at least there'd be a good party and an opportunity for some serious networking.

A fresh week and Mark was determined to bring about a resolution to the Carter v Tillotson case. He rang Tillotson first thing, at 9.10 am on Monday and told him he thought he had a plan that might bring about a result that was an acceptable conclusion for all concerned.

'A plan. What do you mean?' asked Tillotson.

'If it gets as far as court, then the whole business has been a waste of time. All the fees will end up absorbing any cash that anyone gets apart from, perhaps, Mr Carter because the process of reaching a conclusion will have cost so much time and money.'

'So how do you think you can sort it out?'

'Before we go any further, we need to know what your real financial situation is.'

'What do you mean? I've told you the business owes money, but I'm earning enough to pay my way out of debt. Once the finance is paid off, then I'll be in clover. It wouldn't be long before I could clear the mortgage on the house. Then my darling wife can live there, and my life can get back to the point where I start living again instead of walking around like a zombi because I'm always knackered.'

'I understand that, but what is the situation with your wife? You own a house where your wife is presently living with your children. From a legal point of view, we need to ascertain exactly what the legal position is relating to your wife, your house and the children. Only after we have concluded exactly what the *legal* situation is, can we come to a satisfactory understanding of how we deal with all the matters involved with your real financial situation. I can't explain it more clearly than that, other than to say we need every detail of your personal, and financial existence before we can reach a satisfactory conclusion as to how to deal with your case. It is not simple, but the time spent will bear dividends you'd never believe. It's true we can organise things in such a way as to overcome all your financial problems. The first question, how good or bad is your relationship with your wife?'

'In the end, it's all down to the fact that I spend just about all my bloody time working because that's the only way I'm managing to stay afloat. She can't accept the fact that although there's money available, it's only available to pay off the finance on the buildings, the plant, and the house. There's next to nothing left for anything beyond the basics; food, clothes, heating and the cars. We can't do without them to get around and to keep everything running.'

'Are you on good enough terms to get her to our office so we can discuss the situation from the various legal and financial viewpoints that need to be considered? We have legal experts available who can explain the aspects of the case and how we can put together a package that works to the advantage of all concerned.'

'I'm sure I can get her to come to a meeting like that but you'll need to make it plain about how she'll be looked after. She's not daft but once she gets an idea fixed in her head, it's not easy to get her to budge. She's stubborn as set concrete in a busted mixer; you won't budge her with a lump hammer.'

'That being the case, if you find answers to a list of questions we will provide, we will organise a meeting and explain our plan to deal with all your difficulties, as well as ours, and get us all out of the present mess we're stuck with.'

Mark contacted Lydia and explained how he'd like to proceed with the Langton Hotel business. Essentially, a company registered in a UK-administered tax haven, ideally Jersey or perhaps the Isle of Man, with an internationally branded British Bank as backing. That way profits from the Langland deal could be rendered tax-free. The Langland as a business would be registered in Jersey and the profits would accrue in Jersey but the ownership would be in England, though that would not show up in England because the assets of the company would be registered in Kenya where Prama Moise, the President, and Mark had an association through the Junior Minister for Overseas Trade, who could control the profit and loss of the company through published accounts there. The Junior Minister would expect his 'commission'. They already had an agreement through Darius whereby published accounts of the Company would show that any taxes due had been paid in Kenya. Prama would expect a substantial cut but that would be a small price to pay when the profits were so high.

Mark could almost see Lydia rubbing her hands with glee. She told him to come and visit her that evening. He said he would. For the most part, all he had to do now was finish the paperwork putting together the syndicate to buy the Langland. He'd set everybody up with personal accounts in Jersey through a British high street bank. He'd pay Carter out of his cut, make Tillotson an offer he couldn't refuse with all his debts paid and a fixed contract for work that needed doing on the Langland. Tillotson's present company would declare bankruptcy, with the new company buying the stock and buildings for peanuts through a poorly-advertised auction, with ridiculously low attendance. His new company would be registered under the names of both him and his wife as well as a separate trust for the children.

He'd already spoken to a couple of people at the Construction Safety Executive about improving the construction industry's safety record and how a charity structure for its administration might improve the safety record of the industry as a whole, as well as its administration through the appointment of properly-qualified trustees, whose remuneration would be paid from the coffers of IASIA, that would receive a government grant for the work it would be undertaking. The Construction Industry Training Organisation would make a contribution from a general fund created for that very purpose.

Tillotson might well prove a suitable candidate for a position on the board, for a consideration. There would be other work that would certainly need doing when Mark had picked up some other property he already had his eye on. He even thought he might rope in the next PM. He knew the future PM had an eye for a hot deal. Once they were on the right side of the House, the sky had to be the limit. Now it was simply a waiting game while they filled the Langland with refugees and as soon as the place opened its doors, they had some of them working for cash, 'On the nod' tidying up the building.

Tillotson was delighted.

'If English labour worked half as fuckin' hard, we'd still have an empire.'

Mark did not feel happy establishing a relationship with such a pleb as Tillotson but 'needs must'. M A&D took care of security (Again a 'needs must' decision) which was quite difficult at times because British Immigration, after rather insensitively, he thought, occasionally mixing Serbs and Croats together, created an unnecessary nuisance by bringing the war to the shores of the UK. Consequently, they did encounter the odd murder as the immigrants brought their conflict with them; rather an embarrassment.

However, there was a convenient Russian Orthodox church nearby which was, most accommodatingly, willing to accept other Eastern Europeans in its cemetery and not too fussy about exact religious affiliation or other niceties, especially for what Mark thought was a very modest financial consideration. Economic concerns appeared often to sway the clergy of more-or-less all denominations, he seemed to have noticed. No doubt being elucidated in the old saying God will provide! Neither the local police nor the media showed any interest in the proceedings at all, despite some rather awkward coroners' reports that Mark considered a potential source of embarrassment.

Nine

Sara, or Lilith as she now wanted to be known, was having fun spending some of their hard-earned cash on their wedding. Even Darius was making a worthwhile contribution as he saw the occasion in the same light as Mark, a good opportunity for networking. Mark was looking forward to their honeymoon which they'd arranged with Prama Moise to take place in Kenya in an area of Nairobi with the rather unfortunate name of Embakhazi, especially in the light of the "Carry On Films". He booked a trip to Mombasa with Lilith as she insisted he called her. She'd even stopped answering to Sara. He didn't enquire why. If that was what she wanted, it was up to her. They held a reception in London where he had one or two interesting conversations with New Labour organisers, one of whom it turned out was an Israeli who was apparently well-funded and well-connected with people who were realistic politicians rather than knee-jerk left-wingers. Things were moving forward nicely for realists in the Party.

The nuptial celebration holiday was pleasant though quite tiring physically because of all the traveling. On the return journey, all he wanted was to get home, to keep tabs on the Langland project. A general election was on the cards and he wanted to be ready. He'd been confirmed as the party candidate for a constituency in the Midlands quite near home, and statistically, he had an excellent chance of winning. He wanted to start researching the area. Forewarned is forearmed was the way he saw this, and a great opportunity to raise his profile at a national as well as local level. He felt he needed to start raising his profile in the area as a strategic part of a general campaign. He needed to sort out accommodation in London reasonably near to Parliament.

He also needed an agent. He shopped around and found the very man; Sam Stanger, Head of Northern Granite Building

Securities Bank. He was superbly well-qualified with a Cambridge Economics First, and control of enough cash to manage Mark's campaign with aplomb, while investing in a block of houses in a redevelopment area in Midshires City where Mark was about to become the incumbent MP. The rents of these might well contribute to their expenses, while Mark created another complicated offshore legal framework for the Company concerned. Sam was well acquainted with Lydia who recommended him. He also had one of the juiciest arses Mark had ever squeezed as well as a penchant for S&M. They were made for one another.

At the election, Mark cleaned up with the rest of the Party. He won with a swing from the Tories of nearly 25%, one of the best results for Labour in the whole election. Given that the Tory contender for the seat was the man Mark had met years ago upstairs at the 'Black Boy', none other than one step short of an imbecile Noddy, it wasn't really surprising he was able to take him apart at the hustings. Needless to say, Labour policies were designed to increase the welfare of those who developed the wealth of the country. The people with foresight and patience to see investment create wealth. The hoi polloi wasted their money on fripperies and rubbish while the intelligent invested with sound judgement.

Mark was an investor. Under the new PM, John Major's plan to increase the investment opportunities of people with prudence, prescience and patience would obviously improve our country's and Mark's economic situation beyond all recognition. The Private Finance Initiative was putting everything - hospitals, schools and universities, housing and railways and electricity, as well as anything else they could think of - in hock to the banks, at extortionate interest rates. This meant money was flying around for those with the wit to take it, in a bonanza that made the Yukon gold rush look like a chimps' tea party. Even Tillotson, who wasn't the brightest star in the sky, picked up a contract for a complete school for fifteen hundred pupils worth millions.

Mark's wealth and influence were growing faster than Superman on steroids, so far beyond his expectations he could hardly cope. His income was rising so fast that he no longer really had any idea how much he was worth at any month's end. It had now reached the point where he could employ not just one but a couple of secretaries on his expense account. One, a female, to look after his day-to-day office commitments and the other, a male, to organise his diary and act as chauffeur whose name was Leonard, though he responded better to Lena. Mark never wanted to drive and now he didn't have to. Life was growing sweeter by the day. His chauffeur soon became a 'friend'. Mark was young and the world was his oyster. He was still fishing for pearls.

Mark's first new opportunity came through his wife, now known as Lilith. She introduced him to a guy called Leslie Stansfield, the new "Guru for Economic Development." He was a New Zealander of Jewish, Czech origin which interested Mark simply because of its dramatic exoticism. Leslie started in the newspaper business in New Zealand when a small Aukland newspaper was left to him by his father. He had a flair for publishing and soon exercised control over much of the business there.

Mark had heard of him as someone becoming well known for cutting-edge business flair even internationally. This was a very uncommon occurrence for an Australian, let alone a New Zealander. Lilith had family in Wellington and had met Leslie there while visiting. As soon as Mark saw him, he was entranced. There was almost an aura about Leslie, no wonder he'd been such a success in New Zealand, a place Mark imagined as full of sheep farmers and Mauri rugby players drinking beer and stretching their vowels. Mark spoke to Lilith about it saying, thank God he hadn't been there, the arsehole of the world, and no wonder Leslie was aiming to escape!

As they grew a little better acquainted, Leslie explained that he had an interest in exporting printing machinery to the Southern Hemisphere where there was a serious shortage. He foresaw some good trade opportunities. If the right machinery could be acquired in the UK and Europe, he would be interested, for both his own use and to sell on if bulk buys could be found at discounted prices. This stirred Mark's interest and he introduced Leslie to Kevin and Gunter who obviously knew more about the trade in machinery than he did.

Basically, Mark knew very little about printing machines. He had studied so-called arty subjects, politics and law and not really at a very high level. Political philosophy and such matters as the rise and fall of civilisations he considered a waste of time. He did, however, consider tactics in battle important and he had read chunks of Clausewitz's 'On War', and had a limited idea about existentialism and essentialism though he was rather at a loss as to how those ideas related to nuts and bolts economics. As far as he was concerned, people's attitudes to war had changed since the industrial revolution, moving away from the idea that war was inherently about the existence or not of God. People fighting with Napoleon thought that the old-time Church and State leaders were charlatans only concerned for their own welfare. Those who thought the State and Church were put there by God for the benefit of all, were diehards of the old order. Mark's point of view on the matter was, 'It's all a load of bollocks.' Essentially, he neither knew nor cared if God existed or not!

All Mark wanted was the slice of the economic pie he thought he deserved, which amounted to what he could grab. He was not bothered about what anybody else got. He wanted anything he could beg, borrow or steal by any means - not excluding fraud - and get away with. Nothing else came into the equation so long as he could get as big a slice of the pie as he could possibly manage.

He talked about these ideas with Gunter who he thought had more experience of life in another world where these questions must have been discussed a great deal. After all, Clausewitz was some kind of German, wasn't he? Mark got confused when trying to work out who was who among Prussians, Austrians, Germans, Swiss and even some Italians who spoke some kind of German.

Not that it really mattered. All he was aware of regarding Gunter was he knew a lot about printing machines and understood what was good, bad and ugly. The truly industrial-sized machines were big, heavy, complicated, and *very* expensive.

Ten

'She's a girl?' said Mark, phrasing it as a question.

'A girl, A GIRL, yes of course she's a girl, even you must know the difference. Or can't you tell the back from the front of *anything anymore? You get dafter by the hour.*'

'I- well, I just assumed it would be a boy. I-I- never even thought it might be a girl. I- well, I suppose it's OK. I just thought it would be a boy.'

'It could have been a boy. Of course, it could have been a boy! Of COURSE, it could have been a boy! It's what they call a fifty-fifty chance. But you - you only bet on certainties, that's why you're so bloody, boringly successful, but not this time. The odds were wrong, and you were wrong, and you never even considered you might be. You're not God; he, she, it does not make mistakes because, he, she, it does not make silly, stupid, assumptions. Not like you. You think you're more powerful than Henry-the-bloody-Eighth and all he could manage were girls but she's beautiful, not like you, either! You might not think so, but the truth is you're an ugly bastard, just like my dad. You look OK, and you make me want to get into bed with you, but God knows why, cos you're really just like my dad, a right bastard, and you're the father of a daughter.

'D'you want to hold her? YOUR daughter. She's beautiful, unlike you. She's more or less perfect. She's lovely! She's MY daughter, and all you want to talk about is fucking printing machines. I despair.'

Mark took the baby and looked at her face, smiled at her, poked out his tongue then crumpled his face and said,

'God, she's her father's daughter, she just dropped one.' Then laughed,

'I guess she's gonna be OK.'

'Of course, she'll be OK. She's called Mahe.'

'So that's non-negotiable, is it?'

'Bloody right it's non-negotiable. I'm Lilith so she has to be Mahe.'

'Is that so? So what's all this Lilith/Mahe business?'

'Don't ask me, do some fucking research. You're not the only one who's got ideas. I'm one step ahead of breaking shop windows in the West End. We'll be living at the house in Kingston in joint ownership with you, and I want you to set up a separate trust for Mahe with me as a signatory. We'll keep our affairs separate in the UK but with joint overseas accounts. I quite fancy the Bahamas but I'm open to negotiation. You can use the central London flat as yours and I'll be separate from that because then you can have it on parliamentary expenses totally independent of anything else. My business in Kingston will be entirely separate from yours, as will any property it rents or owns. How does all that sound? If we keep proper accounts there won't be much in the way of tax to pay so it's a win for us both. Does that seem reasonable?'

Mark had not faced an onslaught like this since he'd come up with the idea of a charity, and in front of him was Sara. He was dumbfounded.

'Ohh Kaaay, if that's the way you want it.'

Accepting without a fight that Lilith was dominant, he was not really considering what this meant in their relationship. He poked his tongue out at Mahe again,

'You're a proper stinker, just like your mum.' A further admittance that Lilith was dominating. He leaned over the bed, returning the baby to her mother, then kissed Lilith on the cheek, 'You'll be the death of me.'

He laughed, then shook his head in disbelief with a wry smile. He knew something major had just happened, though he was not quite sure what it was.

Gunter had supplied Mark with some printing trade magazines to deliberate over and begin to appreciate the practical difficulties printers faced. Not physically dangerous in the way a transport business might be, or building, but more cerebral than most industries because it influenced how society developed in ways far more subtle than almost anything else. "Publish and be damned," came to mind but also technical development, black and white to colour, and most of all literacy and intellectual development.

The prices and costs of everything were changing worldwide. The price of food was falling for working people the world over as never before. Ignorant peasants were gaining an education that was eroding the power of religion. As a result, the value of everything was changing. The post-industrial revolution was coming to the third world with nuclear power, electricity and mobile phones. The value of communication and its influence on minds were impossible to determine. The whole world was in a state of flux. What did words mean, and how precise were they, especially after translation?

Mark's legal training led him towards publishing, publicity and theatricality. How could words be interpreted? What was it that, that made printers and publishers "Movers and Shakers." He knew that facial expressions were at least as important as words in appreciating nuances in what a person was saying.

When Lilith presented Mahe and her position relating to the baby, their businesses and him, he knew something major had happened, but it was about nuances. He could not put his finger on just what it was, but, *SHIT,* he felt, *frustrated,* even *desperate* in a way he did not understand. The world was moving so fast too. Mobile phones known as bricks that charged in the back of a car had just come out and it was obvious that as the technology improved, they would have a major impact on the way people interacted. At that moment they were just status symbols but if they really caught on then the impact would be enormous. Instant communication anytime anywhere, how would that pan out? Everything was moving faster and faster. How could he manage to keep up? He felt he was losing his grip on reality because it was moving so much faster than his mind could assimilate.

He began the new week making a couple of relatively insignificant speeches in parliament as much as anything to let other members know he was there, alive and generally raising his profile. With an income now of over a quarter of a million a year, he was knocking at the door of major financial players at least nationally and some might argue, internationally. He'd employed a female graduate from Durham University with a 2.1 in Politics and Economics who was well-connected in the political sphere essentially on the other side of the Commons and was to do the bulk of his work at Westminster. He did however have to show up regularly for votes and divisions all of which ate heavily into his time. He was also having to attend events and meet constituents. He was employing two secretaries there to share the load.

He'd been mulling over the idea of making a start at entering the world of publishing but had decided it was too ephemeral for his taste and was more interested in the areas of basic consumption i.e. food and drink or something closely related. He chatted with Gunter whose input into the printing side of the charity business had blossomed. The print works had expanded and moved from No 45 to the newly-built industrial site with better access to the motorway system and bigger, more sophisticated machinery. However, business was slowing due to foreign competition.

IASIA was employing a staff of fund raisers, an office administrator and its own solicitors, and had taken over the whole of the Number 45 building, apart from the flat at the top. He hung onto that, partly as a nostalgic, sentimental keepsake but also for accommodation while he was in the constituency. He also still used it occasionally for some of his more obscure hobbies. He was watching over the process of IASIA's development as a trustee, on what appeared, these days, to be a meagre salary of just six thousand a year but as they say, every little helps, and he still maintained some control as chairman of the committee of trustees.

Much of the print work IASIA had been doing in the UK had, of necessity, gone, either to Eastern Europe or the Far East, as international trade had opened up exponentially with the introduction of containers and ever-larger ships, as well as air freight at ridiculous prices. Annoyingly, the imports of used machinery from the UK to abroad were taxed by the importing countries but at least it was the importers paying the taxes. The secret of managing to make a profit in the UK, he concluded, would be high-volume, cheap basic food products, grain, maize or potatoes. Major internationals were already making crisps and clocking up a serious markup. He discussed his ideas with Lydia, Kevin, Sonny, Gunter and Lilith.

Mark also saw an opportunity in the field of brewing. Not only was the market for beer changing but traditional pubs were losing clientele for various reasons. The quality of beer had declined because there was no longer any real competition between brewers selling to pubs they owned. Television was taking people off the streets in the evenings and consequently, beer sales in supermarkets were increasing as prices dropped, while beer prices in pubs rose because of increasing costs and lower demand. At the same time, small brewers were starting up and making better beer while the new organisation CAMRA, "The Campaign for Real Ale," was improving the awareness of dedicated beer drinkers to the quality of their tipples.

As Mark saw it, there was a move for traditional pubs to close while those with large car parks that served food as well as drink were expanding. The whole ethos of pubs was moving away from the old concept of a local to one where entertainment and food were more important than pubs that represented a local social hub. There was a niche for a new kind of pub where beer was treated in almost the same way as wine, as people's palates became more sophisticated. However, a trend towards small-scale breweries becoming far more common, meant that the demand for small-scale brewing plants was growing fast. Making the machinery required, meant that China was the obvious place to go to have it manufactured.

Lilith it was who suggested he spoke to Leslie Stansfield, with whom, he suspected she had more than a casual relationship. Stansfield's involvement in the media peaked when the underhand and undercover business with Maxwell and Murdoch created a public furore. The influence of newspapers was waning as the internet took off at the end of the nineties. The world economy looked to Mark to be in dire straits even before the great UK bank collapse of 2008-9. Thereafter came a time of opportunity as the economy settled and governments propped up the banks (again) with money taken in taxes from the pockets of working people (again).

Stansfield was operating as an international dealer in machinery, specialising in transporting second-hand European machinery to the developing world, where cheap labour made its use viable. Mark had cash aplenty to set up businesses abroad, operated by managers with remuneration packages that were linked to performance in terms of profit.

In his position as an MP, Mark had access to information regarding major manufacturing firms whose situation demanded they set up operations abroad, to increase or simply maintain profits. Opportunities abounded to sell machinery abroad where it could be used profitably by companies operating with "low wage" workforces. He used the cash from the hotel for asylum seekers from the Balkans to buy a famous manufacturer of heavy industrial electrical switches at the value of the land their factory stood on. This approach even gained a name as a business tactic. They called it Asset Stripping. Mark justified his attitude to this sort of opportunism with: if he didn't do it someone else would.

Through Stansfield, he sold the machinery abroad for what he had paid for the whole company so the land came free, for practical purposes. Consequently, through companies registered abroad, he now owned blighted industrial land he could use to build a state-of-the-art food processing plant with excellent transport links. This he set out to do, creating an organisation to manufacture and distribute a million bags of crisps a week, at a price lower than anywhere else in the country. The cost of the potatoes was almost the same as the bags containing the crisps and the distribution cost was just a little less. He shifted the print plant from number 45 to a new building on the same site as the crisps plant.

Mark thought the world had gone mad, but he was making money, money beyond his wildest dreams. He employed managers to run his businesses. A good proportion of all the crisps his new company sold went to pubs, clubs and other entertainment venues so why not supply micro-brewery plants as well? In conjunction with Leslie Stansfield, who already had contacts in China, he set about diversifying his business portfolio into bar-room supplies and machinery imported from a factory he owned fifty-fifty with a Chinese entrepreneur who was desperate for his financial input and access to Western markets. All this was done operating under a veil of secrecy, with frontmen dealing with the nuts and bolts work on the ground and companies registered abroad so that nobody knew of the wealth he was accumulating. His income soon made him a millionaire several times over, paying no tax worth mentioning and no one the wiser.

He represented the working class in parliament, a fact he found excruciatingly funny, while at the same time, it made him sick at himself for taking the bread out of the mouths of his own class. He was such a cynic. He had to be. He hadn't gone to Eton or Harrow and consequently needed to be twice as slick and crafty as any opposition.

He was employing a young guy, Goran, introduced by Gunter from what used to be Yugoslavia which was presently breaking up and separating into ethnic enclaves. He'd employed Goran as a go-between for his business interests in Eastern Europe. Goran had a top engineering degree from Czechoslovakia and he'd earned it. He was a natural and Mark was using him to oversee his engineering plants in various countries around the world. At times he went with Goran, and despite his being 100% heterosexual, they got on well together.

At Christmas, Mark sent his mother a turkey far too big for her to eat, and maybe even to cook, as well as a disk of Queen's, "We Are the Champions" with a card saying, Merry Christmas - No time for losers - I'll take a bow. He'd done it. She could rub her nose in that, and carry on working at the poxy glue factory. He had decided he didn't care if he never spoke to her or saw her again.

Mark now faced a different problem, he had money such as he'd never imagined possible. When he thought about it, he could not believe the amount of money he had access to. With the cash he got from his job as an MP and other declared income, his lifestyle had changed in a way beyond his imagination. He owned a fancy car, but he didn't even drive, he had a secretary to do that. He regarded driving as a chore and if the secretary wasn't available, he called a taxi. He could fly whenever and pretty much wherever he chose. He stayed at hotels as a VIP, and had a flat 'in town' and a detached house in the Home Counties. He frequently dined out on expenses i.e. against his tax bill. He worked as hard as ever but for the most part that involved networking which, when you came down to it, was a matter of dealing, nod- nod, wink-wink. In essence, backscratching with acquaintances who like himself had one objective in mind, filling their pockets as well as their bellies, and more realistically, their offshore accounts. He employed accountants creating 'Shell Companies' to make his financial situation as opaque as possible to limit his tax liabilities to the absolute minimum. His income as Chair of Trustees of IASIA continued to rise slowly but was puny compared to his other interests. However, it did provide an image of him as a man of conscience looking after the interests of the dispossessed.

Without really thinking about it, his main objective now was to increase his power to do exactly what he wanted; in other words, to manipulate his world to accommodate his every whim and fancy and his whims were growing more bizarre almost by the hour. His wife, Lilith, was becoming more demanding and an increasing annoyance in various ways but worst of all, she expected him to take greater responsibility for his children who he felt were hers rather than his because it was she who produced them with only marginal input from him. His involvement he regarded as insignificant. In short, the older he got, the more insanely irresponsible and selfish he became.

His adherence to the old adage, pride comes before a fall, that he'd lived by in his early days had slipped further and further to the back of his mind. He was beginning to see himself as invulnerable. He was losing sight of Midas and hubris, imagining he'd become invulnerable. Even though he still had to show up in the Commons reasonably regularly for votes and to appear to be making an effort to represent his constituents, he'd become adept at showing his face as infrequently as possible while accruing the maximum publicity for his quite rare public appearances. Everything and anything he thought or did had to be right, and the possibility of failure verging on impossible because *he* did it. It was more or less just as he had reached this feeling of invulnerability that Sara/Lilith rang to tell him that, Tom, his youngest had been taken to hospital suffering from an overdose! His first response was to ask what it was that Tom had overdosed on. Lilith told him it was cocaine, but where Tom got it was something of a mystery.

This caused Mark some consternation because when he'd last seen Tom, some weeks previously, he'd just had a supply delivered by Abdallah. It was in the kitchen and he thought Tom might have known because Abdallah had been around while he was there. Tom and his father had rowed about Abdallah, whom Tom had called a weasel and as untrustworthy as a pickpocket in a jeweller's shop. In his heart of hearts, Mark agreed. He could not bring himself to admit it because he knew that dealing with Abdallah was downright stupid. Ultimately Abdallah would be caught because he was almost half-witted when it came to covering his tracks regarding his business dealings.

Mark felt even more queasy at the thought of how Lilith's voice held an icy aloofness he'd only heard once or twice before, when she was bitterly angry, and the consequences had always been seriously bad for the recipients of her anger. Mark realised that for the first time in all the time since he'd set up IASIA, he was feeling vulnerable and began to wonder if he should not go back to basics looking to those over whom he had power as his defence against what looked like a potentially threatening situation. He knew Abdallah was worried half to death because although he had power in his own community, he faced racism and dislike among the traditional white elite. Abdallah was scared and nervous that the truth might come out regarding his sexuality and activities, essentially blackmailing young gay men in his own community to do things they hated. His future would be bleak. On top of this, his business dealing in cocaine was becoming too public and well known.

Eleven

Mark decided this might be an opportune moment to claim sickness. He contacted a doctor whose name was familiar in particular political circles for supplying evidence of nervous exhaustion. The doctor recommended a nursing home in Jersey that was expensive but had an excellent reputation for its attitude to the privacy of patients. Mark felt that such a period of rest might be a good option, given his present circumstances. He set out to maintain contact with his business partners through Lydia, Sonny and Kevin.

Meanwhile, Lilith was arguing with her father. 'You're a bigger bastard than my fucking husband!' she screamed.

Feigning dignity, her father answered, 'You come into my house where I paid for your education, and your mother looked after you, fed you and brought you up to be a respectable member of the community and now you're here using foul language such as you never learnt from us. Is this any way to treat your parents?'

Lilith, who was at the end of her tether with him, yelled, 'You treat Mum like a sore spot on your arse when you treat her like anything at all, and you've always treated me like a fucking hire car, put on earth as a convenience. A convenience for you! I'm not a fucking toilet. You set me out to sleep with your cronies when I was just a bit more than a kid. I'm your daughter, not your property. You're not living in Mauritania now. Parents who pimp their daughters might be accepted there, but this is the UK. It's the United Kingdom that's neither united, nor a bloody kingdom, but still a whole lot better place for a woman to be in than fucking Mauritania. Rule fucking Britannia. All it really rules are the fag ends of the empire in the Seychelles, the Bahamas, Jersey and the other tax havens run by the shitty CITY OF LONDON with its bloody bent and misogynistic police force, and judges and laws designed to protect the wealth of multinational and home-grown elite thieves and scumbags like you who treat women like shit. You're complicit with my disgusting husband, and I want nothing more to do with you or him, the stinking hypocritical thug! You can all fuck off. The lot of you. Consider me no longer your daughter. I want nothing more to do with you!'

After this tirade, she walked out and drove away from her parents' home. It was a scene that had been brewing for years and now it was done, there would be no going back. She was in a position at last to assert her independence from anybody.

Her law firm in South London had firmly established its position as one of the foremost, if not the leading firm representing women's rights in the UK. That night would seal her position. She was due to present a whole raft of demands on primetime TV asserting the growing importance of women in both the media and politics. The programme would confirm her position as brand leader of the Women's Rights Movement in the UK. It was a position that was paying handsomely. The legal business gained from her high public profile, and her awareness of the law contributed to her credibility as a pundit on the legal position of women, both politically and socially. Her star was in the ascendent. The kids were grown enough to be pretty much independent, and it was Lilith who provided the stability that had allowed them to become stable members of society, she was sure. Tom's latest folly messing around with drugs was as much the fault of Mark, his father, as anyone, though she was aware that he could be a bloody idiot at times, unlike his sister who was a chip off the old block, Lilith herself.

She drove home to prepare herself for her performance that night. Mahe was there to help and provide support in preparation for her mother's big occasion. When Lilith arrived home, the smell of cauliflower-cheese pervaded the kitchen. Mahe was well on the way to laying out a light meal. Some crisp-breads were spread on a serving plate and a small glass of Prosecco had already been poured. They ate the meal together and then went to the bedroom. Mahe had laid out a dress on the bed for her mother to wear, that she had selected for the occasion, hot red and figure-hugging to emphasise Lilith's still athletic body.

Lilith put it on then seeing herself in the mirror, she stripped it off.

'It's too sexy. I want to look attractive, stylish, and smart.'

She donned flared black trousers and a pair of black patent thick-soled, high-heeled shoes to give her as much height as possible. She pinned up her hair to make her look even taller, not sexy but first day at the office smart, stylish. No makeup, the people at the studio could deal with that. She topped the ensemble with a postbox red blouse, 'A-shaped' much like a dress, drawing attention away from her medium-sized breasts but presenting a dramatic flare around her hips as she moved, setting off the flared pants.

'This will let them know I don't intend to be pushed around,' she said, strutting before Mahe.

She was ready. She ordered a taxi making sure she had everything she needed in her simple, stylish handbag, colour-matched to her blouse and shoes. She felt as confident for battle as she ever would. A dramatic outfit for one of the most dramatic days of her life, ready to drop her bombshell!

She arrived at the studio in plenty of time. She'd brought a trendy women's magazine to read, and maybe to provide relaxation or inspiration, should she need it. She felt just nervous enough to be at her best. It was due to be one of the most exciting moments in her life as she dropped her bomb. Her agent had confirmed the interviewer would be a woman though she would not be tied down to exactly who. When Lilith was introduced, she was not particularly pleased, but that put her on her mettle.

The interviewer began with the usual pleasantries, introducing Lilith as, 'The well-known women's rights campaigner and lawyer, supporting women who in various ways have been discriminated against in many well-publicised cases, and wife of MP, Mark Spivey, Lilith Spivey!'

'Before we go any further,' responded Lilith, 'I would like to explain that I no longer wish to be referred to as Lilith Spivey, as I'm just beginning the process of divorcing my husband on the grounds of neglect and desertion.'

Lilith could tell that this revelation had wrong-footed the interviewer as it was followed by a long pause, and another moment's pause, as the woman poured a drink of water and took a mouthful while she collected her thoughts. She then began to fill the space with platitudes as she processed the information and tried to assess the implications of this juicy tit-bit. She instinctively grasped the situation aware that the revelation would inspire comment and gossip in the popular media for days, even weeks, to come. It could even be the interview that saw her rise from a third-stringer to the top of her profession, as the growing scandal developed. From gossip she'd heard, there was plenty of that associated with Labour MP Mark Spivey!

She suddenly realised she'd hit a goldmine and she began to dig. She'd done her research and was aware that Lilith had changed her forename some time previously.

'I believe you changed your first name some time ago. Would you care to tell me why?'

Lilith gave a small grin, 'I wondered if you'd ask me that.' She smiled and raised her eyebrows, then continued, 'The reason was, I found myself! It was a revelation. Always, since I was a child, I'd never had any real confidence in myself; any real natural confidence I was born with was more or less systematically driven out of me by my father, not necessarily physically. There was some of that, but the real damage was done psychologically. He's always been arrogant and manipulative and always treated me as a kind of extension of him. My mother is just a walking cypher; she doesn't understand herself, so no one else can. She's always looking at an image of herself and never quite able to come to terms with what she sees. My mother is a lost soul. I decided to change my position and as part of the change, I decided I would separate myself from both my father and mother. As a part of the process, I changed my name. It's the best thing that's happened to me in all my life.'

'How do you see yourself?' asked the interviewer. 'What you've just said sounds kind of mystical. Do you see yourself as some kind of mystic?'

Lilith adopted an expression of faint derision, as she stared back at the interviewer. 'That's one hundred per cent - and I mean one hundred per cent the last way I see myself these days. My feet are more firmly on the ground than ever before. I'm rock-solid in the here and now.'

'May I ask why you chose the name Lilith? It's rather unusual isn't it?'

'It's interesting you should ask me that. When I told him I was going to do it, Mark, my husband, asked me the same question, and I told him to do the research. I don't think he ever did. He just thought it was a silly whim, but I was already on the path towards divorcing him. We never ever really lived together and he was so arrogant, he thought I didn't have an opinion in the matter, and, in a way, maybe I didn't, but Lilith does.'

'So, are you saying that when you changed your name you became a different person?'

'I wouldn't say that. What happened was a process and processes don't take place all at once or even in a series of steps. The elements of a process flow into one another, and that's what happened to me. As I developed, different parts of me developed more-or-less independently, but then blended together to make a different whole, and at the same time a more concrete whole. I'm happier with myself, more at one with myself and the world, in all sorts of ways, than I've ever been before.'

'I think I understand,' said the interviewer, although in truth she was utterly bemused and failed to understand at all. She was having some difficulty keeping up.

'Well, er, let's get back to what you referred to as the concrete part of you. What made you choose the name Lilith?'

Lilith's derisive expression returned, 'I just answered that question.'

The interviewer understood she was losing control and set about retaking the initiative.

'So, what is the present state of your marriage? Is it terribly acrimonious?'

Lilith smiled, with an ironic expression this time. 'You tell me. I really have no idea. I haven't spoken to my husband for nearly a month but that's nothing new.'

'So, are you estranged?'

Lilith shook her head in disbelief. 'Are you kidding? What planet do you live on? Sorry, you're supposed to as ask the questions. Just try to keep it real.' She felt herself getting annoyed and took a long breath to calm down.

'Do you know where your husband is now?'

'That's easy, I neither know nor care. Look, can we start again? I came here to answer questions about my work with human rights issues relating to women, not to discuss my personal life and any dirty washing you can dig up relating either to my husband, myself, or my children.'

'OK, I apologise if you feel that my questions have related to your personal life rather than your public life but don't you agree that the two overlap and are intertwined?'

Lilith took control again. 'I guess I have to accept that the two do overlap, and why? Because men have always held a dominant position in pretty much all aspects of life. What I want to see is parity in the workplace, from the point of view of remuneration and conditions of employment and in terms of contracts of employment, and health and safety in the workplace. The last element of which is difficult to assess or even define, simply because women are biologically different from men, and men as we all know have dominated the workplace since at least the start of the industrial revolution.'

'So, what exactly are your objectives?'

'Our aims and objectives are quite simple: to obtain parity, as nearly as possible, with men, despite the biological differences and the fact that men are generally physically stronger. Computers have changed our world and many manual jobs have been either eliminated or rendered less arduous by the application of mechanical aids, such as mechanical road sweepers and forklift trucks. Computers are steadily eating into skilled employment to the point where old-fashioned, labour-intensive employment is being replaced with machines that just require mechanical or electrical energy.

'Look, for instance, at the traditional employment of women as seamstresses and the knowledge needed to make the most economical use of fabric. Not only does a good computer programme do it better and more quickly than either women or men, new machines can even sew difficult seams better than the most skilled humans. Computers are making people of both sexes redundant. We would argue that in general the intellect of women is in no way inferior to males, and female manual dexterity is generally better. Why is it that women accept our present position as second-class citizens?

'To support that argument, you only have to look at such women as Marie Curie, Ada Lovelace and George Elliot, to name just a few. There are so few women acclaimed as people of genius, simply because men dominate all forms of media, and consequently, the potential of women has never been allowed to develop and be exploited by society as a whole. Women have been barred from education and most other forms of intellectual exercise. Mary Ann Evans was published under the pen name, George Eliot because to publish her work under her real name would have limited the acclaim she ultimately achieved, simply because of her sex.

'Our objective is to change this sorry state of affairs and gain for women the position we truly deserve. At the same time, we want to have equal access to opportunities available to men, in terms of both education and employment, even though it is our bodies that enable the continuance of the human race. You may not have noticed that although some people are arguing that sexuality is a continuum and surgery can overcome nature, no machine can replace a woman's womb, or is ever likely to.'

'Well, thank you, Lilith. What else can I say, but that I support you whole-heartedly, and I only hope that the producers are listening. I see no reason at all why my income should not match that of our male counterparts, for the same work, despite our biological differences.' And she looked at the camera with a quizzical expression.

Twelve

Mark called Lilith when he saw the news that evening in Jersey. There was no reply. Then he then called Lydia who was aware he was in Jersey. She picked up. He told her he'd only seen snatches of the interview with Lilith.

'Have you seen the whole interview?' he asked. 'How bad is it?'

'You want an honest answer? It's a can of worms and the lid is just coming off. I don't want to be involved. It's your can, and they're your worms. I want nothing to do with it and you won't find many who will. If I were you, I'd make for the hills. The media are already like hyenas on a carcass. I'll do anything I can, within reason, but don't expect a lot. Stay where you are at the moment and wait till the initial furore wears off, is the best I can offer for now. Have a nervous breakdown, and play dumb, don't lose your cool. With any luck, and some greasy palms lubricated, it'll blow over. You're not the first and won't be the last. Stay shtum and think of the three monkeys.' With that, she hung up.

Mark went down to the nursing home bar and sat down with a double whiskey to consider what his next move should be. One thing he was sure of, he needed to move as much liquid cash to his Swiss account as he could get his hands on. He imagined his mother rubbing her hands together, like Dickens's Fagin, and smirking,

'I told you so. You're no more use than your bloody father. What you gonna do now? Take the easy way out same as him?'

No way would he give her the satisfaction. He'd fight with every weapon at his disposal. He closed his mind to his problems, deciding it was time for a little relaxation. He rang for a taxi which arrived within a few minutes.

Before he got in, he leaned down to the driver's window, offered a large denomination note and asked, 'Can you recommend any gay venues?'

'I know just the place,' smiled the driver.

'Give me a card; I'll call you later for the return journey.'

'Jump in,' he said, snatching a second generous note.

It was only minutes before the car stopped by an alley too small for a car. 'Bottom of the alley mate, good luck,' he said, then winked as he took the fare and drove off.

Mark walked straight into the bar, ordered a double Red Bull, sat on a bar stool and undid the top two buttons of his garish, red shirt.

'Warm in here tonight, I'm hot,' he announced loudly to the barman.

Seconds later, a flamboyantly-dressed young man appeared beside him.

'I'm parched and skint,' he said. 'You wanna buy me a drink?'

'Have one on me. I'm new around here. If I call a taxi, you going to show me the sights?'

Mark called the taxi he'd just left and minutes later, having downed their drinks, they were on their way to the local 'knocking shop' hotel. As the car pulled away, a dog chased it barking wildly. Mark with an unusual sense of premonition wondered if it was an omen but shook his head to throw off the silly idea. They were still in the taxi when Mark realised he might have bitten off more than he could chew. His predilection was domination but the guy he'd picked up was approximately as tall as him and a good deal more heavily built; worse still, his body looked powerful rather than fat. Mark needed to think fast. He paid off the taxi and they went into the hotel. He was surprised that it gave the impression of being quite respectable with no air of seediness, and there was a bar.

'Shall we get another drink before we go up to the room?' he said. 'What's your name?'

'You can call me John, but Whatsyourname'll do. Yeah, another drink would be good.'

Mark ordered the drinks, then said, 'I need a piss. I won't be a mo.'

The toilet was by the main door. Mark did a runner. The moment was exciting but unnerving. He was beginning to realise how vulnerable he was as he walked quickly back to the nursing home. Even though he had plenty of cash now, he was beginning to see that his resources were finite and he needed to begin to act with a bit more circumspection. Easy come, easy go was the wrong sort of philosophy in his present circumstances. With that in mind, he was starting to realise that being away from his home turf added to his vulnerability. He went to bed feeling less upbeat than he had for years.

The next morning, he strolled down to the restaurant, only to meet his new acquaintance, Whatsyourname, dressed in a sober business suit and hanging around his neck was his security identification as an employee of the nursing home. The man grinned, licked his lips and said,

'Good morning, sir. Warm this morning. The forecast is for a hot day. Enjoy your breakfast.'

It appeared he filled a management role at the nursing home. Mark simply grunted in reply. It was a long time since he'd wanted to disappear in a puff of smoke.

He ate a quick light breakfast with a double espresso and returned to his room which he decided, must now double as an office. There were things he needed to do and fast. First, he called Kevin who he'd seen less and less of recently, but needs must...

'Wow!' replied Kevin, 'shit and fans aren't in it. Your Lilith sure goes for the jugular!'

'So, what's she saying now?'

'Basically, you brought coke into her house when you knew that your son was there and likely to be vulnerable. It gets worse, the full name hasn't been made public yet but it looks as though she's implicated a guy called Abdhalla, as your supplier. Does that sound right? I get the impression and it's rumoured he's already under investigation. What you may not know is he's already got a record on two counts: one child abuse; and two, supplying drugs. I get the feeling he'd shop you as soon as look at you. That all sounds seriously messy.

'You can't look for any help from Sonny or Lydia either. I was talking to Sonny last night, and as far as she's concerned, you might as well be a hot brick. All she wants to do is drop you in cold water and let the whole business cool down. I have a feeling Lilith may have got to Sonny and Lyd, and now it's all the girls together and nuts to LGBTQ. Up with the drawbridge and off to the battlements. You should stay where you are till someone comes knocking, then off to a bolt-hole somewhere as discreet as you can possibly find, is pretty much your only short-term option, I'd say. You've played more or less straight with me, so anything I can do, without putting a noose around my neck, I will, OK?'

At least that's one more or less, ally, thought Mark.

'Thanks for that,' he said. 'I'll keep you posted always on a private line, OK?'

Next, Mark phoned a Mr Gomez recommended by Leslie Stansfield. He had been given to believe that Mr Gomez was a dab-hand at securing Israeli passports for those with Jewish relatives. Mark's grandmother was Jewish, so acquiring a passport should be relatively easy, or so he'd been led to believe. The only problem would be a matter of proving through documentation that his grandmother was, in fact, Jewish. This was Mr Gomez's forte. Two passports can be a blessing but also a millstone. On the one hand, it's possible to play one authority against the other. On the other hand, if the two begin to work together your problems are doubled. The time and cost were two unknown variables but Gomez estimated he could complete Mark's job in about two months, if Mark could come up with £2,000, up front, with a balance of £8,000 on delivery.

Mark forwarded the two grand cash, immediately. His next move was to purchase a pair of heavy-framed spectacles and some peroxide hair bleach. He then bought a flight to Cork and from there, to East Midlands. This involved an overnight stop-off in Cork which was no problem as he enjoyed the craic there.

Gomez operated from London and Mark liked to meet those he did business with, especially when the business was of a confidential nature!

What had been Mark's horror story was beginning to take on an exciting aspect. He was almost enjoying himself, despite the fact that whenever he left his room he might face the embarrassment of meeting Whatsyourname.

To escape from the "Nursing Home" for a while, Mark slipped quietly from his room and took a walk into the town to book a rail ticket from EMA to London where he intended to stay for a couple of days sorting out more urgent business, as well as the Jewish passport. On his way, whom should he meet, but Whatsyourname. The embarrassment was wearing off and he merely nodded, but the man gave a small smirk, stopped and said quietly,

'I think you might be interested in visiting our annexe sir, while you're here. I think you might find it has a wonderfully relaxing atmosphere after the nursing home and we like to make all our guests' visits as enjoyable as possible. After all, what is a nursing home for, but to relieve the stresses of modern life for our patients?'

Unusually, Mark was a little flummoxed by this turn of events. He stopped and paused while he considered what was, or was not going on, then concluding there was only one way to find out, said,

'OK, nothing ventured nothing gained. Why not?'

'I'll call you, sir, after dinner tonight and arrange the visit,' he replied then continued on his way.

After the evening meal, Whatsyourname moved quietly behind Mark's chair and whispered,

'There's a taxi waiting at the front entrance, sir. If you'd like to follow me?'

Mark moved his chair back away from the table and followed him out to the taxi. Like everywhere on the Island, the journey was short. They arrived at a private school with several buildings set among well-manicured lawns and drove to the rear where stood quite a large building that had much of the appearance of an early twentieth-century, two-storey mansion. At the front, stood a grand porticoed entrance set between two large bay windows topped by dormer windows that reached the apex of the roof. Well-kept flowerbeds graced the front of each bay.

'Call-me-John! Mr Spivey,' said Whatsyourname, as they dismounted from the taxi and entered the building.

They climbed an impressive central stairway, turned left at the landing, and left again to another small staircase and up into converted servants' quarters, so reminiscent of his old flat at Number 45, that it made Mark feel almost at home, even though the stairs were not carpeted. The only other major difference was that the room they entered was so sparsely furnished with a plain table on which stood an old-fashioned desk lamp. Around the table stood four, tidily-placed chairs that matched the table for their bald plainness. In a dark corner, lurked an old-fashioned, iron-framed bed. The bedclothes covering the bed would have been promptly recognised in the 19th Century as something from a better class workhouse, if there was such a thing, straight from a Dickens novel. Coarse but clean cotton sheets and rough army-style grey blankets covered a thin, sad mattress and old Fashioned lumpy-looking pillow. The room was positively spartan.

Mark was feeling decidedly edgy about his situation, especially when he tried the door of the room, to discover he was locked in. But it wasn't long before he heard steps on the stairs outside. A key turned in the lock, and the door opened. A small boy entered followed closely by Call-me-John and another person, a heavily-built, hatchet-faced woman, grey hair pulled up close to her skull, away from her face into a tight bun. She carried a supermarket shopping bag which she proceeded to empty onto the table, simply by pouring out the contents. Having done this, she faced Mark and announced,

'This child deserves chastisement. He constantly wets his bed and displays dumb insolence when questioned about his behaviour. On the table I've placed some articles of chastisement for your use, Mr Spivey. You have the school's permission to approach the punishment of this recalcitrant boy in any way you see fit. If you're happy to deal with this situation, we'd be pleased to witness the way you deal with the correction of this child.'

Mark was enthralled by this opportunity to impose his will on such an unattractive, even despicable, human being. He said quietly but with malice,

'What's your name boy?'

He didn't even think for a second how Call-me-John knew about his penchant for S&M with minors.

'Stephen,' answered the boy, as urine trickled down his leg and a tear ran from his left eye.

'When I ask a question,' said Mark, 'I expect a proper answer. What's your name?'

'Stephen,' said the boy again, beginning to sob.

'What's your full name?'

'Stephen,' desperately repeated the boy.

'That's it, is it, just Stephen? And where do you come from, Just Stephen?'

'Don't know,' said Stephen.

'Get undressed, Stephen and stop crying or I'll give you something to cry about, you silly boy,' growled Mark.

Stephen took off his shirt, then his sandals and socks. More slowly, he dropped his short trousers and stepped out of them but stopped at his dampened pants.

'Why have you stopped?' asked Mark, picking up a length of knotted cotton rope from the pile on the table, and wrapping it around his fingers before whipping it with a crack on the table-top.

Stephen simply stood silent, apart from the quiet sound of suppressed sobs, racking his thin shivering body.

'Take off your pants, and dry yourself with your shirt, Stephen!'

Stephen slowly did as he was told.

Mark, turned to Call-me-john, 'Before I have anything more to do with Stephen, I need to see he's cleaned up after pissing himself. He smells.' Looking at Stephen with an expression of disgust. Is there a bath available?'

'As matron, I don't have the authority to use the baths, only showers. For that, I'd have to ask his housemaster and at the moment he's at the main nursing home building,' said the sinister-looking woman.

'Well, if you're expecting premium payment for premium service then premium service it needs to be. There are baths in this building, I assume?' Mark was beginning to feel the need to assert himself and cash was his only weapon.

'There are baths in the basement, but as you say, that's premium service,' said Call-me-john. 'But I'll see what can be arranged. As luck would have it, the school is out on holiday at the moment, there are only a few special-case kids here at the moment. Stephen is one of the most noxious.'

With that, Call-me-John and the matron left, and Mark made as if to lie on the bed but thought better of it, took off the blanket and threw it to Stephen, saying,

'You can stop snivelling and sit and be quiet. You hear, be bloody quiet.'

Stephen wrapped the blanket around himself and sat on one of the chairs at the table, doing his best to suppress his sobbing.

Mark lay with his hands behind his head simply waiting to see the way things developed, occasionally eyeing Stephen. It wasn't long before the matron and Call-me-john returned carrying a big bunch of keys.

'We can use the baths so follow us,' said Matron. 'That includes you, Stephen, you silly boy.'

Call-me-john led the way, followed by Stephen who was ushered by the matron, followed by Mark.

The little group trooped downstairs to the ground floor and then in a nook behind the main staircase Call-me-john inserted a large key into the lock of a small door leading down more stairs to a big damp basement with low, whitewashed ceiling and whitewashed brick walls, and a rough, old, quarry tiled floor. Along the back of this cellar lay an ancient slate-walled tank, nearly two meters long, and one wide, perhaps half a meter deep above which, at the back, was a rusted pipe and verdigris-covered brass tap; its original use was hard to imagine but now, apparently to function as a bath.

Call-me-john turned on the tap to allow a copious flow of cold water to run into the tank. The matron nodded to Mark indicating with added eye movements, that he should get Stephen into the tank, which he proceeded to do by placing a hand on the boy's back and pushing him in, during which he almost fell over. The matron handed Mark a block of old-style laundry soap, who then passed it to the boy.

'Right!' said Mark. 'Now clean yourself up then we'll decide what to do with you.'

Stephen dipped the soap into the water and began to soap himself as the water steadily rose above his feet, and he began to spasmodically shiver.

'Come here! Now give me the soap Stephen,' said Mark.

The boy handed the soap carefully to Mark who dipped his hands into the water and lathered them well with the soap. He then rubbed the soap block on the boy's hair working up a good lather, then worked his way down the boy's body before turning the child's back towards him in order to ram his finger up the boy's rectum. Stephen squealed.

'Don't worry son, just cleaning your arse! Right! Now sit down.'

Stephen stood rigid with shock.

'Sit!' shouted Mark, putting his hand on the boy's head and pushing downwards.

Stephen sat half-immersed in the cold water.

'Lie down,' said Mark.

Stephen sat frozen with his arms around his knees.

Mark forced him backwards. He opened his arms trying so stop his head from submersion, but Mark was far too strong and Stephen's head sank below the surface of the water.

Call-me-john intervened, 'Take care, we don't want to drown the little twat. That'll do!'

Mark was on a high, not so different from a line of coke, but came down quickly when Call-me-john placed a heavy hand on his shoulder and said,

'Snuff comes dearer than you might be willing to pay. I think that's enough.'

'What do you think Matron?'

She gave an ironic smile, 'That'll do I suppose. I think we may as well get him to bed. If he pisses the bed again, we'll have to decide how we're going to deal with the fucking little runt.' With that, she gave a disgusting belch. 'Come on Stephen, get a move on, wrap this around you.' Throwing the child the blanket and set off dragging a silent, staggering Stephen up the stairs.

Call-me-john followed, turning his head back towards Mark and said, 'It's like a drug, you know. Power corrupts, so the saying goes.'

Back on the ground floor, Call-me-john ordered a taxi to take both Mark and him back to the nursing home. Once there, Mark went straight to his room and pre-ordered a taxi to take him to the airport after breakfast in the morning, ready to catch his flight to Ireland. He then downed a double Glenfiddich and went to bed. Despite the whiskey, his mind was still buzzing with the events of the evening. He didn't sleep well, and arose early, though not refreshed but muzzy. He bleached his hair and eyebrows then packed ready to go, before breakfast, and the moment the taxi arrived, he was off. The less contact he had with Call-me-john the better. He knew the man could not be trusted. Why else would he not even know his real name?

By eleven o'clock he was in Cork feeling better after a nap on the plane. Despite the bleached hair, there was no hassle at passport control, and he reached his hotel before lunch.

Lilith, for her part, was sorting out details for her divorce and looking at angles from which she could attack Mark's ownership of his businesses and property. She was aiming for the jugular. Anything of Mark's property she could get her hands on was hers. Mark had pushed her around for far too long and she was intending to hit him where it would hurt him most, his pocket. She contacted a firm specialising in bugging devices, recommended to her by Lydia. On speaking to a representative there, she discovered that not only did the company supply the devices, they also provided an installation service, and around-the-clock recording of all messages. Added to all of that, the charges for their service were, she thought, very modest.

She ordered bugs to be placed on, not just the phone in Mark's London flat, but also his bolt-hole at Number 45 Pinfold Street, his Party-funded constituency office, and even the car he got on expenses, for his work-related travel, as well as that of his secretary, cum driver. Lydia also provided some basic lessons in collecting embarrassing information and awkward-to-explain financial material on individuals of interest. On top of all this, she suggested ways of discovering events that could be difficult to excuse by searching through publicly-available correspondence. Even further she suggested contacts who might be willing to cause annoyance, provoke, embarrass, and annoy, target individuals. It seemed that Lydia ran an intelligence network that might, in its own small way, rival MI6.

The operation would take time but once the ball began to roll, the media would be making their own investigations "digging dirt to hurt". Mark's future was looking bleaker by the hour. The thought caused her to smile. Her biggest problem might turn out to be her own association with Mark, who she knew had a remarkable innate ability to encourage sympathy. To that end, she set out through every medium possible to distance herself from him and his activities which, to some degree, she had been doing for a considerable time. Her main advantage was that it was she who had brought up their children, even to the point of providing the bulk of the cash for their education and upkeep, which through careful accounting and record-keeping she could easily prove.

Mahe, Lilith's daughter was 100% her mother's child, having caught the women's lib bug early in life. Her mother had encouraged her towards a career in the legal profession, helping her to gain a second-class honours degree in law from UCL. The day she graduated, she had always had plenty of lucrative opportunities in the profession, unlike her father when he was young.

Lydia's instruction course in undercover surveillance had really put the bit between Lilith's teeth, and she was swiftly becoming obsessive. Not only was she setting out to know

Mark's every move, but she was trying to get inside his mind and understand his basic motivations, a task he himself would have found impossible. She managed through the tap on his phone at the Nursing Home, to discover his travel plans, but the events with Call-me-john at the nightclub and school building were closed to her. She was aware he was liquidating assets as fast as he possibly could. She also knew he was coming to London to meet Gomez to acquire a second passport. Essentially, he was 'On the Run', though she had no idea that he'd done his best to change his appearance with the glasses and peroxide. Had she seen a picture, she'd probably have nearly wet herself laughing, imagining him adopting a 'Clouseau' accent, almost as if he intended to make himself look a complete clown.

She was collecting documentary evidence that he was trying to hide the huge wealth he had accumulated which he regarded as his own personal money. As his wife, she was entitled to half, and beyond that a contribution to the upkeep of his children. She was also collecting personal information not just about his unusual sexuality but also his perversions and vicious attacks upon vulnerable, young, homosexual men through his contact with Abdullah, a convicted child molester and drug dealer. She was feeling utterly vindictive, and she was going to make him pay for the treatment he had meted out to her and his children. She'd see the arrogant, slimy, perverted, scumbag, broken, crushed, and burning in hell. She smiled viciously at the thought.

Mark reached his old flat at 45 Pinfold Gate almost exactly 48 hours after leaving Jersey. As he climbed the stairs, his mood changed looking forward to the peace and quiet of his old haunt on the third floor, out of the way of the manic world outside. It was almost six months since he'd last been there, but despite the neglected smell of the place, and dust and cobwebs, it still felt like home. He went to the junk-filled broom cupboard, took out the vacuum cleaner and plugged it in, then went to the kitchen and turned on the tap to drain the pipe of stagnant water and closed the fridge door and switched it on. He decided he'd nip out to the local shop and get some frozen stuff in then take a quick shufti at the pile of trash circulars causing a blockage behind the front door, before dumping it in the bin and sitting in comfort to watch a trash film.

It was almost like stepping back into his old life before he'd gained fame and fortune. It was kind of relaxing to be transported back to looking after himself. He hadn't smoked for over twenty years but suddenly felt a twinge of the old craving. He buried the idea by switching on the vacuum cleaner to suck up some of the accumulated dust on the floor and help eliminate the smell of neglect. He opened a couple of windows letting in some fresh air.

When he arrived at the pile of junk mail by the front door, he switched off the machine and set about gathering up the rubbish. but near the top lay a padded envelope that bore no stamp and looked as though it had recently been hand-delivered. He carried the rubbish to the bin in the kitchen and dumped it, then took the mystery envelope to the sitting room and tore it open. Inside was a cassette tape. He slipped it into the deck and switched it on. He heard his own voice saying, 'Take off your clothes Stephen.' He shivered as the realisation hit him. He'd been set up.

'Christ Almighty!' he said out loud, then 'Shit' as the full impact dawned upon him that Callmejohn, four hundred miles away had him by the balls, as sure as if he were in the flat, there and then.

He poured himself a Glenfiddich. His woes were piling up but he was a long step from finished yet. He thought about his options. His main advantage was cash, and he still had enough to not even know how much there really was, so his course of action was still wide open. It was time to go back to basics. He called the old M&D number. The same old gritty voice answered.

'M&D.'

'Hi, it's Mark, from IASIA, you remember?'

'Yeah. Long time since you called. Heard you got problems.' Sounding a little smug, 'You need somethin' sortin'?'

'Could be. It's kind of delicate.'

'Delicate ain't what we do. Direct is our speciality. You know what we do. Sub-out most of the work these days. Half me joints are bleedin' knackered from me days roofin'. We got young talent though. You got a job needs doin' we still sub' out some 'o' the jobs to one or two good lads but they ain't really as reliable as they might be. If you want a job done right, it's always best to do it yourself.'

'Can we meet? This is serious and there's serious money involved.'

'Whenever y' like. We've got an office now, we rent from Lydia, cheap, y' know but it's OK. Y'can come there. It's number 1, Dawson Sreet jus' round th' corner from yor' ol' office.'

'I know it. How about now?'

'OK. See y' in a coupla minutes.'

Mark set off straight away. On arrival, looking at Mick, he worried he might have become a bloated 'has been'. When Mark first saw him the flick knife had appeared in his hand almost in the way of a conjuring trick. Now his hands, like the rest of his body, were puffy and swollen.

'So what y' lookin' for, Mark?'

'I've been wondering how to go about it,' replied Mark.

'Sooh. Go about what?'

'Well, explained in a careful sort of way, I want someone to disappear.'

'What?' said Mick, 'We're in security. We Ain't fucking magicians. What, y'a talkin' about?'

'Well look at it like this. Last year according to official figures 170,000 people disappeared in the UK and the government admitted the real figure is a lot higher than that. Officially, there were nine non-domestic murders per million people in the UK last year. That's about 600. I've been checking. So I'm looking at making someone disappear. If you get my meaning. If there's no physical evidence then someone has disappeared, so to avoid any proper investigation, the government or the police or whoever declares a person disappeared, otherwise they'd be spending a fortune looking for people who'd cracked up, and gone walk-about. D'you see what I'm getting at? If there's no body, then someone has disappeared, rather than been, rubbed out, as you might say. Putting it bluntly, d'you think you might find a way to make a person disappear?'

'Jesus Mark! You're talkin' serious action here. Premier league' stuff. Sserious, money. It could be organised, but you're talking life sentences, even falling out of the top window of a block of flats. If it wasn't a top professional job, it'd be all too easy to make a right bollocks of it. You'd have to do the rubbing out and disappear the body without any evidence. Whatever way you look at it, it'd be a case of heavy negotiations about fees an' there's no way anyone'd be talkin' chicken feed. Your best option, I'd 'ave thought, would be top-line ex-military. That's the kind of caper they deal in. Out 'o' my league really, but I expect I could rustle up some contacts. Dodgy people though. To deal with the likes o' them you never know where their contacts might stop. You could be stepping on god knows whose toes; even government's.

'You'd probably know more about that than me, these days, you bein' a high flyer an' all that. Embarrassment in high places, lots of nasty consequences, if you're not careful. You might do well to talk to Lydia. She's higher up the shit pile than me. I wish you fucking luck mate, but if you get real stuck. I'll see what I can do but make no mistake it'd cost Big Time!'

'Well, put out some feelers,' said Mark, 'cos I need some action pronto! I'll try Lydia. I don't really think it's her style, but I'll give it a go.'

Then came the idea, almost like the inspiration for IASIA and that had turned up trumps. He was acquainted with a guy from the other side of the House who he knew ran a business doing shady mercenary work. It took on operations commissioned on an undercover, arm's length, basis, to carry out military tasks financed through the back door of national security from the private side of the public purse. For the right remuneration, he might have contacts to carry out the work Mark needed doing. In business terms, it was just another contract after all!

Thirteen

Almost without realising it, Lilith and Mahe were beginning to work as a partnership, though not without some friction. Mahe was influencing her mother, steadily pointing out the failure of the system in dealing with young people and education. She had joined the Green Party, something her mother did not necessarily approve of, but her daughter had a right to her own opinions, and there was a certain logic to what she said. They often discussed the situation in the light of Tom's education and his attitudes to life. Mahe thought her mother was too lenient with him, with his drinking and smoking dope. She often said things like,

'Tom's still in bed and it's nine o clock. He's supposed to be at his first lecture now.'

'We'll get him a gap year and stop his allowance,' Lilith would reply. 'And then he'll have to decide what the hell he wants to do with his life. We know the course he's on is a waste of time, bloody Archeology. Go home, ancient bloody Rome. What's the point? What's gone is gone and done with. As for money, he's probably better off on the dole. Hopefully, when we stop his allowance, he'll see sense. In the end, he'll have to make up his own mind. If he's determined he wants to drink himself to death and spend his life smoking dope and scrabbling around in mud, there's nothing I, or anyone else, can do about it. He's always been a lazy little sod. I've done my best, but his father's been as much use as a bucket with a hole in the bottom, keeping dribbling him cash when he's in trouble with money and nothing else that's any use. I just despair.'

Mahe would argue back,

'That's all very well, but part of the problem has to be government policy. It's the direction that the government is leading all young people to follow. The government is pushing the idea that anyone who's going to get anywhere in life needs a degree. Some of the so-called degrees are beyond a joke. I saw one the other day, a degree in Swimming Pool Management. They'll be offering degrees in flea training for flea circus managers next!'

Lilith's response,

'OK, in the less popular subjects like the sciences, maths and engineering, the quality of students and their work is often improving, although the wages on offer aren't anything to write home about, so don't sound so attractive. If kids have the wit to do the work and take a sensible approach to their future, then they can still do OK.

'Look at courses in computer game design. They're selling like hot cakes and a half-wit would know the market's already totally swamped. Any idiot can see it's just a fad. 'Game of Thrones? A five-minute wonder!

'So, there's a situation where reasonably intelligent students are not really thinking straight. Thinking about the real value of their degrees, but then, what can they expect? Racking up debts, just doing what they enjoy, playing silly, essentially children's games. They need to grow up. Life's not all fun and they'll learn bloody damn fast. There are real consequences for everything we do. They'll find out the hard way. Your father learnt that lesson and was bright enough to see a way out. I have to give him credit for that, the crafty sod. Outsmarted my father, and that's not easy! Paid off his debts in double quick time. Mind you he had the luck of the devil, and by God, that's running out pretty quick, if I have anything to do with it.'

Mahe understood the feeling of frustration among talented young people and their helplessness. They consequently felt desperation when it dawned upon them that anyone with real aspirations was going to meet a brick wall regarding their future. Real opportunities were almost non-existent.

The world was changing, and not for the better, especially in the West where the old order was moving towards collapse. The contraceptive pill, as well as all the other contraceptive devices, had done more for the real liberation of women than all the Votes For Women acts passed by parliament put together. The two world wars had put women into the jobs market, expanding the real workforce available. In 1926, at the time of the general strike, there were a million men employed in coal mines. At the time of the miners' strike in 1984, there were just 180,000 miners left employed. Mechanisation was destroying jobs at an ever-increasing rate. Governments across Europe were setting out to solve the problem by expanding the 'Service Sector' ie tourism, restaurants and entertainment, but the truth as she saw it, was they don't contribute to the economy like a sack of grain or a tank of fuel These are real, like a bag of gold. The North Sea gas bonanza meant coal as a source of basic energy was finished. Coal had taken the place of backbreaking human toil. Coal like so much of the old labouring workforce was becoming redundant. Dirty to use, expensive to extract and expensive to transport. This changed the world beyond recognition.

Mahe knew all this, and more. She was interested in history, every bit as much as in law. She knew history was a matter of happenstance, rather than the clever activities of humans, the will of God, call it what you will. She thought, no one had a crystal ball, that was the way she interpreted how the world worked. On climate change, she wasn't convinced either way. Both sides relied too much on shaky theories and iffy scientific information. She felt to some degree that way about her father. He hadn't been good with his children, there was no doubt, but she knew his life had been a helter-skelter, one thing after another, and now her mother was out to get him, come whatever, for what she saw as her victimisation. Mahe felt that even thinking about all these things was no more use than arguing about whether or not God was Mohammed, Jesus or Buddha.

Meanwhile, Mark called the man he knew who ran the company employing mercenaries used by the government for undercover operations abroad. His name was Nigel Bendt-Schleimaan. Mark had only met him socially in the past in formal situations, and they had no more than a casual acquaintance, so his approach needed to be decidedly circumspect. The questions he was asking were extremely delicate in their nature. Mark hinted to Nigel about his predicament. Nigel suggested they make an appointment for lunchtime the following day at a non-descript small restaurant in Clapham, South London near the Common where they could have a confidential chat while taking a stroll. He, clearly, fully understood that Mark was proposing something illegal when he said,

'So, it's a state of affairs that demands the left hand doesn't need to know what the right hand is up to. Would that sum up the situation?' His eyes opening wide and his head nodding slightly with an expression indicating a question.

Mark half-smiled at Nigel inclining his head in affirmation.

'So, what exactly are you looking for?'

'I'm being blackmailed. I know who it is. I want it stopped.'

'I see, and why are you telling me?'

'Being blunt, I thought you might know where to find someone who could make an individual disappear. Obviously, I could make it worth their while.'

'Nothing like the blunt approach. Say what you mean and mean what you say. It might be possible. No doubt you've considered the expense?'

'Of course, but I don't see any alternative. I've been set up by some very unsavoury people, and the only way I can see to deal with them is, in effect go to war, and you operate with mercenaries through your firm, 'Safeguard Security Support'. I thought you might be able to take on a battle for me.'

'So, where did you hear about us?'

'I don't really know, word just gets around, I guess.'

'I'll do some research; probably the way to go about such a task is to approach it from abroad, maybe somewhere south of the equator. People aren't so... erm. So squeamish there. One of the Spanish-speaking countries where relations with the UK aren't too good. Argentina might be a good bet.'

'How exactly would you expect to make someone disappear?'

'What I was thinking was maybe a fishing boat and lose the target overboard, well weighted.'

'Very Mafia. I'd recommend something much simpler and much tidier, just sort out the paperwork and have the body cremated. When it's gone, it's gone and never to be seen again. Just a matter of crossing the right palms. The most difficult part is creating a plausible story. A plausible explanation of who the cadaver belonged to, that differed convincingly from the truth. Once that's established, and any real evidence is destroyed then no one can prove anything one way or the other. All the concrete evidence is destroyed. Before we do anything else, we need to know who the individual is. Ideally with photo identification. It wouldn't do for a mix-up to take place, would it? Do you think that would be possible?'

'It wouldn't be easy for me, but I know what his job is and where he works, so I should think employing someone to get a photo shouldn't be too difficult, easy even. So, you might be prepared to take the job on?'

'Obviously, we'd need to discover the identity of the person involved then we could consider our options.'

'I'll look into getting photo ID,' said Mark, 'and a name, unless you can recommend someone to do it?'

'We could take that on for a start. Simple enough. Wouldn't even be very expensive. So where does this person work, and what's his job?'

'He's employed at a private psychiatric hospital on the Island of Jersey in the Channel Islands, dealing with security.'

'Fascinating. There's only one private psychiatric hospital on the Island. It's well known among a certain class of people,' he said, looking pointedly at Mark. 'I'm inclined to think I might just be acquainted with the person in question, as well as the place of his employment. Isn't the world a small place? I'll do some research and ring you with a price for the work done and as soon as the cash arrives, I'll start wheels turning to complete the task. OK? Shouldn't take long, maybe a week. All being well should be able to solve your difficulties quite promptly, maybe in a couple of months, perhaps even less. Depends on what we discover on the way. That sound OK?'

'Sounds excellent. Let me know the initial cost and I'll sort out payment any way you want.'

'Cash would be the preferred option. I'll be in touch.'

Mark breathed a sigh of relief. One major problem, apparently, more-or-less solved.

It was clear that people who were a danger to him were aware of his location, and he decided his next move should be to go somewhere nondescript, away from the world he knew. 'Just in case,' as his mother would say.

He had, for quite some time, harboured the idea of joining the landed gentry, buying an estate somewhere not necessarily in the UK. He picked up a bottle of wine and saw the label, Rioja. That would do. He already had the links with so-called 'craft beer' and the processes that making good beer involved. He thought making excellent wine would involve the same sort of mindset. He felt it was an area, outside finance, that interested him.

He sat down to look at ads for vineyards in Spain. There was something about Spain that attracted him. He was not sure why and was pleasantly surprised to see how cheap a small vineyard in somewhere like Rioja or Galicia might be, and on a whim, decided to go take a look. If he was in Spain looking at property, in general terms, he'd be out of easy reach of the UK media whose attention he could do without at present. He booked a one-way tourist class flight to Madrid for the following day, then called Kevin to let him know where he was and get him to instruct his secretary/driver, who was still in his employ, telling him he needed him to do some driving in Spain and to book the earliest flight, then charge it to his account.

The day after he'd first made his decision, he was at Adolfo Suarez Airport, Madrid, shortly before lunchtime. He realised, during the flight, why it was so much better to fly first class. A child sitting behind him spent the bulk of his time kicking the back of his seat. He was patient. He did not make a scene, as he was inclined to do, because, the last thing he wanted, was to draw attention to himself.

Taking a taxi to the city, alone, when offers were made to share, made him realise just how fortunate he was to have built such a financial empire so quickly. At the city centre, he instructed the driver to take him to an area nearby, where the best hotels were. He chose a hotel on a pot-luck basis that looked traditional but well-maintained. He booked in. He was still stuck with using his English passport.

The room was pleasant, slightly away from the centre, where the traffic was thickest, and consequently, reasonably quiet. He unpacked, took a shower then went down to the restaurant and settled for the 'menu del dia,' Which turned out to be a potato and onion omelette. Pretty much what his mother might have described as good, solid, peasant, food, but it was OK, fresh and hot, with a glass of perfectly reasonable local red. It seemed he might be slipping back to his roots.

It only cost 6.5 euros. And his room was clean and comfortable with a shower for just 90 per night. He'd slept in rooms, perhaps even smaller, but no way, really, any better at ten times the price. He sometimes wondered why he bothered. He smiled to himself because he knew where he was. and still would never swap places with that pathetic little prick Stephen, who was simply destined to be one of life's eternally downtrodden until he died. Killing him would have saved the sad little bastard, a whole lot of pain and suffering. Mark would have done him, and the world, a favour if he'd drowned him!

There were winners in this life and losers. Mark, despite anything that might happen in the future, was a winner. He'd already proved that.

He decided to take a look around the local area and see if there were any worthwhile opportunities around Logrono where he might indulge his fancy for a vineyard. He felt he might be able to reinvent himself as a connoisseur, producing wine that he regarded as a suitable product from his own estate, small though it might be.

He called his office in the UK to find out what was happening with his secretary/driver Leonard/Lenny/Lena. It was 8.30 a.m. in Madrid but 7.30 in London and he got the cleaner, Sally, who unusually for a female, he liked, partly because she was so good at her job. She kept his office spotless, without even thinking about it, cleaning came to her as a preferred occupation. She was just clean and tidy by nature and had no feeling of subservience because the rest of the world saw her work as a lowly occupation. Surprisingly, this pleased Mark in a way he did not quite understand. Sally was one of the few women he liked from a sexual point of view. In just the same way as his wife Lilith, as she now wanted to be called. He could have bedded Sally with pleasure and was happy to chat. He asked her what time Leonard/lena, his secretary/driver was likely to be in.

'I'm not sure,' replied Sally, 'but, I think he might have left. I've not seen him for more than a week and he was nearly always early. Mostly no later than quarter to eight. He's usually here by now.'

On the spur of the moment, Mark said. 'Do you drive?'

'I've got a Volkswagen Golf nineteen hundred diesel,' she replied. 'It's a bloody good car, goes like shit off a shovel, and economical, but I hardly use it. The traffic here's so bad, I use an electric bike unless it's pissing down; then I avoid the rush hour and take the Tube. E-bikes are easily the quickest way of getting around in London. I only use the Golf, more or less, when I'm going on the motorway.'

'Have you ever driven in Europe on the right?'

'Been a couple of times, the main roads are pretty good, especially in Spain, hardly any traffic out of the towns there and mostly they're small, anyway.'

'Ever been to Logrono in Rioja?'

'No, don't think so, might have been round the ring road past it, though. I've heard of Rioja that's where the wine comes from but never heard of Logrono as far as I can remember.'

Without thinking, he said, 'How d'you fancy a couple of weeks out here, as my driver? I'd pay you a good rate.'

'Bloody hell, bit sudden. I need to think about it.' Then, 'Go on then. My dad used to say, don't look a gift horse in the mouth, but you'd have to keep your hands to yourself. I'd just be your driver, nothing else, and I'd want my own accommodation.'

'Done,' said Mark.

He'd somehow sensed that Lennard/Lena had deserted when his services were not called upon for a fortnight. He later heard he'd gained employment in Lisbon. It was known as a haven for people with Lena's proclivities, especially during the English winter. The fact neither bothered, nor surprised him. Driver assistants were two-a-penny, as far as he was concerned, and having a woman driving for him would pique people's curiosity. That might not go amiss, even though he was aiming to keep a low profile, simply because it might place a red herring in the narrative that he wanted to create surrounding his persona.

'Speak to Kevin, downstairs. I'll ring him and let him know what's what and he'll organise a flight for you to Madrid. Call me when you get there and I'll get a taxi to the airport. I'm at the Ibera Catalon; just ask for Mr Spivey. They speak good English. Then we'll hire a car. I want to tour the area around Logrono. I want to look around the vineyards there. It'll be interesting being a tourist. I've never done that sort of thing before, except when I got married in Africa, and it's such a big place, it was just too tiring. 90% of the time we were just being driven around on bad roads. My personal opinion was, it was a literal pain in the arse.

'I'm not going to do that again. We won't be driving much more than 100 miles a day maximum. There'll be plenty of stops, giving me lots of time to look around. I don't want to rush, just take it steady and get a feel for the place. Eat some good food and taste some good wine, 'OK?'

'I always thought you were a bit odd, but now I know you're crazy,' she said. 'Should I call you boss, or sir?'

'Call me Mark, or Mr Spivey, not boss, but don't forget that I am, OK?'

He then set about wandering around the area near his hotel, getting a feel for the place just as he'd intended. It reminded him of his days wandering the streets of Bagchester touting for jobs in the legal profession. It seemed such a long time ago, but it was warm and sunny, not cold and raining.

Fourteen

It was forty-eight hours before Sally finally arrived. Her first words were,

'Sorry it took so long. Had to get a new cozzy. Seem to have got a bit curvier since I wore the old one.'

'You're not here on holiday, you're here as my driver.'

'Yeah, but I'll get some time to myself, won't I?'

'No doubt, but where we're going isn't near the sea. It'll be on mountain slopes.'

They took a taxi to Mark's Hotel in Madrid where he'd booked a separate room for Sally. He came with her to her room, while a young male hotel employee brought her luggage. She walked in, looked around, walked to the window and opened it. She licked her finger and drew it along the top of the frame. She held it up for Mark to see the accumulated dust at the tip.

'Not very clean these Spanish are they?' she said, as she winked and smiled at the young man who'd brought her luggage.

'The air's dustier here because it's warm and dry,' said Mark. 'D'you want some lunch? The food is pretty good and I think the wine is better than the stuff they send us in England.'

They went downstairs to the restaurant and agreed to share gazpacho soup with bread, green olives and a bottle of red, a part of which they were told could be kept for them for later if they wanted. After their lunch, they went in search of a hire car. Mark chose a medium-sized Mercedes with input from Sally who then drove them back to the hotel where she asked him what he wanted to do that evening. He asked if she fancied a stroll around Chueca.

'It's the gay area where they say it's the best for entertainment.'

'Sounds OK to me,' she replied.

So, off they went. It was early, just after three thirty so everything was still pretty quiet with just a few sight-seers. They simply wandered around, casually chatting as they walked. They found a bar and sat with drinks and some tapas.

They both came to the same conclusion as Mark said,

'I don't know about you, but I think we might as well go back to the hotel, follow the local tradition and have a siesta.'

'Seems as good an idea as any,' she replied. 'My feet have had enough of walking.'

Mark slept for two hours, waking at six thirty. He walked to Sally's room and knocked. She opened the door and he took her hand, gently but firmly pulling her into the hallway, then whispered in her ear,

'I think we're being followed.'

He then indicated with his finger and a motion of the head to follow him. She responded, indicating she'd get her door entry card. He nodded. She got the card and followed him down to the bar. He bought a couple of small drinks and took them to a table where they sat down.

'I want to leave. Now!'

She looked at him as though he was crazy.

'You may think I'm nuts but in this world, there are wheels within wheels. That's part of the reason you're here. There are things going on you don't understand. The world I live in is a complicated place. Having money isn't, necessarily, all it's cracked up to be. I have enemies. I'm more or less certain my phone is being tapped, and I think there may even be a tracker on the car. I want to get away from here tonight. Are you OK with that? It'll mean we have to take pot luck about where we stay. It might be a bit rough because I want somewhere away from any main population centres. You happy with that?'

'You're the boss, but I'm not staying in any old fleapit,' she said. 'This is turning into something like out of a film. I thought you were crazy, but I didn't expect it to be this crazy but it's up to you; you're the boss, Sir,' she said with a giggle.

'This is serious! How long will it take you to pack?'

'It'll only take five minutes. I've not really unpacked yet.'

'Good,' he said. 'I'll be waiting in the foyer in ten minutes. OK?'

'I'll be there in ten. You're the boss, boss – sorry, Sir,' with another giggle.

Mark almost laughed himself. He could see the funny side of the way things appeared. He'd checked a map and concluded the best route to Logrono would be the A2 then M111 and given the quality of the Spanish motorway network, if divided into two days of travelling, the trip need not be particularly arduous at all. They could stop for plenty of breaks. Despite his foreboding that they might be followed, he was still determined to treat his time in Spain as much like a holiday as anything else. He was not used to the idea of holidays. He'd never really had one before. There was never enough cash or time. Now all that had changed and he was determined to make the best of it he could.

He was trying to relax despite his misgivings. He set out with the intention of a stopover at Siguenza, more or less halfway to their destination, the total trip being around 300 kilometres. His research had shown that there was a Castle and Cathedral as well as other tourist attractions, although the population was small at about 4,500. There were likely to be reasonable hotels with vacancies, especially as they were late in the season. He also had in mind the fact that any undue attention from strangers was likely to stand out like a sore thumb.

He met Sally in the foyer and they walked through to the car park, shoved their luggage in the boot and set off. Sally was well used to using a satnav and although the verbal directions were in Spanish, she could follow the visual instructions without too much trouble. Once they were on the motorway the driving was easy, except for a tendency to look the wrong way at roundabouts but she soon settled to that and the car itself was comfortable and fast, a top-of-the-range piece of German engineering.

They chatted intermittently, while Mark kept an eye on the mirrors to see if they were being followed. He soon relaxed when he was fairly certain they had no tail. They stopped after about an hour for a coffee break and to stretch their legs at a nondescript motorway cafe. Mark looked out for anything suspicious but could see nothing worrying. Then they carried on to Siguenza which turned out to be a small town, centred around the cathedral with several hotels. The largest of these was quite high-end, with 80 rooms, a large restaurant, very Spanish in character, built with local stone and featuring two great arches in the restaurant giving it the feel of a real castle. There was even a suit of armour in the foyer.

It was not what Mark expected at all, but he was quite happy to enjoy the good fortune that fate had laid in his path. There were no single rooms. It wasn't that sort of place. He booked two doubles both spacious and comfortable with all the facilities anyone might want or need, short of a kitchen. They were shown Sally's room first. Her jaw dropped at the luxury.

'God!' she said, 'I've never slept in a bed that big. Bloody hell, I could get used to this kind of living.'

It was Mark's turn to laugh, and he was pleasantly surprised when they told him the price. On an impulse, he booked an extra night thinking that tomorrow they could drive to Logrono in a couple of hours and return later to this very satisfactory accommodation, if they felt inclined, after a reconnoitre of Logrono.

He suggested a quiet drink in the bar before bed. Sally agreed and they sat and chatted for a while before returning to their respective rooms. Mark was casually reading a tourist brochure while lying in bed before sleep when there was a knock at the door. He got up, slipped on a dressing gown, then opened the door. It was Sally. She was fully dressed but looking unusually subdued.

'What's the matter?' he asked.

'I had a quick shower, got into bed and turned out the light and the bed's so big and the room too. It felt kind of creepy and echoey. I knew I wouldn't be able to sleep. You've got twin beds and I thought I'd be happier sleeping here. Would that be alright?'

'That's no problem if that's what you want. Both these beds are doubles though, but it's up to you.'

He slipped off his dressing gown and got back into his bed. Sally swiftly stripped to her underclothes, then slipped into her bed, and took off her underwear dropping it onto the floor beside the bed. They both switched off their lights.

'Is that better?' he asked.

'It's a bit cold.'

'No hot water bottles.'

'You could warm it up,' she said.

'You can come over here if you want,' said Mark.

Sally quickly jumped out of her bed and into his.

'Are these sheets silk?' she asked. 'They're kind of slippery. Not sure whether I like them or not.'

She snuggled up to him as he lay on his side. She put her hand over his arm and felt his erection. 'You gonna use that?'

Which he did, and then they fell asleep together in each other's arms.

Mark awoke first. He quietly crept from the bed to the shower. He showered quickly and towelled himself dry. He was still naked but wrapped in a towel. Sally was just getting out of bed. Mark went to her and pulled her close to kiss with one arm around her back and the other hand on her bum, the cheek of which he pinched quite hard. Sally drew away from him far enough to get a good swing and slapped his face hard.

'You can leave that out, for a start. Shagging's one thing, pinching my bum's another. Do that again and you'll get a knee in the balls. See how you'd like that.'

Sally was clearly quite capable of looking after herself. Mark looked at her in amazement.

'I didn't mean anything,' he said.

'If I stick a knife up your arse while you're asleep, I won't mean anything either, but you might never have a comfortable crap again. Got it!... Boss?' she responded. 'We gonna get some breakfast? I'll have a quick shower. I'll be with you in five. Boss,' she finished with a slant-eyed grin.

Mark surprised himself. He felt like laughing, and oddly comfortable.

She came out of the shower room already dressed. He was sitting on the bed looking at the same brochure as last night. He put it on the bed and stood. She walked up to him pulled him to her, and kissed him on the cheek,

'Breakfast?'

They went to the restaurant, ate a swift meal of croissants and coffee, and were on their way to Logrono by half past eight. Mark had intended to stop at Soria but he felt it had a lot in common with Siguenza and no vineyards. He decided with Sally's consent to carry on all the way to Logrono. He'd been a little disappointed not to have seen any signs of vineyards on the way but was surprised at how mountainous the country was with the road always circuitous following valleys without much in the way of views except up ahead or behind. He still kept something of an eye out for a tail, getting no indication of that either.

When they arrived at Logrono, Mark realised that this was a very different proposition to Siguenza and more like Madrid, not a big village or small town, but a real city, the capital of Rioja, a major centre of wine production world-wide. It was a wine buff's dream city surrounded by world- famous wineries. Wine was the motor that drove the local economy and had been so since the Romans were there 2000 years before. They found a multi-storey car park near the centre and left the car to take a walk around.

Their immediate impressions were that the general atmosphere of the place was different from Madrid. There was the great cathedral at the centre that, although being quintessentially Spanish, somehow had a more European feel. Mark was there to enquire about Vineyards and found a few estate agents but none dealing in land unless it was for building. There were plenty of apartments for sale, but he could find nothing advertising agricultural land and this annoyed him.

They were, however, directed to the small town of Haro. The real hub of wine production in the region. It did not appear to be far on a map but turned out to be nearly an hour's drive. Mark discussed their options with Sally and concluded that their best alternative would be to cancel the room in Siguenza and find somewhere in Haro. They could then investigate the area he was really interested in, more thoroughly. So they drove to Haro and booked into the only four-star hotel.

'Just book the one room, so long as that suits you, but no bum pinching or you'll regret it!' she said.

'Truce,' he said and laughed.

They booked the room. By now it was lunchtime, and as soon as they'd moved their luggage in and parked the car, Mark led the way to the restaurant. They had a light lunch. Mark told Sally he needed to make some calls, so she may as well take the afternoon off. She could stay in the hotel, or she could take a walk or the car. The choice was hers. She chose to take the car.

Mark called Kevin at the print plant just to see how things were going.

Kevin's first words were, 'That copper from years ago's looking for you, and that creepy Muslim bloke you used to see sometimes has been murdered.' The line went quiet. 'You still there?'

'I'm still here. When did the copper come, and what did he say?'

'I just told him the usual. I didn't know anything. Not where you were, nothing. I was ever so sorry, you were still the boss but didn't come here much, and even when we had meetings, they were sometimes done on the new phone system where you could be a thousand miles away and talk between one another on screen. He just said as soon as you were in touch to let you know he wanted to talk to you.'

'Did he say anything about Abdallah?'

'No, just as soon as I see you or get in contact, to let him know where you are.'

'OK. If he turns up again tell him I said I was in Jersey in the Channel Islands, that'll keep him guessing for a bit. How are things otherwise?'

'Oh, just plodding along really, odd hick-ups, late deliveries and stuff like that. Bloody nuisance, but nothing to get het up about. You likely to be around anytime soon? I've got a new flat you can always come and stay for a bit if you get stuck.'

'Thanks, but I'm OK at the moment. I'll stay in contact. Probably see you soon. Bye.'

His next call went to Gomez.

'Hello, Mr Gomez. How's it going with the passport?'

'Call me Alex. My name is Alessandro, but most people call me Alex, it's simpler and easier for people to remember. I guess you're looking for an update. It's going well; I've managed to get a copy of your mother's birth certificate. Her mother's name was-hang on a minute, you want to write it down? Her name was Adina Eva Orvieto, all good Italian Jewish names and they fit with the idea that she came from a family forced to leave Italy by an edict of 1492. Later, Muslims were expelled as well, if they refused to renounce their religion.

'So, we have clear evidence that your grandmother was, clearly, Jewish although growing up in Italy. She was what they call Sephardic Jewish. This is opposed to Ashkenazi Jewish. They came from Eastern Europe to where they were invited under the auspices of the Ottoman Empire. In consequence, your mother according to Israeli law is Jewish. Your grandmother was born in 1896. Quite how she ended up in the UK is a bit of a mystery, but there are records we've traced that show she married a man from Chatham, in Kent, called Thomas Albert Fuller. Fuller's occupation is listed as seaman. So, it's likely they met in Italy, and he brought her to England and married her, giving her English nationality but she retained her Israeli nationality as well. They ended up, as far as we make out, living in the East End of London in Stepney. They had seven children. That's as far as we can discover. The upshot is that if you want to claim Jewish nationality to move to Israel, it shouldn't be a problem. We've applied for your passport, and we're told it should be available within the next three weeks. Congratulations, Mazle tov. Where shall I send the bill?'

Mark's next call went to Nigel Bendt-Schleimaan. The response was cagey,

'Who is this?'

'Hi, it's Mark Spivey. I was wondering if there was any progress?'

'You'll be pleased to hear that there will be no further difficulties regarding the matter of your concern. The individual has not been dealt with in quite the way you anticipated simply because there was no need. He is, shall we say, an indirect employee of people who have concerns in matters of mutual interest. You have my assurance that it has been dealt with discreetly. I'm afraid the individual concerned became over-ambitious. You operate a charity I believe. Our organisation is in the charity business too. We'd be grateful for a one-time contribution of, shall we say 75K, and nothing more said regarding the matter.'

Mark was silent for a moment considering what the guy had just said and then asked,

'What guarantee would I have that the matter had been dealt with once and for all?'

'Clearly, publicity regarding the matter we're discussing would be of disadvantage, to either party, if it became public. The money donated would be going to a charity of our choice, and a matter of public record. That would be your assurance that the matter was concluded to the satisfaction of both parties. I hope you understand our point of view. While obviously, we are fully cognisant of yours. Should anything relating to the matter reach the public domain, all concerned would be seriously embarrassed. That's the only guarantee we're in a position to give. There you have it, in a nutshell. Any embarrassment to anyone involved has been dealt with in a confidential manner.

'As the old saying goes: no names, no pack drill. I hope you understand, and you're OK with that, it's the best we can offer. I hope that our services at the rest home were satisfactory, and should you feel the need, you would be happy to return there, without any qualms. Individuals there who acted in a way breaching confidentiality regulations imposed by the employers have been dealt with most severely. I hope that answers any questions you might have.'

Mark was not entirely convinced.

'I can't see any real reason why I should make any donation to any charity when the truth of the matter is, that a company allowed its employees to run riot over any sort of security or confidentiality enforcement within its organisation?'

'How about we say a 10k donation as a gesture of goodwill when both parties have made er transgressions?'

'Fair enough,' said Mark. 'I can accept that.'

Next, he rang Sam Stanger at Northern Granite.

'Mark Spivey, as I live and breathe! How are you? I hear you have some domestic problems. Comes to us all, but you can do without it getting out to the media arseholes. So, to what do I owe the honour?'

'How d'you know it's me?' asked Mark.

'Ah, fancy phone with some sort of computer recognition feature. It's really handy, anyone you can do without speaking to, just either hang up or give a not available message like,' he continued in a gruff voice, 'The person you are calling is not available at present, please leave a message, and we'll call you back as soon as possible. So, what *are* you calling for?'

'I'm thinking of buying a vineyard. There's a big outfit based in the States that's advertising stuff in Spain, the US and Chile at extortionate prices. I wondered if you had any contacts. I'm in Haro in Rioja, Spain at the moment. Thought I'd have a look around while I'm keeping out of sight of the media. I'm gonna go to the wine museum here and go on a couple of tasting tours. Maybe taste some of the proper local plonk at local prices, and see if I'm still interested. I just wondered if you might have any ideas regarding wineries and vineyards?'

'Not an area I've had any experience of. Mostly hotels and holiday lets are my speciality, but I'll put out some feelers and see how we get on. Give me a week, and call me back. Stay out of the way of the Fleet Street hacks, and good luck.'

Following that, Mark decided to take a walk and weigh the situation regarding wine tours, and get a feel for the business. To a degree, as he saw it, the biggest problem was harvesting the grapes. Making beer overcame, and more or less eliminated, the problem of harvesting the raw material for the product, with the combine harvester that cut the corn and threshed it. From then on, it was a simple matter of getting set up to carry out the processes of malting, boiling, fermenting and distributing. The difficulty with grapes was, as Mark saw it, that they needed picking by hand, and that meant a step back into the nineteenth century.

He didn't want Sally around while he was at the museum because he thought she might be a distraction, with little or nothing to contribute to his investigations. In consequence, he decided to take a taxi. He was quite surprised, when, on arrival at the museum, the first thing he saw was the car he'd hired in Madrid. He made his way to the reception desk to ask if he could take a wander around the museum. The receptionist pointed out that the museum only operated on the basis of bookings with guides because some of the exhibits were of high value, and there were some situations, in, and about the museum that could put visitors at risk.

Mark pointed out that his driver was already at the museum, and he would like to join her. The receptionist asked him to wait while she made enquiries. Mark was beginning to get annoyed by the time she returned. He'd waited more than ten minutes.

When she did finally arrive back, she explained that the museum was very large, covering a total area of 4,000 square metres. However, she had found the party he was looking for, and if he was willing to pay the full entry fee, which included a meal with wine, and further wine tasting as well as the tour, some of which of necessity he would miss simply because of the time available, he was welcome to join the party that was part way through their tour. Mark grudgingly paid the hundred euros requested and was conducted to the place the party had reached. When he arrived, he was shocked to see not just Sally, but also Mahe. There were half a dozen others in the party so he was in no position to make any sort of fuss without upsetting almost everybody there.

'What's going on?' he whispered to Sally,

'We can't talk now I'll explain later,' she whispered back.

The atmosphere among the whole party grew tense as everyone involved realised a "situation" was hanging over everyone present.

The time came when they sat for the meal. The table was laid for a dozen people though there were only ten in the party, including Mark. He waited until everybody was seated, apart from himself, Sally and Mahe. The atmosphere had improved as time passed and people relaxed. There were two seats unoccupied at one end of the table and one opposite. Mahe sat nearest to the rest of the party and Sally at the end opposite Mark. The rest of the party were Americans. They began chatting among themselves, more or less inviting Mark and the two women who were obviously acquainted to sort out any differences they might have between them. The atmosphere was still strained. Sally opened the conversation by saying,

'I thought you'd be longer with your calls.'

'Obviously.'

As she looked at Mark trying to present a relaxed front, he asked Mahe,

'Why are you here? There's no way you'll convince me it's a billion-to-one coincidence. How did you know where I was?'

'Of course, it's not a coincidence,' replied Mahe. 'Sally and I have known each other since I was a girl, and Mum got her the job with you.'

'And how did your mother get Sally her job with me?'

'As far as I know, Mum knows Gunter, and he took Sally on, as a good worker on Mum's recommendation.'

'And I do as good a job as anyone else would,' interjected Sally, 'and almost certainly better, your office is as clean as anyone's and sometimes, I take messages, and carry out errands no one else would because it's not part of my job, but I like it there, it's convenient and relaxed. I like Gunter, and you and I get on OK too, and the pay's pretty good for what I do, as well.'

The Americans were beginning to listen in because the situation had an air of drama about it. A big man with a big belly, who, through sheer size tended to dominate the table, said,

'This sounds like somthin' outa' one'a them soaps. You Guys wanna soak up the amm'biance. Aint that what we're here fur? And som'a this fa'ine wine. Take it easy, Guys. The food ain't that spacial. Gi'me barbeque ribs an' a faine Southern sauce any day. Though Ah guess th' wine does take sum beat'nn.'

Even Mark had to laugh. Much of the tension fell away.

The meal ended, generally, in a festive way with more wine. This time a strong cheap white joven and the party were beginning to be extremely convivial. Mark's mood, however, was slipping steadily towards aggression. Sally was taking it easy because she was driving, and Mahe was carefully maintaining a clear head. She could see a storm brewing. The three English members of the tour group left the wine museum together, in the car hired by Mark, but driven by Sally. Mahe sat in the back. The atmosphere was tense. Mark opened the conversation,

'How's your mother, Mahe?'

'She's fine, no thanks to you. You know the media are looking high and low for you, and the bloody police aren't far behind. What do you know about the Abdallah guy's murder?'

'The simple answer to that is nothing. Does your mother know you are here and exactly why are you here? Is your mother tailing me? It's been OK since I've been here, but when I was in London, I had a feeling I was being followed. Did you and your mother have anything to do with that? And Sally, have you been in contact with Mahe while we've been here? Or her mother? What the fuck's going on? I'm beginning to feel like I'm some sort of pariah like I was some kind of social leper. OK, I've done some dodgy deals in my time, but that applies to almost any politician. It goes with the job. We don't put ourselves on the line in public for fuck all. We do it for all sorts of reasons, and, OK, most do it, not least, for cash, but there's a price for that, and by God, I'm paying it at the moment. I'm sick and tired of it, but I'll not buckle. You can bet your life on that. Got it, the pair of you?

'I think I deserve an apology. I spy on people, I make no secret of it. It goes with my job, and I'm no family man, that's just the way I am, but at least I don't shit on my own family. Got it? I feel like I'm being shat upon, and you can take that or leave it. I'm not pleased. What are you going to do, the pair of you, you gonna apologise, 'cos, if not, you can both piss off here and now.'

Sally kept her mouth shut, but Mahe let rip too.

'You're my dad and I hardly know you. You're almost a stranger. You'll cough up some cash if we more or less blackmail you, but beyond that, how often do we see you? We're not like a family at all, we hardly know one another. You've got problems. OK. Some of those problems rub off on us, but you never think of that. We've got lives too, and whether you like it or not our lives are linked. You and Mum are two of a kind and only think about yourselves. Me and Tom are your kids as well as Mum's and she's gunning for you, big time, and we're involved whether we like it or not, and we don't like it. What do you expect?

'Tom's going off the rails and that has to do with this family, if you can call it that. You treat us more or less as though we don't exist. It feels to me as though in your eyes, I'm just a slightly inconvenient, mild, nuisance, like a sodding gnat bite or a pimple on your face. It's not fair.'

At that, she burst into tears, half in anger, half in frustration.

The car continued to hum, just like the machine it was and apart from Mahe's suppressed sobs, it was faceless and noncommittal. Sally stayed silent concentrating on driving more carefully than usual. Mark stared out of the window. His mind was in turmoil. He'd seldom felt less happy in any situation. The journey back to Haro seemed twice as long as the ride out, for all involved. When they arrived back at the hotel, Sally parked. The three stood together by the car. Mark asked Mahe where she was staying.

'I've not booked anywhere. I've not had time.'

'Well, I'd better see what I can do. We're just getting to the busiest time of year for this place because of the grape harvest. You OK with that?'

'So long as you've no problem with your daughter staying at the same hotel as her father?' she replied, pointedly.

Both Sally and Mark were looking and feeling a little uncomfortable because it was becoming apparent that Mahe would soon learn they were sharing a room and neither knew exactly how she would react to the news.

Mark went straight to reception and told the story that his daughter had turned up unexpectedly and needed a room. He was informed that fortunately there had been a cancellation minutes before so there was a room available. He paid there and then. Mahe stood behind him.

'We're in luck,' he said, 'you have a room.'

'I'll get my things,' she said, looking at Sally.

When Mahe and Sally went out to the car together, Mahe asked,

'You shagging him?'

'What's it to you? Your mum wanted me to keep tabs on him. That's what I'm doing. Doesn't mean anything to me. I'm just enjoying myself on holiday, and getting paid for it. It's up to them, I couldn't care less just having a great holiday free. Why wouldn't I? Wouldn't you?'

'Fair enough, shall I tell Mum?'

'Up to you. It's no secret. I expect your mother's guessed anyway.'

She pulled Mahe's luggage trolly from the boot and left it for Mahe to lug to reception. Mahe then went to her room, showered and went to bed. It had been a long day.

Fifteen

Sally went to the room she'd occupied with Mark who'd managed to get hold of a couple of yesterday's English newspapers, the Times and an Express. He sat in an easy chair and was thumbing through the Times looking for articles relating to him. He found nothing.

'I guess I'll shower,' said Sally, 'and may as well go to bed. I can't make any sense of the stuff on the box. Viva Espana is all very well but the language is Spanish and I don't really want to learn it. Good old England.'

'Getting fed up, are you?' asked Mark.

'Been a bit of a pain of a day, really, hasn't it?'

'I don't see it that way,' he replied. 'I've learned quite a lot about wine and grapes and something about myself and my relationship with my family and my philosophy. How do you fancy a trip to Romania?'

'What?'

'I'm thinking Romania might turn out to be a better deal for a vineyard than Spain. Wages are lower, the climate and soil are just as good and the business isn't so well-developed there. Transport would be a bit dearer, but not a lot, and there's plenty of room for development. I'd have to check to make sure, but I have a feeling we'd be getting in nearer the ground floor, developing a marketing strategy based on one of the oldest wine-producing areas in Europe. More opportunity all around. There are wineries there already at less than half the price of anything here. Here the labour for pickers is coming from all over the place. In Romania, it would be local, making things simpler and good for the national economy, so the government would be happier and more keen to help. Also, there are proven supplies of oil that equal the country's present consumption for a few years to come.

So, energy is likely to stay relatively cheap at least for a while. So d'you fancy a trip to Romania?'

'What about Mahe? Asked Sally. 'It'd look as though you're running away from her.'

'No problem, she can come if she wants. I can book her in with us. She already knows we're sleeping together. I've not talked to her about that but I don't think she's too bothered. Lilith and I never lived together even when we had the kids. Mahe was a shock and Tom just kind of happened. Lilith's more involved in all of that than me, the kids just kind of turned up as far as I was concerned. I'm not even 100% certain they're both mine. We're not living in the nineteen fifties. So, are you willing to take on the driving in Romania, if I decide to go there?'

'Ok, I don't suppose it's much different from here when you come down to it. The weather can't be much different, otherwise it would be no good for grapes. D'you know what the roads are like?'

'From what I can make out, the roads are pretty near the worst in Europe. The motorways are OK but local roads can be not much better than our cart tracks so a four-wheel drive might be in order. Would you be OK with that?'

'Never driven one, but there has to be a first time for everything. Might even be quite fun. I'm not sure I'd want to be a passenger though but that's up to you. Like you said, you're the boss,' she said, smirking.

'You take it steady,' he said, with a threatening glare.

'I'll have a word with Mahe in the morning.'

The next morning, Mark was up first, shaved and showered, before the girls appeared. He went downstairs to see if any papers had arrived, but was too early. When he arrived back at the room, Sally was in the shower. He went and knocked on Mahe's door. It opened promptly. She faced him with a dirty look. He smiled, almost ready to laugh.

'Good morning,' he beamed. 'How are you, sleep well?'

'Well enough, thank you.'

'Are you ready for breakfast?'

'I just need to get finished dressing. I'll be ready in ten minutes.'

'OK, see you in the restaurant in ten.'

He returned to his and Sally's room and told her he was going down to the restaurant, and that Mahe was due down in ten minutes so probably no need to rush. He went back downstairs, bought yesterday's Times and took it to the restaurant to read while he waited. On page 2, he found an article by an investigative journalist who claimed he had evidence of Mark's involvement in a money laundering scam operated through a corrupt African politician who was the Minister of Finance of Gzamba. He was staring at the article when Mahe arrived, along with Sally. They both sat opposite Mark who folded the paper to show Mahe the article.

'You know anything about this?'

Mahe began to read but was interrupted by a waitress waiting to take their order. She ordered then asked,

'Where's Gzamba?'

Mark smiled, 'It's more or less in the middle of Africa and is now called Bahmzahgaba. It's been a democratic republic since 1979. They're implying I was involved in corrupt dealings with the then finance minister there before you were born. It's where your mother and I had our honeymoon. The guy, who's behind it is a Tory bigmouth, who will get his comeuppance in double quick time if he doesn't stop shouting his mouth off. He's a chancer out of nowhere, who is out to cause trouble for those who are happy with the status quo. His days are numbered, though he might cause me a certain amount of nuisance. As the old song goes, We shall overcome. He's a nobody setting out to hang himself. Big-mouthed idiot. I'm suspended from

Parliament, because of him shouting his mouth off for a month over allegations of wrongdoing regarding payments, that weren't even made to me, but to your mother, and it all happened before you were born. It's a bloody joke.

'On a totally different subject, I'm intending to go to Romania. D'you want to come? We'll be in the east near the Black Sea, the best climate, warmer in winter and cooler in summer. I think the vineyards there are a better deal than here, ready for development, and the place is one of the oldest wine-producing areas in the world. They were making wine there long before the Roman Empire existed. I want to taste some of the stuff they're making. I have a feeling it'll be really good, and underrated.

I've spoken to Sally, she's game. You could even call your brother. If I buy a place there, he could take over the management, or I guess you could even share it if you wanted to. That might help get him back on the straight and narrow. Give him some real responsibility, and see if he can deal with it. If he falls by the wayside, he'll have no one to blame but himself. You can only do so much to help people, no matter who they are, if they can't hack it, then it's out of anybody's hands, bar God maybe, and I can't say I've ever had a run-in with him. So, what more can I say, d'you want to come?'

'I'll call Mum and see what she says. She might want to talk to Tom. You're like a jumping jack, bloody firework. We never know what you're going to do next.'

'We only get one life, might as well get on with it while we've got the chance. Ring your Mum and decide what you want to do, then I can book the flight to Romania. Have you got any friends you want to bring? If my retinue gets much bigger, they'll be saying I'm turning into someone akin to a flaming oil sheikh. That's all for now. I've told Sally to book a couple more wine tastings. You can come if you want, it's up to you, but let her know what you want to do.'

After the last couple of days, the two days that followed were more or less uneventful, just the sort of days any average tourist might have spent, apart from a small parcel arriving at reception for Mark, that he was pleased to discover was his Jewish Passport. Sally looked into a flight to Bucharest for just the three of them. Tom did not want to come. Mark called Lilith to see just how the land lay in that direction. Lilith was guarded in anything she said, committed to nothing, and Mark was left even more puzzled about her attitude towards him.

The following morning, he began making enquiries about the choice of routes to Bucharest, whether it would be best to return to Madrid or fly from Bilbao. He concluded the best way would be through Madrid which meant they could return the car to the airport at Madrid. As they had to drive back to Madrid, and he'd been so impressed with the hotel at Siguenza, he booked rooms there for an overnight stop, and then an afternoon flight to Bucharest. It would be a long day, and the hotel would be a potluck matter, but it was the off-season so there should be plenty of vacancies.

He told the girls his plans. They both seemed reasonably happy at the prospect. He confirmed the bookings. The three of them spent the day pottering around as regular tourists. They began to settle into one another's company in the foreign environment which forced them into a closer relationship than might be normal at home in the UK. The stop-over in Siguenza was a major success because the facilities, ambience and food at the hotel were truly excellent. Even Mark was impressed. It was with mixed feelings that they left after just one night, their experience of the hotel had been so pleasant, but there was a plan to be followed and they were off to Romania.

They returned the car and caught the plane without hassle. The flight was quite boring. On arrival, they took a taxi to the centre of Bucharest and booked into the plushest hotel according to the taxi driver. The price was cheap, half what Mark had paid in Spain and the facilities were good, though the furniture and decoration were by English standards excruciatingly ornate like something from a Louis 14th French palace that Mark found so grandiose as to be almost funny, but it was clean and comfortable and ridiculously cheap. He thought to himself, if the vineyards were as cheap in relative terms to Spain then he'd reached the right conclusion. They settled in and then went to the restaurant for an evening meal which involved a good deal of meat which did not please Mahe who ended up having vegetable soup and a bread roll.

Again, Mark was stunned at the low prices, especially the wine. The following day he set out to make a serious tour of the wine-making area near the Black Sea. The low price of everything was seriously exciting his interest. He felt that as long as the political situation remained reasonably stable, this was a real land of opportunity. He had no faith in high-tech businesses long term. In his opinion, they were what he thought of as whiz-bang industries that went up like balloons and then burst with a resounding pop rather than a bang. His brewery business was doing well, whereas the Langland Hotel where he really got his start was in the process of redevelopment turning into crumby apartments to be let at extortionate rents, that he thought would not last, because he for one would not want to live in such a dump.

Food and drink were long-term. He could envisage a well-run vineyard and winery becoming an institution. Marketed well, it might one day have a reputation as strong as Scotch or Champagne. He liked the idea of the permanence of a well-run, long-term agricultural investment. He was on a quest again. His days as a politician had sickened him with the whole business. He wanted out and a quiet life away from the limelight and the shitty arseholes, he'd been dealing with for the bulk of his working life.

Sixteen

Mark was back on a mission. He was going to search out an area where he could develop a vineyard and winery that was world-class. It was in his mind to move the brewery there and export the beer to the UK. Some taxes would have to be paid but in his mind's eye he could see there were long-term profits to be made, and with three hundred days of sunshine a year it had to have a better climate than the UK. Even if the winters were colder, at least they were short. He picked a town on a map, Lasi, population of a quarter of a million with a history that went back a thousand years.

The drive time from Bucharest was around 7 hours so he decided to stop part way there just as he'd done in Spain with the stop in the fantastic hotel in Siguenza. He chose Focsani, a medium-sized town of around 50,000 people and famous for cheap wine and earthquakes.

He explained his plan to Mahe and Sally and met no dissent, so off they went and arrived just about lunchtime. Mark was impressed by the area in just the way he had hoped. They passed some vineyards on the way and the land was generally undulating rather than the steep slopes encountered in the Rioja area of Spain, although they were at the base of the Carpathian Mountains. Picking grapes would be easier. It might even be possible to use machines, though he wondered quite how well they really worked.

The little party had a meal at a small restaurant that was cheap and sustaining, though not to Mahe's taste. Almost everything on the menu involved plenty of meat.

Mark went in search of a good accountant. He'd discovered that foreigners were not allowed to buy agricultural land, but could buy companies, so there was a way. It was just a matter of finding the right contact. As always, this required hard cash and the right man. Mark was certain he had enough cash. He was surprised too, at how many people spoke some English. It could be explained partly, he was told, by the fact that many American and English films were shown on TV with subtitles. He thanked heaven for "Top Gear" and found his way to Tourist Information. It was in the town hall, and when he explained what he was looking for, a representative from the council was brought to speak to him. He thought he might have struck gold. The man spoke good English and his name was Romeo, so only too easy to remember.

Romeo told Mark the town Council was actually in the middle of a programme to promote investment in the area's wine production industry, in tandem with the promotion of local tourism. If Mark had the necessary capital, the local authority would look favourably at any proposals he might wish to discuss.

If you can't be rich be lucky! Thought Mark. You can't go wrong if you're both. It looked as if the old days might be coming back. Romania's fortunes were on the up. Could it be that Mark was in the right place at the right time again?

He walked back to the hotel. The sun was shining. He was feeling better than he had for some time. When he went to his room, however, he found not just Sally but Lilith and his son Tom all sitting side by side on the bed. He stood looking at them for a second then said,

'Bloody hell, it's the three unwise monkeys.'

'I'm no fucking monkey,' snapped Tom. 'If I am what does that make you, a chimpanzee or baboon, or what?'

'Fair comment. What do apes look like?' said Lilith.

'Happy families, Ooh, ooh Hooo!' laughed Sally, then stood and curled her hands to scratch her armpits. 'Anyone fancy a drink? I could certainly do with one. I might even buy 'em.'

'Have you lot got a start on me already?' asked Mark.

The situation was already so silly, that all any of them could do was smile, even Lilith. What could have been an explosive situation settled into farce.

'Things are looking up,' said Mark.

'What things? Bug-eyed monkeys?' asked Tom.

'Not exactly, only the local council!'

'Are there any bleached blonde monkeys?' asked Lilith laughing.

'I was trying to travel incognito,' said Mark. 'Now I've got a flaming retinue. Have you told anyone you've come to join me? I know journalists were after me like a pack of hounds. How did you know where I was? Have you been in contact with Sally from day one? What the hell's going on? I'm obviously the only person here who thinks I'm making any sort of successful effort to cover my tracks. Who knows if I've got the police trying to contact me?'

'Your problem,' said Lilith, looking him straight in the eye, 'is, you think you're too clever by half. Hardly anyone believes anything you say. You talk so much nonsense that even when you tell the truth, people think it's rubbish because you're so often telling half-truths, and half the time things you say don't make any sense.'

'Does this make sense?' he retaliated, 'I've just had a chat with a guy at the town hall who's indicated that if I come up with investment cash and a half reasonable business plan for a vineyard combined with a wine-tasting tourist attraction, they'd be willing to provide help, especially if it creates employment for locals and improves the local economy. It's a long-term thing, not a flash in the pan. I've always tried to build up capital to create something stable. Food and drink couldn't be more stable. Computers might be fashionable now, but in the end, they're just like films or radio, a big deal for a few years then something else comes along to keep consumers buying the latest fad, but food and drink never go out of fashion. That's why I'm here. I'm done with politics, I've made enough of a pile to build something permanent. It'll take time and steady work but I'll have something I really value. I just want a quiet life. I'm fed up with chasing my tail sucking up to a bunch of super-rich scumbags from Eton and Winchester, and being self-indulgent. I'm ready to settle and this place is out of the way, and that's where I am at the moment.'

'Well I'm delighted to hear it, Blondie,' said Lilith, 'cos with that hair you look a right prick. Anyone seeing you is going to think, God what a dickhead. Pansy Potter the Beano fairy. MP and Minister for Economic Development, but I doubt for much longer.'

There was a knock at the door. Mark opened it to see Mahe standing there.

'Here we all are, our happy family, and how's my lovely vegetarian daughter?'

'Mother! When did you arrive? How did you know where we were?'

'Ah, so it wasn't you shopping me to your mother?'

'It's not just you who plays tricky games,' said Lilith. 'There's a bug on your luggage. It was easy. I've known exactly where you were for the last three weeks. Have you got the Israeli passport yet?'

She's a bigger cow even than my effing mother, he thought.

'So why are you here, the lot of you? What is it you want? Or are you just here for a happy holiday?' he asked, walking to the mini bar. He opened a Glenfiddich miniature, slurped a mouthful straight from the bottle and flung it in the bin. 'Christ, I was having a good day till you lot turned up. I'm gonna get something to eat.'

He set off for the restaurant with Tom following him. Mark selected a table and Tom sat opposite. They picked up the menus.

'I'll just have the house special with a soup starter. God knows what we'll get,' said Mark.

'I'll have the vegetal supa and tochitura,' said Tom.

'So, what's tochitura?'

'More or less ragu with bolognese sauce, I think.'

'How d'you know that?'

'Dunno really, just know.'

'So, you're a bit keen on foreign food, or you wanna be a chef?'

'Neither, but I do like good meat. Mahe thinks I like meat to wind her up, but I love a nice pork pie. She goes crazy about me liking black pudding. Says just the thought of wanting to eat curdled blood is disgusting. Makes a fuss cos it's fashionable being veggie. I think it's a load of poncey crap, just trendy girlish bullshit.'

'Fair comment, but she's not stupid.'

'I didn't say she was stupid, but she's a bit 'Nah nah, nah, ne nah! If you know what I mean. Just gets on my wick. I get fed up with her. She's always right. Even if that makes everybody else wrong. I don't think she does it on purpose, it's just the way she is. Mum's a bit like it too, but not as bad as Mahe.'

'You've never met my mother have you? You think Mahe's a pain, living with my mother was like living on a bed of nails or even needles. Nothing anyone ever did was right. I hated her.'

'Isn't she still alive?'

'Yes, she's still alive as far as I know. I haven't had anything to do with her for just about twenty, even thirty years now. I haven't missed her one bit, either. Glad to be shot of her. Best thing that ever happened to me, getting out of her clutches. For practical purposes, she killed my dad. I think she drove him like a car over a cliff. She killed my father, sure as eggs is eggs. We've never talked like this before. Is there something you wanted to ask me?'

'You were going to go to Lasi but it looks as though you've kind of fallen on your feet here, from what you were saying about the bloke in the tourist information, but I quite fancy going there. It's a proper old city and the library is famous. I'd like to go there. The history of this area is wild. You might think England's history is crazy, but here it's downright mad. Like the difference between the Black Sea and the Southern Ocean. A Black Sea wave might reach three or four meters. In the Southern Ocean, it's not uncommon for waves to reach thirty-five meters. Really scary.'

'So, you really are interested in archaeology and history. Can't say they're my favourite subjects, but each to his own. If you want to go to Lasi, that's up to you. You want me to pay?'

'I was hoping you might. Mum might start moaning.'

'Tell you what, I'll pay for you to go there for a week, but if you go, I want you to bring me back a list of accountants and land agents, with comments about how you feel about each one. Let's say three of each. Pick the best, and point out why you think so. At the same time, I'd like you to write, I guess you might call it an essay, about where you went, and how you felt about it. Does that sound like a reasonable deal?'

'Sounds a bit like you want me to go back to school, in a weird sort of way, but I suppose I can't complain if you're paying. Don't expect a book though. I'll just write general impressions.'

'Just write what you want to. One other thing, don't tell your mother.'

'Why not?'

'No particular reason, just don't say anything to her. Another thing, if you think you want, or need longer, give me a call, OK?'

'What shall I tell Mum, then?'

'Just tell her you want to go and I've said I'll pay if you check out accountants, and that's all. You got that? You're going to check out accountants. When you get there, you can tell them you're involved with someone who's thinking of setting up in business here from the UK, but don't mention me. You got that? Don't mention me! Understand? Don't mention me! We'll nip down to the bank after we've eaten and I'll get you 5,000 lei OK? I'll want receipts.'

'Thanks, Dad, I'll tell Mum and take a bus tomorrow.'

'OK, mind how you go. Don't go messing about with substances.'

It took no more than ten minutes before Lilith was at his door.

'What are you doing?' She did not yell but she was definitely vehement.

'I was just going to get a shower,' he answered, not setting out to wind her up - much!

'Are you completely daft, or what? You know he's been doing silly things. Are you setting out to encourage him to do something really stupid?'

'You want him to grow up, you need to give him the chance to do it,' replied Mark. 'In two weeks, he'll be old enough to join the army and get himself killed. Who knows what will happen this week but whatever it is, he'll be the one responsible. You just need to let go. He's more or less a young man. He'll start making his own decisions and all being well, start to act like an adult. If you keep interfering, you'll screw him up for sure, and I'm quite certain he's perfectly capable of doing that, all on his own. You want to stop him having a week on his own, in a foreign country, that's up to you. I've just given him the option. What you do is up to you. D'you fancy a drink?'

'Go on then, maybe you're right.'

They went to the bar.

'If he fucks up,' she said, 'it's down to you.'

"If he fucks up, it doesn't matter who it's down to. He's fucked up for the last time as far as I'm concerned.'

They tested some local vintages and got very relaxed then went back to Lilith's room and renewed their acquaintance. It was morning when they awoke.

The first thing Lilith said was, 'God, you're a sly bastard.'

'Sticks and stones. Give us a kiss.'

Lilith laughed and kissed him. They stayed in bed for another half hour, chatting, among other things. The subject of Tom never entered either's head.

Tom had decided to take a bus. He'd discovered he could go by train; it would be quicker, though a little more expensive, however, he chose the bus, not because it was cheaper but because he felt he might get a better insight into the local people and the way they engaged with one another.

The bus station was a good deal bigger than he'd expected. He was having difficulty finding the bus bound for Lasi. He'd tried to make himself understood by various people. He was having problems until he found an information office and a young woman who spoke good English.

'Follow me,' she said. 'I'm going there too.'

Tom did as instructed and followed the girl onto the bus then sat on the seat behind her. She turned to him and asked,

'Why are you going to Lasi?'

Tom smiled, 'Why are you?'

'I'm studying languages and tourism at the university.'

'Then maybe you can show me the way there, too. I thought I'd take a look at the library building. The architecture is supposed to be quite special, and I'm interested in European architecture. My uncle has sent me to check out accountants. He's thinking of starting a business here. He wants a real professional who's up on international law for tax and business stuff. I don't know anything about it really, but he's given me the job as a sort of exercise, I think, to see what I'm capable of. Focsani is a bit small for the type of accountants he's looking for, I think. Sounds a bit weird, I guess, a bit kind of crazy, but I'll do my best. He's paid my fare and I wanted to get away from my mother. They're both here in Romania at Focsani. She didn't want me to go. I don't know why. She thinks I'm still a kid, and can't look after myself. She can be a real pain.'

'What does your uncle do?'

'He's in business, all kinds. I suppose you might call him a wheeler-dealer. I think he's interested in getting involved in the wine business here. He thinks there are opportunities for making serious money and it's getting more difficult in the UK.'

'Some of my lecturers have business links with accountancy, I think. I could ask if there's anyone they would recommend.'

'Are you getting neck ache?' asked Tom. 'I could come and sit beside you, or you could come and sit beside me?'

She got up and sat beside him. 'What is your name? I'm Michaela.'

'Thomas,' he said, holding out his hand to shake. 'They just call me Tom.' He was surprised when she squeezed his hand quite hard. 'Good grip. D'you play sports?'

'I like to play tennis.'

'I'm not very sporty, but I'm doing archaeology so a fair bit of digging at times. Not quite a Horney-handed ton of soil, though.'

'Pardon? I don't understand.'

'Sorry, it's a kind of joke. It's based on, Horney-handed son of toil. I was trying to be funny and your English is so good, I wasn't thinking. Have you lived in England?'

'I spent the second year of my degree course at Warwick University. I had a wonderful time there, I loved it. Where do you live in England?'

'We live in Purley in Surrey, more or less a suburb of London. It's not bad, but kind of boring, usual shops, pubs, and stuff. Ordinary middle class, characterless, bland, a faceless place, poncey shops, bars and restaurants that change every couple of years with trends and fashions. I'm looking forward to seeing parts of Romania because England is going down the pan, I think.'

'Down the pan?'

'Oh, lavatory pan, toilet. To be blunt, there are some real shit-hole places especially in the north of England, now, where the main occupation is shutting out reality by taking drugs. Places where there are no proper jobs, and no future, no matter who you are, and what you've got or do. Overall, I think it's a depressing dump. How do you feel about what's going on here? Is it good or bad?'

'Here, it's some good, and some not too bad, but worrying. Things are getting better, and more stable, but the future is kind of in a balance. Will it get better or worse? We just don't know. We just cross the fingers and hope.'

They chatted on and off for the next couple of hours, mainly concerning Tom's questions about the country they passed through before a stop at Vaslui, a non-descript place catering for those travelling between cities. They had a drink and a snack at a place where Michaela had been before. Tom paid the bill and they re-boarded the bus. For the next two hours of the trip neither said a great deal, but they were already relaxed in each other's company. On arrival at Lasi, they were travelling more or less as a couple.

'What do you want to do?' asked Tom. 'Have you got somewhere to go?'

'I have a student room near the university,' Micheala answered, rather coyly. 'There's still time if we go straight there. I can drop off my luggage and we could walk to the University. I could show you the way around. Then we could visit the Library.'

'There are taxis just across the road there. We could get a taxi?' he said. 'What I saved getting here by bus will pay for it.'

'I can pay half.'

'Don't worry about it. My uncle is paying and I need to get accommodation anyway. Shall we find a reasonably-priced hotel, and get me a room first? It'd help me, especially if the driver doesn't speak English. I never trust taxi drivers.'

'That sounds sensible,' she said and kissed him on the cheek.

Michaela took over as they got into the taxi explaining to the driver that they were looking for a good, reasonably priced hotel. She turned to Tom and told him what she'd done. He took her hand and gave it a squeeze. Within a few minutes, they had stopped at a hotel. Tom explained to the receptionist they wanted a room for a week. They brought in their luggage and were shown into a double room.

'I think I need a shower,' Tom said diffidently.

'I do too,' she answered. 'We should maybe shower together?'

They did, and needless to say, one thing led to another, and they finished up testing the bed. It was adequate. They stayed in bed for hours talking and touching, until Michaela decided she was getting hungry.

'I think we should celebrate with a meal to be remembered. Get up, and I'll take you to my favourite restaurant in Lasi. I'll introduce you to our wonderful food. Traditional dishes here are so much better than traditional food in England. Fish and chips, Huh!' she laughed.

They dressed and were soon strolling, quietly hand in hand, on their way to the restaurant of Michaela's choice.

The celebratory meal was a modest success. Afterwards, Michaela took Tom to see her room, and then they walked back to his hotel. It wasn't long before they were back in bed. In the morning, they went to the university and Michaela showed Tom around, finishing at the library, which he found interesting, though not exactly stunning, then they parted and agreed to meet at his hotel in the evening. Tom spent the time until the evening getting his bearings in the city centre.

Mark phoned Tom, just after lunch, the day after Tom had arrived in Lasi.

'Hi, Dad.'

'How are you getting on? Get there OK?'

'Got here. No trouble. Had a bit of bother sorting out the right bus at your end, but there was a girl there who speaks perfect English, even though she's Romanian. She was on the same bus as me. She sat next to me and pointed out stuff on the way. The bus was dead slow, so it took nearly six hours, with an hour's stop in the middle of nowhere. When we got here, it was gone three o clock and we found a hotel that's OK, and not expensive, then we went for a meal.'

'Oh? Did she stay the night?'

'Yeah, well it seemed silly for her not to.'

'Yeah, well it's OK, but be careful.'

'She's alright, Dad. She's in her third year doing Tourism and Languages at the university here. She spent last year at Warwick as part of her language course studying English and German. She's not crazy about English fish and chips. We went to a restaurant last night and the food was great, would have cost a bomb at home, but here it was dead cheap. Her family live where you are.'

'Have you asked her about accountants? What's her name?'

'She's called Michaela Dascalu. I've not said anything about accountants.'

'Well just ask her about accountants, be careful and keep in contact OK?'

Next, Mark called Kevin.

'How's it going, Mark? Things have quietened down here. There's been nothing in the media about you that I've seen. That copper, Standing, has phoned a couple of times but I just tell him I don't know anything about anything. He gets a bit snotty, but I think he's just sick of the whole business. He knows it's in everybody who counts' interest to keep their mouths shut, and trying to break through the wall of silence is like Canute holding back the tide. He seems most bothered about that Abdallah character that got murdered. Sounds to me as though he got what he asked for, but I don't really know anything, and that's all I keep telling him. Blind, dumb, daft and stupid that's me. I've not had any word from him for over a week now. Things here are just ticking over. I'm gonna have a week off myself next week so don't bother calling then. I'm going to Lisbon. I think I've earned some time off. I fancy visiting the fleshpots, I've heard there's a lively scene.'

'I guess you've earned some time off,' said Mark. 'How are you getting on? You OK?'

'I'm OK, just feeling a bit down. There's something wrong with my back. It just aches all the time. Bloody doctor's a waste of space. His suggestion was to have a rest, take some time off, and take it easy for a bit. If it doesn't get any better soon, I'm gonna see a specialist, even if I have to pay some extortionate money.'

'Go see a specialist. Charge it to the company as expenses, that'll be alright with me.'

'I'll do that. It's been nagging at me for months now. I think there might be something really wrong.'

'Look after yourself. I expect to be back in the UK in a week or two so probably see you soon. Look after yourself.'

Then he phoned Goran. 'Hello Goran. Where are you?'

'Bei Jing. The outfit making the brewing equipment has a problem. There's a union started up and they're asking for more wages. Might have to shut down here and go elsewhere, even back to Europe.'

'Ah Interesting,' said Mark. 'I'm in Romania, and as long as the politics remain stable, it could be a good place to establish a serious presence. When do you expect to be back in the UK?'

'Just waiting to see how things develop here, so not too sure. I don't like it here, the language is a big problem, and they just don't think like Europeans. Difficult to put your finger on, but that's the reason it's so difficult.'

'I've never really had faith in setting up there, Goran. I've always thought they've never forgotten the opium wars, and want to even the score. The atmosphere here is good but not stable, but that's just s sign of the times; everything is changing. Recent history indicates that there is room for a more enlightened approach to development. The climate and resources here are generally good. I'm thinking seriously of investing here in a vineyard and winery. I've had indications there might be state support available. Stability is a worry though, but wherever you go, life's a lottery. No one has a crystal ball; we can only look at the situation, guess the outcome, and hope.

'It's a bit like being a general. Napoleon was a great personality to be able to raise the vast armies he did, but when he went to Russia he had no real idea of the enormity of his task, and losing there was the beginning of his end. Same with Hitler. Wellesley, Lord Wellington finished Napoleon off with the help of Blucher by the skin of his teeth, but it was a close-run thing. Wellesley knew his job, but if the truth be told, I don't think he had the panache of Napoleon. In the end, the outcome might have been down to the flip of a coin. I think I'm gonna take a gamble. I've done it more than once and been lucky.

'Recently, I've pushed my luck, and I'm gonna stick rather than twist. I like the feel of this place and at least the weather here is good. I'm going back to London soon to do some sorting out, then, if all goes well, I'll settle here. I'm done with swimming against the tide. I'll have to learn the language; that shouldn't be too difficult even if I am getting a bit old. It'll be part of the challenge. Let me know when you're back in London, and we'll have a chat about how we organise for the future. I've got to get sorted out with my wife and kids first. When that's done, I'll decide on the best way forward, and finally make some big decisions.'

Mark then went looking for Lilith. He found Mahe in her mother's room, lying on the bed and reading, supported by pillows and cushions and asked her where Lilith was.

'She said she was going into town to have a look around. She asked me if I wanted to come, but I've got a good book I bought at the airport and want to finish it. She's gone on her own I think.'

'Maybe I'll do the same,' he said, 'and see if I meet her. I'll see you later.'

Off he went with no real objective other than finding Lilith for a serious chat alone with her. He wandered aimlessly for half an hour and then found a shop selling papers from abroad. He then went to a restaurant, with tables on the street, for a coffee, a snack, and a quick search through the Times. He found nothing of interest. But Lilith found him. She sat down opposite and he folded the paper.

'We need to talk.'

'Agreed,' she said.

'I've more or less decided this is where I want to set up and stay. I'll keep the old flat at 45 Pinfold Gate, but I'll set up to live here. I've even started to pick up a bit of the language, even though English is more or less the lingua franca, even if it is a bit pigeon. The weather is good, everything's cheap. I like it. I've got the two passports so can use them to play games with the authorities if I feel the need, and I've had enough of the shambles and backbiting throughout British politics, I think the UK's on the ropes. I'm ready to settle for a quiet life, and I need to settle with you about how we organise things from now on, vis-a-vie the kids, and a settlement that's to the advantage of all rather than trying to cut each other's throats.

'You see what I'm getting at? We've done it for other people, now let's do it for ourselves. We did it for Tillotson that builder clown and his dreary wife now let's do it for us. Does that sound reasonable? Theoretically, there's cash by the bucketful but liquidating it takes time, and in the end, the reality doesn't match the theory. What I'm saying is we need to play our cards sensibly. I was talking to Goran earlier, who I think you've met, but he watches my managers abroad, and he's good. He tells me the business in China is looking iffy; there are major labour problems, and the political situation is getting worse. So, I need to see the best way of moving forward on that because it impacts the business in the UK, a lot.

'The outlook there is looking pretty bleak as far as I can see. The costs of the crisps' plant have nearly doubled in just a year. Transport costs have gone the same way. Things don't look as though they'll improve anytime in the near future without a war. Sales are dropping off something awful. So, we need to be sensible if we're to come to a sensible conclusion for all concerned. How are you feeling, about the way things are going for you?'

'Things are going a whole lot better for me than they are for you,' she replied.

'Is that so? How is it you reach that conclusion?'

'It's simple, just about all the people who helped you on the road to success are looking at you now as a liability.'

'And who specifically are we talking about?'

'Lydia, for one, and Sonny. Neither of them wants anything to do with you, and it was them that got you your start in politics, and me your start in business. You thought you'd left us behind, but you're mistaken. Between us, we know enough about you to drop you right in the shit.'

'Is that so? Birds of a feather flock together.'

'What do you mean by that?'

'I mean that by dropping me in the shit, you'd be cutting your own throat. In real terms, I know as much about you and your route to success as you know about me. The same applies to both Lydia and Sonny. We've all got skeletons in the cupboard if that's what you want to call life as it presents itself. The same goes for anyone in the public eye. No one's perfect, so we need to come to a mutually satisfactory conclusion about how we're going to live together, without bringing any of us down. If any of us starts stabbing another in the back like that maniac kid did killing Abdhalla, then we're all dead.'

'So, what is it you're proposing?' she asked.

'I'm proposing we all put our heads together and plan to work together for the benefit of everyone. Sounds a bit socialistic, but when you get down to brass tacks, it's the only sensible answer for all of us. We've all worked our socks off one way and another. Hard work, luck, intelligence and a whole lot of other things have got us where we are, and throwing away everything we've worked for, at our time of life, is plain stupid. We need to get together to sort things out, and preserve what we've fought and worked for all our lives.'

'Hmm, I'll think it over.'

Mark went back to his own room to shave off the beard Lilith had derided so much then trimmed his eyebrows too, to remove the bleached part. He then set off to find a barber to remove his bleached hair. Looking at the result in the mirror, he decided that the effect was almost as good as the original disguise. He wasn't too bothered either way. He'd decided he was going back to the UK to face his future there. On the way back from the barber's, he managed to pick up a two-day-old Daily Telegraph. Thumbing through it he found a small headline: "Briton found dead on French coast" and the following article,

"A man identified as Daffyd Wyn Jones, last known address on the Isle of Jersey, has been discovered on a beach at St Lunaire a short distance from the Port of St Malo.

The body was discovered by tourists walking along the beach. The identification was made when police on the island of Jersey contacted their counterparts in France after Mr Jones was reported missing from his place of work at a private hospital on Jersey. Mr Jones had been warned against swimming from certain beaches on the island by lifeguards on more than one occasion in the past. The tides around the island are among the most powerful in the world and although Mr Jones was a notedly powerful swimmer, it appears that he got into difficulties and drowned. His death has been recorded as - By Misadventure. The Island's police have asked that any relatives of Mr Jones contact them for reasons undisclosed."

Back at the hotel, Mark called Nigel Bendt-Schleimaan.

'Bent-Schleiman's Office,' said the secretary.

'Can I speak to Mr Bent-Schleimaan, please? It's Mark Spivey.'

'He's out of the office at the moment. Can I get him to call you back?'

'At his earliest convenience please.'

'I'll do that.'

'Thank you.'

Nigel called back at about 5 o'clock UK time, 7.30 p.m. in Romania.

'Hi,' said Mark, 'a Welsh guy has been found on a beach in France near the island of Jersey. You know anything about that?'

'Nothing whatsoever. No idea what you're talking about.'

'Thanks, Nigel, enough said.'

'Good luck. Bye.'

The phone went dead. Mark repeated to himself, 'Enough said,' and smiled. One big worry was eliminated, and quite a few vulnerable backs covered. Then he booked a first-class ticket back to the UK for the following day and went in search of Lilith. She was in her room.

'I'm going back to Heathrow tomorrow. There are a few things I need to sort out. I'll be back in a couple of days.'

'What happened to you, baldy?' she mocked. 'You look almost normal.'

He laughed, 'Thank you, madam. That almost deserves a kiss.' Then bowed as if she were a medieval queen.

She came to him. He hugged her gently and kissed her cheek.

'I'm gonna get a meal,' he said. 'You coming?'

'You get a table and I'll follow you down.'

They ate the meal and had a couple of drinks with Sally and Mahe, then went up to bed again, together in Lilith's room.

Seventeen

The next morning, he rose early, leaving Lilith still asleep. He was interested to discover that he could still programme his head to tell him to wake early. He'd always had a dislike of alarm clocks, they made him feel tired throughout the day, being woken that way. Whereas if he programmed himself, he'd feel OK, as long as he didn't do it too often.

He'd booked a flight from Lasi to Bucharest leaving at six thirty-five. He planned to be back in less than a week. He'd told Lilith of his travel plans though not his objectives for going. He reached Bucharest shortly before eight and was on board a flight to Heathrow, using the Israeli passport without question. He was scheduled to arrive in London at six in the evening after an hour's stop in Warsaw. It would be a gruelling, boring day, but he simply wanted to get his business done and return to Romania within the week.

Lilith had told him she intended to go to the UK the following week, so he would see her in Lasi before she returned to London. He'd told her he would resign from his seat in parliament before the next election. Powerful figures within the Party had warned him that his days were numbered if he stayed because there was a general feeling that his presence had become an embarrassment. He was happy with that. He'd become disenchanted with the whole business. He'd felt out the PM about putting forward Lilith in his place, and it had been tacitly agreed that would be a satisfactory arrangement for all concerned, if Lilith was willing to accept the offer, and Mark made a significant donation to Party funds.

On arrival at Heathrow, he took a taxi to his flat near Westminster, drank a couple of fingers of Glenfiddich and went to bed.

He awoke as it was growing light. He was feeling rough. He wasn't too sure which day it was and realised he was suffering from jet lag. His body clock was beginning to suffer from all the travelling, even though in general he'd been enjoying himself. He decided a day off was in order; apart from making phone calls, he'd stay where he was. He needed to let his body catch up. He showered, dressed and walked down to the local mini-market for something to eat and a carton of milk. A woman at the checkout recognised him.

'Morning, Mr Spivey. You're up early.'

'No peace for the wicked.'

'Oh, I dunno,' she said.

They smiled at each other, knowingly, as he left.

He returned to the flat, ate some muesli, drank a coffee, and went back to bed. It was lunchtime when he awoke. He picked up his phone and called Kevin. He got an answerphone.

'Hi Kevin,' he said, 'it's Mark. I'm back in the UK for a few days. Give me a call.'

Next, he called a taxi to take him to Westminster. The Commons was closed for another week for the summer recess. He went to Bellamy's to assess other members' attitudes towards him. It was quiet but he was discomforted to find he was being effectively cold-shouldered by all and sundry. He left promptly after just a small Red Bull. He was not terribly concerned though, because the bulk of his business interests representing the major part of his real income were now elsewhere. He'd already agreed to stand down at the next election.

He returned to his flat, repacked his few belongings and set out for St Pancras for the train journey to his old haunt at No 42, Pinfold Gate. On arrival, he did not unpack, but walked to the pub and ordered steak and kidney pie and chips with green peas and a glass of best red. He was looking forward to some old-fashioned English food. The pub was almost unrecognisable. The car park was full and the decor looked bright and fresh. The food arrived promptly. Mark was pleasantly surprised, it was delicious. He had a second glass of red and returned to the flat. He picked up the phone and called the policeman, Detective Inspector Standing. He got through immediately.

'Ah, Detective Standing, you wanted to speak to me I believe. It's Mark Spivey. What's it about?'

'There are a few things, actually.'

'Right, fire away.'

'I believe you knew a local Imam whose surname was Abdhalla?'

'That's true.'

'What was your relationship with him?'

'How do you mean?'

'Were you friends or did you do business together?'

'Well, he was a member of the local community where I'm still the MP, as you are no doubt aware. He was a religious leader in the local Muslim Community and as such we met on various occasions as representatives of our respective communities, as I have no doubt you know. And there were various aspects of life within our communities where communication was and is of paramount importance. Racial tensions can arise from all sorts of perspectives, and community leaders clearly function as a conduit of communication between various interest groups within an area. As a consequence, there were quite a few occasions when we both felt discussion regarding various aspects, both political and social elements of interaction between various members and groups of our respective communities were very necessary. Not least between ourselves.'

'Would you regard Mr Abdhalla as a friend, Mr Spivey?'

'No, I would not. I would describe our relationship as a function of representatives of our particular social, racial and political positions within the overall fabric of our society.'

'Are you aware that Mr Abdhalla was killed recently?'

'I am.'

'Does that worry you?'

'I'm sad and sorry to hear he's been killed, and I suppose that I'm, shall we say, rather disconcerted that he's been stabbed in what must be horrible and dreadful circumstances. It's shocking, literally.'

'Where did you hear that he'd been stabbed?'

'I'm not sure, I think I probably read it in one of the papers. I've been away a lot recently on business as I'm no doubt you're aware.'

'Did you spend some time recently at a psychological rest home In Jersey?'

'I did, as you obviously, well know. It was in the papers. I've watched the papers a great deal recently they've been printing some slanderous material about me. It has caused me a great deal of stress and worry. I went to Jersey for a rest. Why did you ask that question? It's none of anyone's business but mine. That can have absolutely nothing whatsoever to do with the death of Abdhulla which has absolutely nothing to do with me.'

'We are concerned that there may be links between the two events, and a young man named Anil Karani. Does that name ring any bells?'

'I have no intention of answering any more of your questions without legal representation or formal charges. If such is not forthcoming, I have nothing more to say. As far as I am concerned this conversation has not taken place, and cannot in any circumstance be used in a court of law. I have nothing more to say to you about anything. Do not try to contact me again or I will be obliged to take this matter further. You're hounding me. The way you keep following me around amounts to harassment. Good day.'

Mark put the phone down. He picked up again and rang Kevin's number. He got the ringtone and then, 'I'm not around at the moment leave a message and I'll call you back.'

He called Gunter at the print works and got a secretary. She explained that she did not know where Gunter was at that moment, but if he'd like to leave a number, she'd get him to call. He gave her instructions to tell Gunter he'd called and tell him to ring back. He was beginning to wish he'd stayed in Romania. He then called Lilith. No answer. As he looked out of the window, he saw it had begun to rain. That seemed to confirm he might have been better off staying in Romania. A spider crawled up its web in the corner of the window frame and rolled itself into a ball apparently to protect itself from the wet. He thought he knew how it felt.

He went to his drinks cabinet, opened a jar of olives, fished around in it and found a small vial. He dried it on a paper serviette, pulled out the plug, poured himself a line of coke and sniffed it, then put the vial back in the olive jar. Next, he set out for the Earl of Granby for another pie and chips. He was feeling better already. After his meal, he returned to the flat. It was still raining. Dusk was closing in and his dismal mood was returning. Gunter had rung and left the following message,

'Bad news, Mark, Kevin's in hospital they think he's got cancer of the liver. Call after nine tonight.'

Mark decided he'd call Fr Timothy with whom he'd had no communication for around ten years. He rang the old number wondering if it was still functioning. He got the familiar response,

'Father Timothy at St John's.'

'Hello Tim, it's been a long time.'

'Indeed, it has. How are you? Moving in different circles to me these days. To what do I owe the honour?'

'There are questions I'd like to ask in private about certain activities of a very private nature. Would that be possible?'

'Well, I don't know. I like to keep myself to myself these days. How private could we make it?'

'Well,' replied Mark, 'there are questions concerning mutually important matters, I'd like to discuss in total privacy. It's quite urgent for me because I'm flying out again before the end of the week. It's kind of personal and delicate.'

'Fair enough, how about a coincidental meeting at the little Anglo-Saxon church at Bridesthorpe off the A6 at lunchtime, 12 o'clock tomorrow? If it's raining, we can go inside. I have a key.'

'That would be perfect. Thank heaven for the church,' Mark said with a chuckle.

'If only that were a common sentiment,' Timothy replied with chagrin.

Mark picked up a history book he'd been threatening to read for he didn't know how many years, to read in bed for a while. He awoke at gone two in the morning. The bedside light was still on and the book had dropped to the floor and woken him. He got up, made a cup of tea, drank it in bed, turned off the light and went back to sleep.

He woke in the morning at gone eight. He felt energised after his best sleep for some time. He showered, shaved, dressed, breakfasted and set off to walk to the excellent local library, intending to do some research on Romania, its turbulent history and the present-day difficulties it faced, and needed to surmount. He managed to find several books on Romania, both modern and historical. He read indiscriminately for a couple of hours then took a taxi to the Bridesthorpe church. He paid off the taxi and strolled around the churchyard, waiting for Fr Tim who arrived in a battered, dirty, old Ford Focus. As Tim stepped from the car, Mark was surprised at how old he looked.

'How are you? Excuse me for saying, but you don't look very well?'

'Oh, I'm OK, life's just wearing me down, a bit that's all. What have you got me here for?'

'The police are asking me about Abdhalla. They seem to think that somehow I have some involvement in his murder. I had nothing to do with it. I think I may have been at the party where he was killed, but I left earlier in the evening. You were there, weren't you?'

'My situation is the same as yours, Mark. I was there earlier in the evening. The whole business was getting out of hand. Those boys had had too much dope, mixing poppers with coke. I got out before things got really out of hand. I guess you went before me. There was violence in the air, with and about the drugs. I could see things were getting silly. I left before the situation got really nasty. Thank God I did. As far as I can guess, one of the boys went crazy. Abdalla was stabbed multiple times. I don't know how many, but a lot, ten or twenty or so. The boy must have just gone completely berserk. I want nothing to do with any of it.

'I'm just sorry I was there at all. Abdalla was asking for trouble and the way he got it was almost too predictable. If he hadn't been killed, the police were closing in because of the supplying, and one way or another his days were numbered. I think he knew, and he was scared to death of going to jail because a prison sentence would have been a death sentence. There was no way out for him. He'd almost put the noose around his own neck. If he stayed out of jail, he was headed for trouble because of supplying the drugs, and he dared not stop. If he went to jail, he'd have been killed for being what he was, Asian and queer. All we can do is keep quiet, and hope the whole episode fades away.

'I hear you're going abroad. That sounds like as good a plan as any. You're lucky, you've got assets. I'm as near broke as makes no difference, and the church is all but dead in this country. I sometimes feel like taking an overdose myself. My wife and I are living apart-together, and now the kids are gone, our relationship is poisonous.'

'I thought I'd got problems,' said Mark. 'All I can say is, thank God I'm not religious,' raising his eyes and brow towards the roof and almost laughing. 'At least I know where I stand now. Have you met Detective Inspector Standing? He's been poking around since my son overdosed in the town and was taken to the Infirmary. He was lucky, he came out of it OK. I think he found my stash and thought he'd try it. He didn't realise what he was doing and took too much or something, silly little sod.

'Now he seems to have hooked up with a girl in Romania where I'm planning to set up a new business. I'm aiming to be a gentleman landowner, a bit like the old-time English Whigs. New money and satisfied with the status quo, that's me. I've not met her but she sounds as though she might be OK. I have the impression she's a bit older than him but not that much. I'll be interested to see.

'If the worst came to the worst, I guess you could come there so long as it all pans out for me. We might be able to sort you out with something. I'll keep in touch and let you know. If anyone asks about me, you know nothing, and I'll do the same for you, OK? I don't suppose you could drop me off at the edge of town? It would be handy if you could.'

Tim did him the favour and Mark was glad of the lift but was also glad to exit the car. For some reason, the smell reminded him of the smell of his dreadful room over the Chinese takeaway. It came close to making him gag.

As for helping Tim out, he thought he'd rather cut off his hand. The guy made him feel sick. He walked home and then went to the drinks cabinet. He found the vial in the olive jar and flushed the contents down the toilet, rinsed out the vial and threw it in the bin. Whether he'd take recreational drugs again, he wasn't too sure, but at that moment, he vowed to himself he never would. He smiled as he poured himself a Pimms with lemon and ice to take away the horrible memory of the smell of Tim's car.

He sat in his favourite easy chair and called Gunter again. The secretary picked up and said,

'Mr Steinman is here today. I'll pass you over.'

'Hi, Mark, how's it going with you? You OK?'

'Hi, I'm fine, got back here the day before yesterday feeling a bit jet-lagged, but stayed in bed half the day yesterday and I'm right as rain today. Bit worried about Kevin though. How is he?'

'To tell you the truth, I think he's got cancer and he's known for some time. He went into hospital nearly two weeks ago. They kept him in. I went to see him a couple of days ago and he was yellow. He's got jaundice, and they think his liver is packing up. They're still doing tests, but he looked awful and he's lost a lot of weight.'

'God, that's awful. Give me the details of the hospital. I'll go and see him.'

Mark waited till the visiting time Gunter had given him and took a taxi to the hospital. When he got there, he was shocked to see how terrible Kevin looked. He was cadaverous, his skin had a blueish-yellow hue and his eyes were sunken.

'Thanks for coming, Mark,' he said in a feeble voice. 'I don't know how long I've got. I think I'm fucked.'

'Don't be so negative. They told me you've only been here just over a week and they're still doing tests.' He leaned over the bed, took Kevin's hand and kissed the back of it as he gripped it gently, with tears in his eyes. 'You've got to fight! We got together fighting for our lives. You've got to keep on fighting.'

'You're wasting your time, Mark,' he said with a weak laugh. 'My fighting days are over. I haven't had a shit for a week, and I haven't got the strength to get out of bed. I'm fucked.'

'Don't talk like that. Has Sonny been to see you?'

'She's been a couple of times, but I think it upsets her seeing me. She knows I'm fucked. It doesn't hurt, they're giving me morphine. I feel quite good.'

At that, his eyes closed and Mark called a nurse. She took Kevin's pulse and pulled screens around the bed.

'He's asleep,' she said. 'You can stay a little longer if you want.'

Mark sat for a few minutes. Then he stood, pushed the chair away from the bed, picked up Kevin's hand again and slowly kissed it again. Kevin didn't move. He died that night of cancer of the liver. Mark walked home in a pensive mood, deciding what he was going to do next. On arriving, he picked up the phone to call Lilith and Mahe answered.

'Hello, Mahe. What are you doing with your mother's phone?'

'I'm in her room and she's gone downstairs and left the phone behind. Is there anything particular you wanted her for?'

'No, not really. I'm pretty well sorted here, and if I can get a flight OK, I'll come back there tomorrow. I just thought I'd let her know I expect to be back a bit earlier than I originally intended.'

'Right, I'll tell her that. Is that all?'

'How are you getting on? D'you expect to be coming back here with your mother?'

'Of course,' Mahe replied rather brusquely.

'Right. It's Thursday, isn't it? I get confused. Tell your mother I'll be back either late tomorrow or sometime on Saturday. I'll see you then. Bye.'

Mark was getting the hang of secretarial work and managed to book the necessary flights to arrive in Lasi late on Friday. It would be a squeeze to make all the connections. It meant an early train to London, a taxi to Heathrow, and then the drag to Bucharest, but that would be a fast flight. Just three and a half hours, then a two-and-a-half hour flight to Lasi. It would mean another long, hectic day, but he wanted to get away from England. The whole atmosphere of the place had gone sour for him. He'd send flowers by the bucket-load for Kevin's funeral, but he really did not want to be there. He felt it would be depressing, and he'd had enough depressing news lately.

After a long, draining day, Mark was back in Lasi, just wanting a cup of tea, and to collapse into bed. There was just one small problem, he wasn't too clear which room he'd be sleeping in. He had an entrance card to Sally's room, but when he'd left, she was sharing with Mahe. He went to Lilith's and knocked. She opened the door after a few seconds, wearing a dressing gown.

'Back already?'

'I was still at the Pinfold Gate flat this morning. I'm shattered. Who's sleeping where at the moment? What time is it here?'

Lilith looked at a bedside clock. 'It's nearly 3.30 am. Come in. You can share my bed if you want. You want a drink or anything?'

'I'll just brush my teeth,' he said.

He did that, undressed and got into the bed. It was already warm. Within minutes, he was dead to the world.

The next morning, unusually Lilith was up before Mark. He heard her get up, but just rolled over and went back to sleep. It was nearly lunchtime before he got out of bed. By that time, he was ready for brunch. Lilith was missing so he had a quick shower and shave. He was about to go down to the restaurant for something to eat when Lilith came in.

'Sleep well, did you?' she asked. 'I had to put the maid off. She wanted to make the bed.'

'Slept like a stone,' he said. 'What time is it? I'm more than ready some something to eat.'

'It's eleven thirty.'

'Have you had breakfast?'

'About two and a half hours ago. I could manage a coffee and a snack though. If you have a shave, we could go for a walk around and find somewhere for something to eat.'

'I showered and shaved already.'

'Are you sure? You've still got a twelve o'clock shadow. Was the blade blunt or something?'

Mark looked directly at Lilith with raised eyebrows. 'Did I say or do something? Or did I just stop you from getting out of the right side of the bed?'

'Did you do any research into Lilith yet?' she demanded.

'No! Why? What the hell's up with you? Are you wanting to fight? What the hell are you on about? Have you gone crazy?'

'I told you to do the research.'

'What's the matter with you?'

'D'you think I'm made of plastic?' she scorned. 'I came here to sort you out and what do I find? You're shagging that tart, Sally. I wouldn't have been so bothered if you'd brought your other bit on the side, Kevin, but no, it's just the office bike. How d'you think I feel?'

'Kevin's fucking dead!'

He went to the mini bar took out a Johnny Walker miniature, wrenched the lid off, threw it at the waste basket, and missed. He knocked back the whiskey in a gulp and threw the bottle after the cap, hitting the target. At least he could get something right.

'When?' she asked, looking shocked.

'The day before yesterday. I think I must have been the last person to see him alive. He looked as though he was dead already. That's why I came straight back. England just depresses me. I don't care if I never see the white cliffs of fucking Dover ever again.'

'Let's go and get something to eat.'

She put on a jacket and walked out with Mark following. They found a small restaurant nearby, hardly speaking en route. They ordered coffee and croissants.

'So, what is all this Lilith business?' he asked while waiting for their order.

'This Lilith business is about me growing up! Lilith was the Babylonian Goddess of the night. The name comes from an extinct language; nowadays they call it Akkadian. There's no real way of knowing how it sounded because the only evidence of its existence is baked clay tablets, mostly from a sort of library, that was burned down about three thousand years ago. Lilith was some kind of goddess. She represented the spirit of the night. She was said to have the soul of a whore. She was probably invented by men. She was the first woman Adam had. She was banished from the Garden of Eden for having sex with Adam and producing children. All her daughters were tainted with their mother's brush of evil because the two aspects of their appeal to men cause men to fight for their favours. You asked, now you understand why I changed my name. Women want men, but as often as not men make them sick to their stomachs. D'you understand that? You know my father's a bastard and you're not much better, but at least you're more or less my bastard. God knows why. Stand up!'

She stood herself and drew him to her. He drew her close to him so they felt the warmth of each other's bodies mingling. They kissed and sat down smiling at each other.

'I think I understand,' he said. 'What about Mahe?'

'You tell me! I don't think she's ever had a bloke. It's nothing to do with me. God made us all, and he was probably a bloke because he must be as big a bastard as my father.'

They drank their coffee and ate their croissants. Mark paid the bill and left a good tip. They strolled to the town centre and found a big covered market. They went inside to discover both a vegetable market and a separate general market selling almost any everyday item you might want. Lilith bought a pair of fluffy real lambswool slippers for a quarter of the price they'd have been in the UK. They strolled back to the restaurant they'd been to on the way out and had another coffee each.

Back at the hotel, they found Tom and his new girlfriend sitting in the bar. On the table before him, Tom had a beer and

Michaela had some sort of cocktail containing fruit. Both Michaela and Tom stood up. Tom made the introductions. Everyone was slightly edgy because both Tom and Michaela were wondering how things would go. Mark set about helping everybody to relax, offering his hand.

'Well, what a pleasant surprise. What a lucky young man my son is. Since I've been here, I've found almost everyone I've met to be pleasant and friendly, but not many have been as delightful as you Michaela. Did I pronounce it properly?'

Michaela gave something of a cross between a bow and a curtsey, saying, 'You pronounced it quite properly. I'm glad to meet you.'

'Take no notice of him,' said Lilith. 'He's my husband and Tom's dad, but he's still just another man. How was the trip?'

'The train journey was OK but not as quick as it would be in England,' replied Tom. 'You complain about the trains in England, but they are faster than trains here, but often more crowded, more like our, cheap fare, local ones. Things are more relaxed here though and people are more sociable when they're out and about here, more than in England, especially London. The people here seem to be more like people in Northern England only more so. In the end, it's just different. The people are different. The atmosphere here is more, kind of homely, apart from the touts around the stations. I suppose, I've only been here a week, but those are my impressions. Generally, I like it.'

'Living here is slower,' said Michaela, 'and that's nice. England is busier. There's more buzz and that's nice too. I think that in many ways it depends on your mood.'

'I've said I'll go and meet Micheala's parents,' said Tom, breaking the thread of the conversation, 'but before I go, I need to do something with my luggage, and really I need to get a room?'

He phrased it as a question without it being a question. He was gazing at his father.

'How did you get on with accountants?' asked Mark.

'It's more difficult than you think. One of Michaela's lecturers does business studies and he's recommended a couple, but one in particular, and she has an uncle who is an accountant, but he works in local government, and her family is still trying to get back land that was requisitioned under a government programme when Ceausescu was collectivising agriculture in the fifties, and it's never been used properly ever since. There's legal wrangling because the government is trying to sort out the problems caused by putting land back into the private sector. Houses are a different matter. I'm not too sure how it really works, but as far as I can make out, all buildings are dealt with as being separate from the land they stand on. They're still trying to sort out some kind of system that really works. Possession is important though. Once you're in, you're well on the way to ownership. As I understand it, no buildings are owned. Everything is leased and the length of leases is a whole other question. All in all, land ownership law in Romania is a legal minefield. So I'm told.'

Michaela stared at the ceiling her face blank. Saying nothing.

'God almighty,' said Mark. 'The world we live in. I thought the Commons was a madhouse. I suppose we'd better get you a room. Come on then.'

Michaela followed a couple of steps behind, her face still expressionless. They reached the reception desk and Mark explained he needed yet another room if there was one available.

'How long are you staying?' asked the guy, smiling. 'Perhaps you should take a floor and be done.'

'It'll be another week at least,' replied Mark, 'but my wife, daughter, and the other lady will be leaving in a couple of days, then we'll see. If that's OK?'

'That's fine. We are pleased to accommodate you.'

Tom was holding Michaela's hand looking awkward. She turned to face him and smiled.

'Will you send someone to show this young man his room?' asked Mark, then turned on his heel, leaving Tom and Michaela to sort themselves out, at their leisure.

For the evening meal, the party was provided with a table large enough to comfortably seat them all. Following local tradition, the meal did not begin until 7.30 p.m. Mark and Lilith were the first to take their seats then came Tom and Michaela. Tom sat beside his father with Michaela on his right and finally Mahe sat next to Michaela with Sally on her right. They began discussing the menu with everyone except Tom asking for advice. Mahe was insistent about vegetarian food, and Michaela was rather dismissive.

'There is not really much choice for vegetarians or vegans, because in Romania all food is looked upon, more or less as the bounty of God, no matter whether it be meat, vegetables, or seafood. People in Romania are simply glad to have food on the table.'

Mahe remained silent in the face of what she saw, essentially, as a rebuke.

Sally joined the conversation, 'That's the way it is where I come from. Thank God there's food in front of you. There's plenty on the menu. I've never eaten so well in all my life as in the last couple of weeks.'

'For what we are about to receive, may God, and my bank balance make us truly thankful,' said Mark.

'I'll drink to that,' said Tom. 'Thanks, Dad. If there was wine on the table I'd drink to that too. Shall we take Michaela's advice on wine? Her family used to make it.'

'I'm not a connoisseur,' she said quickly. 'I like our local wine but connoisseurs wouldn't approve. I like that it has a character of its own. The wine that wins medals is the stuff they sell all over the world. It has no local character. I still think our local wine is as good as any of the fancy expensive stuff that's approved of by connoisseurs, so-called. They give out the medals at the shows in Paris, and other places, where they tell people they're the experts, but the people who make it should have a say. People here were making wine long before the French. If I'm asked to choose, I'll go for a local red, fermented in fresh oak. The big producers are trying to make people think they are buying the best. They call it 'Marketing,' but I think, really it's a trick.'

'I'll play safe and keep my mouth shut,' said Tom.

Mahe followed this plan as well, looking po-faced, possibly even sulking. Mark ordered two bottles of local red. One of the cheapest wines on the menu. Lilith was unconcerned, tasting the wine which she found quite acceptable and just as Michaela had said, rather different with its character just as Michaela had indicated. She happily enjoyed her meal. She was surprised at how much she'd enjoyed her break in Romania.

She was not looking forward to the next couple of days, knowing that she and Mark needed to negotiate a commonly acceptable plan that would lay the foundation of both their futures, for the latter part of their lives. Some confrontation seemed almost inevitable but how far would it go?

The meal was finished and the group went to the bar for a few drinks, chatting with one another reasonably amicably, even though there was a slight dissonance in the atmosphere as might be expected when strangers are first introduced. As the group separated to return to their respective rooms, with normal "Goodnights" and other pleasantries, exchanged, Lilith said to Mark,

'Well, I thought that went off OK. Generally speaking. What do you think of Michaela? She's a bit older than Tom, and been around a lot more than he has, I should think, but he seems smitten.'

'No snap judgements,' he replied. 'Let's meet her family. If I'm gonna buy a vineyard, and that's my plan, I couldn't really give a shit about anything else. I've always had faith in supplying food and drink. You can live without cars, phones and films and all the other crap people chase after these days, but you're dead without food. That's the only thing we know for certain about any economy. It can't function without food. Politics, anyone with any sense knows, is about bullshit, until food runs short; then people know the truth.

'That's when money counts and the real foundation of money is land to grow the food on. Here the state controls all land, and to me, that when you think about it, is just. I got my start through trickery, that's all a charity is. I started with a charity. Most people think charities are a good thing. Having run one, I think they smell. I think they even stink. Anyone who thinks differently is crazy. No one does anything for nothing. People giving to charity are conscience-stricken about the fact they're better off than a half-wit sitting in a closed shop doorway, begging. In the end, life's a lottery. Individuals who are good at manipulating the lottery are winners and the rest are losers.

'Let's see if Michaela's lot are winners or losers, then we'll be able to come to a conclusion about Tom. He's had the advantage of an easy start, now it's up to him. Michaela seems all right to me so far as I can see. Her head's well screwed on. Picking Tom up on a bus seems to me as good a way as deciding whether you fancy someone, as any other, so now all we can do is wait and see. Her family seems to be reasonably well-connected, let's have a look at them, and see how we get on. If I'm gonna buy a vineyard here, I'll need someone local to give me the nod when I'm setting out to do something the locals can't accept. Michaela and her family seem to me, to be as good as any. I like that she's proud of their local wine. That seems like a good emotional position to me.'

'When are we going to decide how we divide your property?' asked Lilith. She was surprised when Mark laughed. 'I don't think it's a laughing matter.'

'So long as you leave me the brewery and the pubs, you can have the rest,' he laughed again. 'Obviously, I'll want enough to buy 200 hectares of good winery land and enough to develop it to a good standard, you can have the rest, so long as you agree to put some in trust for the kids. From what Goran tells me, the plant in China's up shit creek because it's losing money because the workforce is on strike. So, it's getting to the point where it's a liability.

'I've got an idea that Tom might be interested in helping to run the vineyard if things turn out well with Michaela, and maybe even if not. She's doing a degree in tourism so she's being trained to develop that side of the business. Looks like all the pieces of a puzzle dropping together like they were made to fit.

'The Langland is yours for sure. It's always been a heap of crap from the day it was built, but it's been a goldmine for me. Where there's muck there's money. I want to leave that behind and settle in as a benevolent, old-fashioned squire, basking in the sunshine in my declining years.

'You've all but got the job in Westminster, I've sorted that, with the right palms greased as you're no doubt well aware. Good luck with that! You're welcome to it. I'm sick of it. I've reached the point where I'd as soon shovel shit, as suck up to the scumbags there, the way I have for the last twenty years, thank you very much. In a way, I've enjoyed it, but the more I've seen, the worse it's got. You want it, you're welcome. I've had enough.'

Mark thought he was up first for a shave a shower and then breakfast, so he was surprised to see Tom and Michaela already in the restaurant. As soon as he joined them, Tom launched,

'I've got news for you. This is a small town and there are rumours going around that someone with serious cash is interested in setting up a vineyard locally. D'you think the rumours have anything to do with you?'

'Morning,' replied Mark, giving himself time to think. He raised his eyes towards the ceiling. 'So, who's spreading the rumours and who's listening?'

'Local people who hear things and local people who listen,' said Michaela, smiling.

Mark laughed, shaking his head from side to side. 'You have the prettiest ears. Not very big, but they work well enough, Hmm?'

Michaela simply grinned, and raised her eyebrows a little, saying nothing.

'You've been asked to dinner tonight at Michaela's parents,' said Tom, 'and we'd like to take you for a walk this afternoon if you're free. I've been there and I think you'll like it.'

'Walk! Where, why?'

'Come and we'll show you,' said Michaela.

'How far.'

'Not far at all. Ten minutes, maybe a quarter of an hour.'

'Well, if it's that near, why not after breakfast?'

Tom looked at Michaela.

'Why not?' She nodded with a shrug.

'OK, a walk after breakfast. What could be better?'

There was little conversation while they ate. They concentrated on the meal.

'Are we ready then?' said Mark, taking a last mouthful of coffee.

'We probably need more appropriate footwear,' warned Michaela. 'Good walking shoes or boots would be best.'

'So, we're on a bit of a hike, are we? OK, Tom where are we going?'

'Michaela's got something to show you. Get the best walking shoes you've got and we'll go.'

They went to their respective rooms and put on clothes and shoes best suited to walking that they had with them. They set off, following Michaela who set a good steady pace. In ten minutes, they were out of the town and the road they were following slowly degenerated into a gently rising track. The nature of the fields changed on either side of them, from small patches of assorted vegetables with the occasional ramshackle hut, to vineyards stretching in undulating folds far enough away to begin to disappear in the morning haze. Michaela stopped and gestured to all the land around.

'All this was the land of my family until after the last war. The vines were planted four years ago by a man who is a politician, but he is too lazy or busy to concentrate on looking after the vines. He does not have the interest or the foresight to see what a wonderful opportunity this is. He lives in Bucharest and is rich. He works for the government. He has realised that he needs to be here to look after the vines and make sure they are tended properly. He owns the lease on the land and wants to sell it, but although the price is not high, no one has the sort of money needed to buy the place.

'Our family has a claim to the land because it was taken from us after the war, but we need more money than we have to buy the lease. Also, there is a need to build a winery to make it into a properly viable business. It needs significant investment. The government will contribute financially and with technical help to develop the business, if an investor who can convince them that he will properly commit to the business, can be found. The government would want to monitor progress and might demand things that the investor did not like, but with sensible negotiation, those sorts of problems could be overcome.

'It has been done in western Romania. Done well here it could be better. There is a better tradition of winemaking here. The climate is better, as well as the soil. It is a real opportunity for someone with the time, money and interest, to create something lasting. It is not a short-term project, but if developed well, it could be a wonderful business, with an international reputation. We can walk around. The owner has lost interest, and the work that has already been put into the project is considerable. If work is not continued, the work already done will be wasted. It's a wonderful opportunity for someone with a vision to create something really memorable. Our local wine is a match for anything in the world. Wine has been made here for more than a thousand years. Do you want to see more?'

'You're doing a great job of selling it,' replied Mark. 'Having got this far, you may as well give me the whole tour.'

Michaela's enthusiasm was infectious, but the pace at which she began to move was beginning to cause Mark difficulty. The effects of his sedentary life and approaching middle age began to show. He was flagging. Tom was managing rather better.

'Don't worry, Dad,' he said. 'Last week she won the university ladies' lawn tennis trophy for the third time running. She usually runs five miles, three times a week to keep in training. This is a gentle stroll by her standards. I'm getting fitter already, I nearly kept up yesterday.'

Michaela stood waiting at the next stage of her tour.

'This is just a barn where the tractors and trailers are kept. I don't have a key and what's inside is in poor condition. There are three tractors and one of them is really not worth keeping. Some of the spares could be useful but it's really just scrap. The optimum level of production varies from year to year but we expect, on average, to achieve around 25 tons per hectare.'

'Bloody hell,' said Tom, 'that much. So, in an average year, you get 500 tons of grapes from these vines?'

'That's an average year. In this area five years ago, we were up 15%. This land would have produced nearly 600 tons. At present the grapes have to be transported to the nearest winery that can cope with that sort of volume. In a good year, they can't cope with the volume because they deal with grapes from other yards. The longer you keep them, the more the grapes decline in quality and value. This yard needs its own winery to improve its viability. It would be better if it had a proper cellar too with temperature and humidity control. All of that would be expensive and would only give a return on investment over the long term, maybe as much as ten years, but once it was producing profits, the return on investment can be as high as 20%. No other agricultural investment can produce those sorts of profits.

'Managed well, there can be other opportunities in terms of tourism and general improvement of infrastructure to support the basic industry of viticulture. At present, we need three tractors to transport the grapes to the winery which is 20 kilometers away and doesn't do our grapes justice. This vineyard needs a modern bottling plant too, to deal with 500,000 bottles a year. You can see the levels of investment needed are considerable and this is why getting this vineyard up and running to a standard it has the potential to reach is a significant project. It is a project that I would love to be involved with at every level and stage.'

'Are you trying to sell me this vineyard, Michaela, when it's not even yours?' asked Mark with a quizzical expression.

'I'm just explaining how I would set out to turn this vineyard into one the most outstanding anywhere in the world. I would love to make it famous. I would love to know that I was involved in creating something magnificent.'

'Well, I can't make any promises. I need to look hard at all the aspects you've pointed out, and then we'll see. I've got some money; it's easy to spend, but not so easy to get. I'm sure you know that already, as does your government?'

'I could not agree more. It's easy to get when you don't need it, and hard to get when you do.'

'Exactly. One hundred per cent. I couldn't have put it better myself,' said Mark.

When they returned to the hotel, all the others had gone. Tom and Michaela went off into the town, and Mark set off to the town hall with the intention of checking out what was going on there, with reference to the exchange he'd had with the guy from the tourist information office. He went there and explained he'd spoken a couple of days before to a guy called Romeo about the prospect of him as a foreigner setting about creating a vineyard in the area. The receptionist made an internal call to Romeo who shortly appeared. Mark explained that anything he said today was in the strictest of confidence. The first question he asked was,

'Are you acquainted with Michaela Descalu whose family live in the town?'

'I know of her,' said Romeo. 'She was in a class a couple below me. She lived a few streets away.'

'But you don't know her particularly well?'

'No, our families are acquainted, it's not a big town. Your being here expressing interest in vineyards is news. Things here are changing fast. People know that recent history has left Romania behind. People are aware that even in Poland, wages and living standards are much better than here, and that people in England are rich compared to us, and having a rich Englishman here who casually rents half a floor in one of our best hotels is certain to arouse the interest of local people. There are rumours, but that's all really.'

'I see,' said Mark. 'This morning Michaela Descalu took me for a walk. We went more or less straight up the hill to a big half-developed vineyard almost directly up from the hotel where we're staying. She said it was for sale but that the government was involved in seeing that it was developed well. The idea being to make it almost a showpiece for this whole area of the country. Does that sound right to you?'

'I'd say that is a reasonable expression of the situation.'

'Do you have any idea of the sort of price the owner of that half-developed yard is looking for?'

'The asking price is 18,000 Euros per hectare.'

Mark took out a calculator. 'Three point six million euros? Does that include everything? The vines themselves, the barn and anything else?'

'I'm led to believe that's the asking price.'

'I see, what about services?'

'There is an electricity supply but it is just domestic, not industrial. Also, there is a domestic water supply. There are the remains of an irrigation system but the value of that is not determined. It may not meet modern standards if it were functioning. A technical investigation would be required to conclude its viability if brought back into use.'

'I see,' said Mark. 'Plenty of food for thought.'

He walked back to the hotel, ate a light lunch and strolled back up to the vineyard with a feeling of excitement. The day had grown warmer and sunlight shone brightly over vines rustling in a light breeze. It was early September. The vines just four years old were just beginning to produce viable grapes as far as he could see. He'd learned more in that one day listening to Michaela and starting to feel involved in the business. He was hooked. The money wasn't peanuts but compared with deals he'd done in the past, it would not squeeze his bank balance, even if Lilith took a slice more than half of his assets, and he knew that the truth was a significant slice of those assets existed on paper, but if push came to shove, their real value could collapse in no time.

Here was a real concrete asset. At a pinch, he could involve Tillotson in building a cellar. Goran could sort out the winery and bottling plant. There was a picking machine sold in America but its reliability was suspect and the damage it could cause to the grapes had made its value suspect. He'd read they were improving but were horrifically expensive. He guessed it might take five years before turning a worthwhile profit. By that time, the vines would be reaching full maturity, and then, with a transport subsidiary, if he decided that bringing the brewery to Romania was a paying proposition, that might represent another income stream. Romanian milling barley he knew was about half the price of that in the UK, so that might pay earlier than he'd thought.

The whole puzzle seemed to be dropping together the way things did when he started IASIA. Was he missing London or the

Midlands constituency? He felt almost as happy as when his psoriasis went. Especially after the last couple of years. Now all he had to do was sort out a deal with Lilith. He put off the moment and went to Tom's room to see if he was in. He knocked and was greeted with.

'Who is it?'

'It's your father.'

'Hang on, Dad, I'm in the shower.'

Mark waited. Seconds passed that began to seem like minutes. The door opened. Tom stood there, in shorts, drying his hair.

'Oh, I began to wonder if Michaela was still here.'

'No, she went back home after we got back here. She wanted to help make preparations for the meal tonight. You haven't forgotten or anything, have you?'

'Of course not, especially after this morning. She's quite some girl, isn't she? God knows what she sees in you.'

'Maybe she's a bit like Mum, and what she sees in you,' said Tom with a snicker. 'What did you think of the vineyard? Michaela's set on it. She planted a lot of those vines and there are nearly two million. She planted thousands. Apparently, it's a long, boring and physically draining business, laying out the fields alone with big tractors and special ploughs. It can take days. There's more to it than you might think. A chunk of Michaela's university course was devoted to viticulture, because, here it's a serious part of the economy and is regarded as a major part of the tourism business.'

'What time does she want us there?' asked Mark.

'Eight o'clock or a bit after. Eat slowly, the more you eat the more they'll put on your plate. If you don't eat much, they're likely to think you're not happy with the food. Not eating much is close to being an insult, take your time and eat plenty. We don't want to be causing offence.'

'How much does Michaela eat? There's not much of her is there?'

'She eats plenty. She burns it up like a furnace; she's all wire and gristle.'

'OK, maybe I'll take another walk up to her vineyard and see how long it takes me to walk around it.'

'You try that, and I doubt you'll be back by eight o'clock. I don't know how many miles. I do know it's a bloody lot. How are you feeling? It's likely to be a long evening. They don't go to bed early, especially at the weekend. You'll need plenty of food to soak up the booze as well.'

Mark went back to Lilith's room. She was sitting at a desk typing on her computer. She stopped what she was doing and faced him.

'Well,' she said, 'where do we go from here?'

'What do you suggest?' he replied.

'First of all, we both need to put together a list of our assets and look at the way we can work out an arrangement most advantageous for all concerned to deal with our mutual finances. How does that sound?'

'Sounds reasonable to me. Like I said there's no sense in fighting. From my point of view, all I want to do is begin to enjoy the money I've made. As they say these days, life's too short. I've put myself through the wringer to get what I've got, and now all I want is to have the satisfaction of doing something real and honest. I don't want to live on a knife edge anymore. I'll show you mine, as best I can, if you show me yours.'

'Stop messing about,' she said.

'OK. As of this moment, I've got just about ten million that is liquid that I could put on the table tomorrow. I've worked out that I'll need virtually all of that if I take on this vineyard. I want the vineyard. I've pretty well decided. I'm more or less certain. I think it's a bargain at the prices I'm hearing. I'm certain I can make it pay but it'll take at least five years before I start getting a real return, and it'll mean spending more or less all my time here and spending every penny I can get my hands on. I want to hang onto the brewery and pubs because managed properly, they'll always make money. People need drink, even if it means drinking themselves to death. I need an outlet for my energy, to maintain an interest in life. Brewing is really just a bit more than cooking on a massive scale, and watching the brewery grow has been satisfying, but I really feel that it's reached the point where it's just a business. It's not so different from making the pies in the factory where I lost the end of my finger. It has changed.

'The beer we make now is as good or better than it's ever been, but for the most part, it's all down to chemistry, cleanliness and computers. Wine isn't like that. There's more risk to it, with the weather, diseases of the vines, and all the other things that you don't get making beer. The way brewing is now, you might as well be making cars or other manufactured crap.

'Beer's better than that, but not like wine. Wine's riskier, more of an adventure as to what's produced at the end, and I think that's part of the kick. In a way, part of the buzz I've got out of everything I've done is taking a risk. That's a good part of the pleasure for me, gambling and winning based on my instinct and knack. So, there you are, you can have everything else but the brewery and the pubs and the vineyard. Which I have every intention of buying with or without Tom. He can have a real part if he wants to get involved with the management because I think we could work together. I don't want to have Mahe involved because I don't think she's interested and hasn't got the temperament for that kind of business anyway.

'I've made the deal with the Party regarding my seat in the Commons, and that's worth 90 grand a year, That's yours to develop in any way you like, but count me out. From now on, you're on your own with that. Bugger it up and it's your problem, and look out for the bastards from Eton, Harrow and Winchester. I'm sick of watching my back for knives aimed at it.

I don't want anything more to do with the slippery, bent bastards there, as I've said, more than once before.

'It'll be a breath of fresh air not having to go back to that place every week and listen to their banal wind-bagging bullshit and nonsense, dissembling and deceit. I may not be one hundred per cent honest, taking chances when they come, but I'm not a downright, liar, murderer or thief. Calling Palestinians who've lived on their land for a thousand years, murderers for defending their homes and children isn't really on when Israelis are killing them and imprisoning them for fighting back. The UK is going backwards and this place is moving forward. Only forty years ago, they had a dictator here, now they're trying to sort out the mess he made. I like that and fancy being a part of it.'

'What about the crisps factory, and the Langland, and the transport fleet?'

'All yours if you want them, they're going downhill anyway. I've been neglecting them for a while; just too much like hard work and hassle. The competition is getting tougher and I've lost any fire in my belly. The best thing, I think, is to sell them off, especially the Langland. It was always a dump and, once a dump, always a dump. Get the refurb finished and flog it to the poor sods destined to live in it. I might need to borrow short-term to get the Vineyard going. They're asking 7 million for it as it stands. It's a snip at that. It needs a lot of investment but get it up and running and it's a long-term winner is my guess. There's some risk but that's part of the excitement for me, and a new challenge in a new place, where I'll be creating something to be proud of, as well as providing for the future. How much you want to be involved in that is up to you, obviously, but in my book, I'm feeling more stable than I have for years.

'I've enjoyed the last couple of weeks, apart from seeing Kevin die, obviously, poor sod. He was alright, Kevin. As good a mate as you could hope to have. These last couple of weeks have been better than the last couple of years. If you still want part of what's here, I'm more than happy with that. I have a feeling that

Tom's slotting into this place, and settling down like it was made for him. Have you noticed he's picking up the language already? And his accent's changing a bit too, when he's speaking English, I find that fascinating. We're getting on better than we ever have, not that I've ever had much to do with him. Never had the time, but if we work together the way we have the last couple of days, everything could pan out really well. I don't know, what do you think?'

'I think we'd better start getting ready for this meal with your son's, young lady's family.'

Mahe elected not to go to the party although she was invited.

'It's up to you,' said Tom.

When she answered, 'I don't think I'll bother,' he wasn't in any way displeased. He didn't think her insistence on a vegetarian menu would go down well. Sally wasn't invited.

They dressed smart and casual. The weather was still warm though there was the beginning chill of winter in the air. They rejected the idea of a taxi because the Descalu apartment was just a ten-minute walk from the hotel.

When they arrived, they discovered that the apartment was over a chemist's shop. They had to climb stairs to reach the landing upon which were two doors leading to separate apartments. The Descalu's apartment was on the right. Tom knocked and the door was quickly opened by Michaela. She was dressed in flared jeans and a loose white garment that left her arms bare to just above the elbows. The neck was round with no collar, and a two-inch deep, narrow v, cut into the front. Around all the hems was sewn an embroidered traditional style bright red ribbon picked out with yellow detail. She wore a matching headband threaded around her shoulder length hair.

'Wow!' said Tom. 'You look like a traditional hippy peasant.'

He hugged her and gave her a traditional double kiss on each cheek, which she returned quickly before separating and bowing slightly, saying,

'Mr and Mrs Spivey, you are welcome.'

She led the way to the dining room. The table was set for eight, and two seats were already taken. It was not a big room, maybe four meters by four, so there was not a lot of room left with the table set for eight, though when everyone was seated it would be comfortable. Michaela made the introductions.

'This is my friend, Tom, from England,' she said, holding his hand. 'Tom, this is my Uncle Radu.' Gesturing across the table, 'and my Aunt Andrea. And this is Mark, Tom's Father, and his mother, Lilith.'

Andrea's eyes opened wide, 'Ea esta numita demon.'

Michaela looking both shocked and puzzled said to Tom, 'Your mother is called a demon?'

Tom laughed. 'It's crazy stuff from thousands of years ago. She calls herself a demon to keep my dad in order, and to stick to the idea that women are as good as men or better. It's a kind of English thing, mixing up all sorts of old religious ideas. She thinks it's the only way she can keep him in order. It's not a joke, but it is a joke. In France, people think the English worship in temples, but in England, people think the Pope is a fraud and a crook. That's why English people pulled down the great monasteries and abandoned the Pope. Because there were two Popes, so one *had* to be a fraud. This is a mad way to start an introductory dinner!'

Michaela translated what Tom said for her aunt. At first, she looked bemused but as she considered what he'd said, her face broke into a grin. She looked at her husband, nodded and smiled at Lilith, then laughed out loud.

'Si e as vrea sa fiu nemit demon!' she said. (I would like to be called a demon, too!)

What an icebreaker it was for the women. Michaela turned and said to Tom, 'You should be careful. This might turn into a women's lib evening. You men won't have a chance. Us girls are all turning into vampires.'

'God knows what's going on,' said Tom, looking at his father.

Mark looked at a loss, opening his hands palms up, as if in supplication. Much as to say, 'I'm damned if I know.'

Very appropriate, thought Lilith. The devil take the hindmost.

Things settled down, but the women, as the meal was served, continued to nod and grin at one another, like schoolgirls winding up the boys, so the atmosphere was lightened, but in the oddest way, with the men all the while wondering what the hell was going on, simply mystified. The food came, ferried in by the women looking at one another with knowing expressions. The men were introduced to one another by Michaela speaking to Tom, beginning with her father, Stefan then her uncle, Radu, then pointing out Tom's father, Mark, to them. The drink flowed and the food was consumed while pleasantries were exchanged. Despite the odd beginning, the evening passed pleasantly. Mark discovered that Radu worked as an accountant for the town council, and Michaela's father as a chemist, for a petrochemical company. As far as Mark was concerned, everything had gone well. It had been a pleasant evening. The three of them left shortly after midnight, walking back to the hotel in the cool of the early morning. They moved quite quickly and were all in bed before one in the morning.

The next morning, Mark and Lilith arose together. Mark showered first, needing to freshen up after the drink, and late night, then went downstairs to the Restaurant and ordered for the pair of them. Lilith arrived just as the breakfast was brought to their table. They chatted reasonably amicably. Mark asked about what was going on between the women in the kitchen the previous evening.

'The women here are just catching onto the idea of women's lib' she replied, 'and they thought me changing my name to Lilith was a riot, because the understanding of the word Lilith is simply "female vampire." When they understood, they liked it and thought it was really funny, because it would mean vampire in their mythology. To have a name like that here would be a kind of insult almost but at the same time, it does have a connotation more or less as "witch" in English. I get the impression it could be used as a noun by men. If used by a man, the equivalent in England might be "vicious bitch", that's it as far as I can understand it.'

Mark's response was dismissive, 'Ahh. What are you going to do today? Are you going back tomorrow?'

'What are *you* doing today?' she countered.

'First, I'm going to the town hall to have another chat with the guy there. He's called Romeo. I want to find out in more detail about the vineyard at the top of the hill. I want to meet the owner, be clear about what he's looking for, and sort out exactly what kind of deal the council will find acceptable. I intend to buy the place as things stand, but I want to investigate all the ins and outs of any deal, so I don't get any nasty surprises when I've spent the cash. I'll put a house up there or as nearby as possible, as soon as possible. It'll be a great place to live outside the town but just ten minutes away. You want to come along? Two heads might be better than one and maybe we could put a part of it into a trust or something for the kids? Looks like Tom's developing a real interest in the place. If he decided he wanted to get involved, that could be a bonus that's good for all of us.'

'I think I'll have a better look around the town,' she said, 'and meet you back here at one o'clock. I've got to sort out the journey home, and I'd like to explore the town, OK?'

'That's fine, you do what you want. I'll be back by six. Can you sort out Sally to come back with you? I'll pay obviously.'

'What?! You're the end! You piss off and piss her off. I'm not your bloody slave. I'm LILITH! and don't you forget it. I've enjoyed this week. You've hardly been selfish at all, and then you come out with that. You brought the tart here, YOU get rid of her!'

Whoops, he thought, looking sheepish.

'Sorry, sorry. I'll get rid of her… today. I'll do it now.'

'About bloody time,' she said giving him a filthy look.

He had to admit it, he'd been pretty thoughtless, stupid even. So, he went and found Sally, explained that he no longer needed her, and told her to sort out the earliest flight home she could get. He'd pay, obviously, with a bit of a bonus. He then walked down to the town hall and asked the receptionist if he could talk to Romeo. Romeo came after a few minutes, asking exactly what Mark wanted. Mark told him he'd made up his mind regarding buying the vineyard, there were just some, 'i-s' that needed dotting, and 't-s' crossing, and then he'd supply a non-refundable deposit of five per cent until the deal was complete. In essence, he needed to meet the vendor to make sure exactly what the deal would entail. Get it down in black and white, and work from there to completion.

Romeo said he'd be back in a few minutes. He needed to speak to the vendor. He invited Mark into some sort of boardroom and asked if he'd like a coffee.

'Thank you, that would be good.'

An attractive young woman brought coffee and biscuits, for which Mark smiled and bowed to indicate his thanks. After she left, he looked around the room. Against one wall stood a display designed to sing the praises of the council, setting out its efforts to solve problems and generally improve the situation of local residents. Mark was unable to understand the language, especially because of the unfamiliar alphabet, but the pictures gave a fair indication, he guessed, as to the problems facing the local population. They made him smile simply because they were universal, and if printed in English could have been on a wall in Leeds, Birmingham, or London. After a short time, he was ushered into Romeo's office. It contained Romeo's desk and three others, one occupied by another man, apparently Romeo's junior. The other two by women, one young and the other middle-aged.

Romeo's junior was sent away and Mark was offered his seat and his phone. Romeo gave Mark a piece of paper with a telephone number on it. He said it was the number of the man who wanted to sell the vineyard. He should ring the number and the two of them could speak directly to one another. Mark rang and they quickly agreed that Mark should come to Bucharest where they could meet and speak directly. He would be supplied with accommodation at the expense of the Romanian government and a chauffeured car to carry him to his room from the railway station or airport whichever he chose. It was agreed that Mark should arrive the next day.

He thanked Romeo and shook his hand, then walked back to his hotel. He found Tom in his room and explained what was happening. Mark gave Tom the option to stay or go back to the UK with his mother and Mahe. Tom opted to stay. Mark explained he needed to speak to Michaela's uncle about legal and accountancy matters relating to the vineyard because he needed to set up a company to make it legal for him to own property in Romania. If Michaela and her parents wanted to come, that would be good, because it would create a party occasion, expressing gratitude for accepting strangers into their house while returning the gesture with humility and pleasure.

It would be the last opportunity for Mark and Lilith, Tom and Mahe to be together for some time. It would be a chance for Mark and Lilith to bury their differences, even if only for a limited time, to get on reasonably sensibly and amicably for the benefit of all concerned in their mutually dependent future.

Everyone invited came. Everyone enjoyed the evening apart from Mahe who still felt left out as the only vegetarian among them. This was something both Tom and Lilith remarked about to Mark afterwards to which he replied,

'One of those things. You can never please everyone.'

Radu agreed to meet Mark regarding the matter of sorting out plans to make his ownership of the vineyard legal, and Mark accepted that Radu and Stephan should be junior shareholders in the company, with special interests in the lease of the land itself.

Michaela would be included as having an interest through a trust that would mature into a share on her twenty-seventh birthday.

Five years passed during which time the vineyard prospered. It gained a growing international reputation for exceptional quality wines with its own world-renowned expert and journalist, Michaela Descalu, regarded as second only to Jancis Robinson.

Thomas Spivey became became Professor of European languages at the University of East London, having discovered a natural flair for languages in Romania and roaming throughout Europe for the following five years, working at vineyards in various capacities from tractor driver to director. Lilith, after deciding that the life of an MP was not for her, continued to work as a solicitor dealing with women's issues, and a television presenter dealing with subjects related to the same issues.

Mark settled into the life of a respected local vineyard and winery owner, with what some doctors considered to be a significant drink problem. A suggestion he emphatically denied, often while holding a glass of best red as he swirled it around and held it up to the light before contentedly swishing it around his surprisingly good teeth.

Mahe continued working as an unexceptional solicitor in an unexceptional dreary town on the south coast of England. One of her pet hates being, what Pope said about women in '*The Rape of the Lock*'.

'With varying vanities from every part,
They shift the moving toyshop of their heart.

Printed in Great Britain
by Amazon

37585490R00142